Rosi's Doors (Book III)

Rosi's Company

Edward Eaton

Young Adult Novel Published by
Dragonfly Publishing, Inc.

ROSI'S COMPANY
Rosi's Doors (Book III)
Young Adult Fantasy
Released in 2013

Hardback Edition
EAN 978-1-936381-23-4
ISBN 1-936381-23-0

Paperback Edition
EAN 978-1-936381-24-1
ISBN 1-936381-24-9

eBook Edition
EAN 978-1-936381-25-8
ISBN 1-936381-25-7

Story Text Copyright ©2013 Edward Eaton
Cover Art Copyright ©2012 Dragonfly Publishing, Inc.
Dragonfly Logo Copyright ©2001 Terri L. Branson

Published in the United States of America by
Dragonfly Publishing, Inc.
Website: www.dragonflypubs.com

Dedication:

The author would like to dedicate this book to his wife, Silviya, and his little man, Christopher.

Sine quibus non.

In addition to the people at Dragonfly Publishing, he would like to thank Brian Triber for his assistance, encouragement, and enthusiasm.

PROLOGUE

"ANDY?"

"Yeah, Dan?"

"That was, uh, *weird.*" Dan Meadows thought for a moment. "Is that the right word?"

"You're telling me," Andy Montrose said. "Weird would be a good word."

"You have any clue where we are?" Dan was not quite ready to sit up and look around.

"Nope." Andy opened his eyes. "Well, we're outside."

"I figured as much." Dan could smell the sweet scent of grass and he felt the soft breeze. But if he had not sensed these things, the leaves above would have given it away. "Would you like to be more specific?"

"*Outside* is all I've got at the moment." Andy realized he was holding Dan's hand. He had grabbed it when the door had swung open a few seconds ago. He did not want to let go. "Branches. Trees. Sky. Cloud."

"That's about what I got." Dan pulled his hand free. "You want to get up and look around? Find out some more?"

Andy thought for a moment. "Nope."

"You're supposed to be inquisitive," Dan pointed out. "Maybe you should."

"You're supposed to be brave," Andy countered. "Maybe you should."

Dan and Andy lay on the ground among the trees. One minute they had been talking in Rosi's room. The door had opened, and suddenly they had been in the middle of a lot of trees.

Andy started to say something, but Dan waved him to silence.

"Do you hear that?" Dan asked.

"What?"

"Shut up and listen."

Andy heard a series of sharp staccato pops. "Firecrackers?"

"Could be."

"You going to look?"

"Are you?" Dan challenged.

Andy thought about it for a second. "No."

"I better then."

Dan sat up and poked his head around one of the trees. They were at the edge of a wood.

"What do you see?"

"I'm not really sure." Dan continued to look. "I mean, I know what I see."

"Fireworks?" Andy wondered.

"Nope." There was another round of snaps and pops. Dan scrunched down a bit. "Gunfire."

"That's not funny, Dan."

"I'm not kidding."

"I'm not looking."

"Andy, you'd better look."

"Just tell me. If I need to look, I'll look. I don't want to." Andy did not think it right how they were beamed from one place to another without so much as a *by-your-leave*. He was, though, somewhat concerned with Dan's worried tone.

"Fair enough. Here is what I see. Soldiers. Red Jackets. Tri-cornered hats. Ring a bell?"

Andy sighed. What was this nonsense? "You should know that one as well as me."

"I do. I just didn't expect to actually see them," Dan said.

Andy paused as he chose his words carefully. He knew Dan was one of the top students in his grade, though he certainly did not advertise it. "What else do you see?"

Dan glanced at him with a frown. "Soldiers wearing red jackets," he repeated.

"Okay. Okay. I'll look." Andy crawled over next to Dan. He

was right. Across the large field were soldiers in tri-corned hats, red coats, and carrying guns.

"Dan?"

"Yeah?"

"Do you think this could be some sort of reenactment?"

"Do you think so?" Dan did not think so. He had seen reenactments before, but they usually seemed stiff and awkward, like a chess game using people. This was sloppy. It was not as loud as he would have expected.

Andy shook his head. "Well, to begin with, no one dresses that way anymore."

"You got a point there. Someone could be making a movie."

"I don't see any cameras." Just to make sure Andy looked around. No cameras. If they were making a movie in the area, everyone in town would know about it. "So, of the two options before us, some sort of reenactment would be—"

"The most likely," Dan finished for him.

"I was thinking along the lines of *the more likely*."

"Whatever." Dan scowled.

"And some of them are lying down. They must be resting."

"You ever hear of casualties," Dan pointed out smugly. "They do that in reenactments."

"Of course." Andy scowled this time. "Maybe we should go ask them what's going on."

Neither of them moved.

They watched a while longer. Several more men lay down. The British-looking re-enactors appeared to be winning.

"Andy?"

"Yeah, Dan?"

"I don't think that they're napping."

One man lay down, followed by a small cloud of red that rained down on him.

"You might be right," Andy observed.

One of the redcoats on horseback almost decapitated another man.

"Or acting," Dan ventured. "Perhaps, we should *not* go and

ask them what is going on."

"You have a very good point," Andy conceded.

"Thank you."

They watched for another minute.

"Do you think they might come in this direction?" Andy asked.

Dan pointed out that the redcoats were chasing the others towards the woods in the opposite direction from the two of them. "We're probably safe here. For a while." He did not sound very convinced.

"Agreed." Andy's eyes widened when he spotted the building off in the distance where the fighting was taken place. "Is that The Castle?"

"I think so," Dan answered.

"There are quite a few men in red jackets."

Dan nodded. "I guess we can safely assume they are British soldiers from the American Revolution."

"It seems as if quite a few of those British soldiers are going into The Castle. Perhaps—"

"We should avoid The Castle," Dan finished for him.

They watched the soldiers move across the open area, chasing an unseen enemy into the woods.

Dan turned to Andy. "Let me get this straight. We were in Rosi's room in the middle of the night, and now we're outside watching soldiers kill each other in the middle of the day?"

Andy thought for a moment. "That's seems to be about right."

"Theory," Dan said. "We fell asleep. Someone moved us into the middle of the woods. There are men in costumes shooting each other."

"That would explain what we are seeing." Andy looked up at the sun. "What time do you have?"

"Two forty-five a.m.," Dan said.

Andy pointed up. The sun was fairly high in the sky. "Your watch must have stopped."

"Not for what my dad spent on it." Dan sounded outraged at

the idea.

"You're wearing your father's watch?"

"He has three just like this." Dan held it up. It was a beautiful gold watch that glittered in the morning sun.

Andy grabbed Dan's arm and pulled it down. "Glitter," he said.

Dan nodded. "Dad will never miss it. Sandra told me it was okay."

"Sandra?"

"My stepmother. Kirk's mom."

"Ah." Andy felt that this explained why Dan and Kirk were about as similar as a Ming vase and a clay ashtray made by someone's kid in kindergarten. Andy thought the analogy apt and thought about telling it to Dan, but then thought not. "Even if your watch has not stopped, the visual evidence strongly suggests it is not 2:45 a.m., but rather sometime in the late morning."

"My point is," Dan explained. "That it should be right. Unless...."

"Unless?"

"Someone changed the watch while we were asleep."

"That would be a rather elaborate deception," Andy pointed out.

Andy saw Dan pull something from his pocket and start waving his arms around.

"What are you doing?" Andy asked.

"Trying to get some bars on my phone. Where's yours?"

"On the table in Rosi's room. Any luck?"

"None. I was hoping to get my GPS working, but I can't seem to open it. That is, it opens, but doesn't read anything. There's no satellite reception here."

"But we know where we are," Andy protested. "We are near The Castle. Besides, how regular is your satellite reception around here?"

"No better than yours." Dan stopped to think for a moment. "Somehow we were transported from inside The Castle to the outside of it. The time of day has been changed, I don't know how, and the time of day is about ten hours off. Might it be possible that we've been transported to some place that look like The Castle?"

Andy shrugged. "Yeah."

"Or maybe The Castle and the Carol estate have been transported with us?"

"It's possible," Andy conceded.

"If I can use my GPS."

"You should be able to find our location within a few meters." Andy wished he had thought of it.

"Within a few what?" Dan sounded a bit miffed.

"Meters?"

"Yards or even feet. We Meadows are Republicans," Dan stated. "There is no satellite connection. I can't make any calls." He turned off his phone and carefully put it in his jacket.

"Have you noticed that it is quite chilly?" Andy observed. "Indeed, I might suggest that many people would say it is actually cold. Not at all like late August."

"Perhaps we were asleep for a long time," Dan suggested.

"I don't think so."

"Ockham's razor, Andy."

"If you eliminate the impossible, whatever is left, however unlikely, must be the right answer."

"A+. If you can come up with a better theory or somehow disprove mine, we will assume I am right and that we are the objects of some sort of deception."

Andy could not really argue with that. "Though, the deception is made even more elaborate by the fact that the soldiers appeared to really dying," Andy ventured.

"All right, brainiac. You try." Dan motioned for Andy to follow him and slipped further into the trees. "Whoever the soldiers are, we don't need them see us."

"Okay," Andy started. "Epistemologically speaking—"

"Epistemologically speaking?"

"Right."

"You like those big words, don't you Einstein?"

Andy ignored this. "Epistemologically speaking, perhaps what we are seeing is exactly what it looks like we are seeing. We see men in red coats fighting and dying. A bunch of men who are not in uniform, apparently rebels, have been chased from the grounds. Our senses tell us that they are indeed fighting and dying."

"Accepted. Conditionally," Dan conceded. "Our eyes and ears suggest this. Note, however, that we are some distance from the actual fighting."

"Do you intend to go out into the field and test this hypothesis?" Andy asked.

"Further observation might be warranted," Dan pointed out.

"True," Andy said. "However, if indeed they are actually soldiers in red coats—"

"Which, I will stipulate for the moment."

"And if they really are shooting at people," Andy went on. "Might they shoot at you? Should you wish to gather more empirical data?"

"Empirical?"

"It means *practical*," Andy said a bit too smugly.

"I know what it means, doofus. I am a year older than you are. I do, however, appreciate your observation."

"So, we agree that those men are indeed using real bullets and that they can result in what could be referred to as a premature mortality."

"Agreed," Dan said.

"Now, I am unaware of any military forces who currently wear red tailcoats, tri-cornered hats, and use muzzle-loading rifles."

"More likely muskets, wouldn't you think?" Dan smirked.

"I stand corrected." Andy could have hit himself for making such a basic mistake. "Can you think of any?"

Dan could not and said so.

"Furthermore, even if there were a military group so armed, chances are they would not be supported by a seventy-four gun sailing frigate flying the British flag." Andy pointed out to the sea.

Dan had not noticed the ship until Andy pointed it out. It was magnificent with its billowing sails and puffs of white smoke as it fired somewhere at an unseen target.

"So," Dan began. "You're suggesting—"

"I'm suggesting," Andy said with exaggerated patience. "That we might possibly actually be seeing what we think we're seeing."

"A British attack on The Castle," Dan said.

"Right."

Dan thought about this. "Correct me if I'm wrong—"

"I certainly will," Andy said.

"I'm only aware of one time where British military action was taken in this area. The Revolutionary War."

"To be more specific," Andy said, beginning to get excited. "April 8th, 1780."

"I guess that would explain the soldiers and the frigate."

Andy nodded. "Exactly."

"There is one minor point your theory fails to adequately explain."

"And what is that?" Andy asked perplexed.

"How the hell we got here!" Dan snarled.

He had a point.

"How long have you lived in New Richmond, Dan?"

"Ten years, I believe."

"Are you aware of the stories about the area?"

"Not very."

"A lot of strange things happen here," Andy said.

"That, I am aware of."

"Even stranger things are often associated with The Castle and the Carol family." Andy explained. "People appear. People disappear. Strange things go bump in the night. Lights flashing at odd hours and noises we should simply forget, we're supposed to forget."

"If the old wives' tales are to be believed." Dan said. "I'm not sure they should be. There is a rational explanation to most mysteries. There are no ghosts that go bump in the night."

"Oral tradition often has a basis in fact."

"I have heard." Dan sighed. "Let me get this straight. You are suggesting that we not worry about the method of our...." He could not think of the word.

"Transference? Right."

"You're suggesting that we accept it as *a priori*, our presence in 1780?" Dan asked.

"Exactly. We behave exactly as if we are where—"

"When," Dan corrected.

"*When* it appears that we are and act accordingly." Andy nodded in acknowledgement of the correction. "If we are right, then we should be careful. If we are wrong, we merely look foolish."

"And you," Dan said. "Are not unused to looking foolish and few people would ever laugh at me, no matter how foolish I might appear."

"Exactly."

"I need a drink." Dan reached into his jacket pockets and pulled out two bottles of beer.

"You generally carry beer with you?"

"I thought Rosi might need a drink. To be honest, I thought a beer or two might lighten the mood." He twisted off the top of a beer and handed it to Andy, then did the same for himself.

Andy sipped at the beer. It was warm, but he was thirsty. "You know Dan, you're a pig."

"Indeed."

They were both thirsty. Andy felt oddly important. He never thought he would be downing beers with Dan Meadows. He kicked back, pretending everything was great, at least for the moment. Soon both bottles were empty.

Dan prepared to throw them away.

Andy held up his hand. "Wait."

"What?"

"You should bury them," Andy said. "Twist top bottles from microbreweries have yet to be invented. We don't want to interfere with time."

Dan used a stick to carefully dig a small hole about two feet deep and put the bottles in it. As he pushed the dirt back in the hole, he had a thought. "Haven't we already interfered?"

"How so?"

Dan smoothed over the top layer of dirt and put some pine needles over it. "There's a theory that says observing an incident changes the incident. The Heisenbach theory."

"Heisenberg's theory?"

"You know, Andy." Dan produced two more bottles from his seemingly bottomless jacket pockets and handed one to Andy. "You may be as smart as you look."

Andy blushed. He felt bold. "You know, Dan. You may be smarter than you look."

"Thank you. You know I am going Ivy?"

"Harvard like your dad?" Money could buy just about anything.

"Yale. We go to Yale." Dan took a deep breath to hold his temper. "I let the pig comment pass, but I can't really let that one slide, can I? Harvard!"

Andy sighed. "I guess not." He closed his eyes and waited. "Ow!" He rubbed his arm where Dan hit it. Not too hard, but hard enough to make his point. "Anyway, Heisenberg was wrong."

"Was he?"

"Certainly. If you send someone into a situation and the observer actively participates in the event, a journalist in a battlefield who eats and sleeps with the men, then there's a point. What happens, though, when you watch a meteor shower or a supernova with a strong telescope? There is no possible interference, especially considering the event has happened long before the observation is made."

Dan had not thought about it that way. "Yet," he started defensively. "He has a theory and all you have is a sore arm. We cannot just observe from a safe distance. We are in a new situation. It appears we are in a different time. You yourself said that strange events are often associated or linked with The Castle and the Carol family. If we are here because we came through that door, and if Rosi and Angie went through the same door—"

"They did," Andy said.

"Accepted. Then it stands to reason that they will be—"

"Or have been," Andy interrupted again.

"Somewhere in the same physical—"

"And temporal."

"Locale," Dan finished.

"Your point being?" Andy was not quite sure what Dan wanted them to do.

"My point," Dan said. "Is that we can't stay here in the woods. If nothing else, we should find out if Rosi and Angie are here. We help them, if they need help. Then we should probably figure out a way to go home."

"I suspect if Rosi Carol is here, she'll be the one helping us," Andy said.

The battle was dying down.

"There is a slight problem," Andy said.

"What is that?"

"Whatever Heisenberg might say, everything I've read suggests that the British were routed. It is apparent that the British have won here."

The British had stopped their advance towards the far tree line and were collecting their fallen.

Dan shrugged. "I guess it goes to show that you can never be certain about anything," he said smugly. "If the British won then the British won. We certainly had nothing to do with any of that."

"Someone must have." Andy started looking at his hands.

"What's wrong?"

"History has been changed. We should cease to exist."

"Yet, we're here."

"There seems to be another problem, Dan." Andy pointed at The Castle. "There's your stepbrother."

He was right. There was Kirk, walking to the front door of The Castle, accompanied by a flashily dressed older man with a swagger. The older man said something to Kirk, ruffled the boy's hair, and went to speak to some other men. Kirk was dressed in a loud tailcoat and knee britches. He looked ridiculous, Dan thought.

"Half brother," Dan said absently. He started to rise. "There's someone we know."

"Wait!" Andy grabbed Dan by the arm.

"What is it?" Dan snapped quietly.

"Realize that Kirk is with the British. He's clearly on good terms with them."

"Yes?"

"The British are the bad guys, aren't they? Also, I have heard you on more than one occasion refer to Kirk as a bit of a—"

"Cockroach!"

Andy was going to say worm, but cockroach sounded fine, too. "Perhaps he interfered."

"Clearly he interfered. I'm gonna kick his...." Dan started to move.

Andy had to grab one of his legs and hold on. "He's surrounded by men with guns. We should observe, evaluate, and then plan."

Reluctantly, Dan sat back down.

After a while, a carriage pulled by four elegant horses, drove up. A well dressed older man in a white wig stepped down. All of the men stopped and saluted him. Kirk and his friend rushed out of The Castle, bowed low, and ushered the man inside. Ten minutes later, the man came out and left in his carriage.

Andy said that he thought the man was Admiral Cromwell, because who else would merit such a carriage in the middle of a battlefield? "But what does he, or Kirk, want in The Castle?"

"Kirk probably wants the same thing we do," Dan offered. "To find a way home."

Andy did not think it was that simple.

Things quieted down fairly quickly. Most of the soldiers left the area, moving in the direction of New Richmond. Every once in a while, Dan and Andy heard a fresh outburst of distant gunfire, but they happened further and further away and further and further apart.

Neither Kirk nor his friend came out again.

The sun passed noon. After a while Andy guessed it was about one.

"As they say." Dan stood up and moved a few feet away. "You don't buy beer. You rent it."

Andy grinned politely at the feeble joke and kept his eyes on The Castle.

"Andy?"

"What?"

"I think we may have a bigger problem," Dan said in an odd tone.

"What's that?"

"Come over here."

Andy turned around.

Standing in front of Dan, who looked rather silly with his pants around his ankles, were four people. Three of them were inordinately tall.

"Indians?" Dan asked.

"There aren't supposed to be Indians around here. They all died off around 1700. Disease."

"These guys don't look dead. What kind of Indians were they?"

"Fula'puli."

The four strangers started at the word and spoke to each other softly.

"That one is a woman," Dan said.

Andy took the moment to look at the newcomers carefully. The three men wore tight outfits of hardened leather that seemed to look like armor. They were not painted or decorated. They had close fitting gilded bracelets completely covering each forearm. They had long black hair. One of them, the youngest looking one, had on what appeared to be a Mohawk made of twigs.

The woman was shorter, very slight, and wore what seemed to be a long flesh colored dress. Both Dan and Andy noticed at the same moment that she was actually wearing a short tight fitting vest and lightweight ankle length skirt that revealed as much as it concealed. She looked to be in her late teens and was the spitting image of the younger man.

"I think I might like it back here," Dan said as he looked the woman up and down.

"May I make a suggestion?" said Andy.

"Go for it."

"Pull your pants back up."

"Oh." Dan fumbled with his pants and belt, but eventually got them back in the proper position.

Watching him, the young woman giggled.

"Fula'puli," the oldest looking man said. He carried a long spear, had what looked like a broadsword shoved in his belt, and a musket slung over his shoulder. The other men were similarly armed. The woman openly carried a long knife.

Andy was about to hyperventilate. He started wheezing. He pulled out his inhaler and puffed on it a couple of times. The Fula'puli looked at him curiously. "I need it to breath." He laughed nervously.

They merely looked confused.

"Allow me," Dan said, stepping forward and looking at the young woman. He began waving his arms around strangely.

"What are you doing?" Andy asked.

"I'm trying to speak with them."

"I doubt they understand International Sign Language."

"That's all right, I don't either. I saw this in a movie."

"What are you asking them?"

"I think I'm asking where the post office is."

"That will be useful," Andy said, sarcastically.

"It wasn't a very good movie."

The Fula'puli looked more confused.

"Perhaps they speak French," Andy suggested.

"Go ahead and try."

"I don't speak French. I thought maybe you did."

"Nope," Dan said. "Dad doesn't believe in foreign languages."

"Really?"

"Really. He feels that English is the *lingua franca* of modern business. Further, if I speak a foreign language, it will put the foreigners in a superior position. Allow them to speak English poorly and I am in the dominant position."

"Your family isn't very politically correct," Andy said.

"I have a cousin who's gay."

"That's a start."

Dan thought for a moment. "I think I have an idea."

"What?"

"I met an Indian in Las Vegas." Dan took a deep breath. "Me Dan, live in big wigwam on mountain. We come many moons from now. We use magic door. We are heap plenty powerful. Take us to big chief."

"What was that?" Andy asked.

"That's how the Indian I met talked."

"On a reservation in Nevada?"

"At the casino. She was a bartender."

"May I say something without getting hit?"

"Go for it."

"You're an idiot."

"Perhaps, but I don't see you trying anything." Dan said, as if that proved his point.

These Indians did not seem to understand Dan.

"Go ahead, Andy," Dan insisted. "Impress me and speak with the Indians.

"Looks like we're at something of an impasse," Andy said with a resigned shrug. "I got nothing."

The younger man stepped to one side and gestured for Dan and Andy to follow them.

The two boys looked at each other. That was a sign they understood. They shrugged and followed. If nothing else, they were being led away from the British.

PART I

The Gathering

CHAPTER 1

WITH a sigh, Rosi looked again at the old pocket watch. She had to shift the angle of the watch several times and move it around before she found a strong enough shaft of light to read the Roman numerals.

One o'clock. She was not happy.

Who would stick a fifteen year old girl alone in the middle of the woods in enemy territory in the middle of the night?

I Would, she reminded herself.

She carefully closed the watch. She liked the sound and feel of the gentle click as it shut, and often found herself opening it and shutting it just for the double effect.

A foraging party had brought back the watch a couple of days ago and proudly presented it to their young captain. Ben, a boy Rosi suspected was even younger than her, had bowed grandly when he handed it to her. It was a shiny silver watch with gold inlays that looked to Rosi to be a family crest. She knew little about heraldry, but saw that the top of the shield had a Unicorn in front of a fiery sun. The watch itself was old, but inside the cover was a fairly recent cameo of a rather plain woman and an even plainer baby. The officer her men had taken it from had been killed when the foragers had ambushed him and three other men. The British had not had time to fight back, so Rosi knew nothing about the bravery of the previous owner of the watch. He had been fairly young and a lieutenant. Presumably the picture was of his wife and baby and he was the scion of some wealthy family. The watch was clearly valuable.

"Why give it to me?" she had asked Ben. "You could sell this and buy a new farm."

"What'd I do with farm, miss." Ben had blushed. "Pardon, I mean, Captain. 'sides, who'd I sell it to? Only ones here with money'r th'redcoats. Them's enemies. Most likely shoot me and take watch anyway."

So Rosi got a nice watch. She felt guilty about throwing away the lock of baby's hair tied with a pink ribbon that had been inside the watch. But only for a moment.

She was the only person in her company who could tell time on an analog watch. Ironically, few of her friends at home, at least those in the city, could tell time on an analog watch either. *Perhaps*, she thought, *the past is not that much different than the future.* Or would that be the present?

So now she had a nice watch. Rosi felt sorry for the wife and child of the dead officer, but then she wondered how many 'husbands' and 'fathers' the young lieutenant might have killed.

She had only been involved in this war for a couple of weeks and already Rosi had lost loved ones. She was angry. She let her men think her anger was with the British, but it was not.

The leader of the British in this area was an Admiral Cromwell. Rosi understood that Cromwell had some sort of personal reason for being involved in the attack on New Richmond. However, he did not start the war. Nor did he set military policy. Whatever his intentions and motivations might be, his overall plan was approved by someone higher up. It was not *his* army. It was not *his* navy. Those belonged to the King.

No. Spending time being angry with the Admiral was futile.

Being angry with the King was even more pointless. The King might have power and influence, but Georgian England was far from being an absolute monarchy. The King probably had less power than the President did. He was certainly bound by more rigid rules. What would she do were she King and her colonies rebelled? She would probably fight to keep them part of her empire.

George III might have his problems, but porphyria made you mad, not bad. Besides, the King and his ministers probably saw New Richmond as little more than a splotch on a map. If the British government really had any idea of the power that could be tapped in the area, it would not be a renegade Admiral and a few hundred men. Rosi did not know how much input the British government had in the tactics of the war. She suspected not much. People in London were too distant on several levels to be angry with.

The officers and soldiers in the area might be cruel masters. The reports and rumors coming in daily suggested they were. They were probably also scared. If they could keep the local population under heel, they would probably be safe from them. So, they had terrorized a few farmers and burned a handful of barns. This certainly was not nice, but understandable. People who aided and abetted her rag tag company of men or even the more military and *official* militias fighting the British were arguably guilty of treason. The occupying soldiers might not follow due process. Then again, even Rosi's men had burned a couple of farms this past week because those farmers were dealing with the British and her men had not asked a lot of questions or allowed the farmers to explain themselves.

Yes, the British soldiers were killing American soldiers. As Rosi understood it, they were doing a very good job of it. She had heard that they were often somewhat enthusiastic about it. When she took the time to think about it, she thought maybe their enthusiasm was not driven by wickedness, so much as, adrenaline and fear.

She, herself, had been through one battle and knew how that felt. There had been no patriotism flowing through her veins that day. There had been no fervor. There had been no philosophy. There had been ice so cold it made her core shiver. There had been fear. There had been a desire to live, whatever the cost.

When she had finally escaped the battle, she experienced a surge of energy with no outlet. In her case, her arm had been wounded before the battle, but the battle damaged it more. After nearly being crushed by a horse, Spartacus, her First Sergeant, had to straighten the bones. The pain alone knocked her out.

For the rest of her men, the energy had been fear, pure and simple. Only a couple of them had kept their heads.

Then again, Rosi's men had lost the battle.

The British had won. Even then, whatever excesses they were responsible for were tame compared to the way victorious armies often treated the local populaces after battles. Even the greatest, most popular generals, rarely tried to curb their men after a great victory. A more modern general would most likely have been cashiered, imprisoned, or even hanged were he to allow his men the license Wellington allowed his men after the storming of Badajoz.

Rosi had recently been able to hand her men some small victories. She had sent out squads to watch the roads and keep them clear of British supply trains and messengers. This had only been successful for about two days. After that, the British went everywhere in force.

No, Rosi could not hate the British soldiers. As long as they acted like soldiers and did what soldiers do. She could no more hate them than she could hate the members of a rival baseball team.

Her job, and the job of her men, was to beat the enemy. More often than not, that meant killing them. So Rosi did not bother trying to discuss the nature of hatred with her men. She did try and stoke the fires of hatred whenever she could.

Rosi knew whom she could hate. She knew whom she had to destroy. Kirk.

Kirk was not a soldier. He was not a general. He was not a politician. He should not have involved himself in this war.

He was just a jackass.

Rosi never liked Kirk. He was the worst kind of bully, the kind who liked to pick on *her* friends. If it were only that, she would be able to treat him like bullies should be treated. She could ignore and despise him.

But Kirk was not a *simple* bully. He was smarter than most.

Rosi knew about her family's role as Guardians of a cluster of doorways in space and time. But she was still half wallowing in shock at being dragged through one of the doorways. And she had done it several times with her uncle, the current Guardian.

Kirk had not only been tossed into this new time, but he

apparently picked himself up and had come up with a plan, a plan he put into motion without skipping a beat. He could have tried to find the then Guardian, Beatitude Carol. It would hardly have been a great logical stretch to go from being transported through time while in The Castle to figuring that the owners of The Castle might have a clue as to what was going on. Had Kirk gone into New Richmond, it would have taken him only a few minutes to recognize The Dancing Cavalier and Young Captain Sam.

Rosi was not yet sure what Young Captain Sam and the Dancing Cavalier had to do with the time doorways or the Guardians, but he was somehow connected. It could not be a coincidence that the man was thriving in both revolutionary New Richmond and modern New Richmond. According to Angie, Young Captain Sam seemed older now that he would in their time.

Young Captain Sam probably would not have helped him out, but Kirk could have tried. Kirk could have used his knowledge of history and made a small fortune. He also could have set himself up in a mountain palace filled with wine, women, and song. Instead, he had, intentionally, rewritten history. It was not some minor change. Kirk had, in fact, arranged for the British to win the Battle for New Richmond. The battle, previously a British defeat, had barely even been a footnote to history. A British victory, however, could not be ignored. His actions would certainly rewrite the histories of North America and the British Empire.

Rosi had managed to gather together a handful of local farmers with muskets to help her. They would most likely follow her to the very gates of Hell if she asked them, or they would go home when it came time to plant their crops.

Kirk had managed to put himself in the middle of one of the strongest and best trained armies in the history of the world, and somehow to get it to work for him.

Rosi and her men were sleeping in ruins and eating any food they were lucky enough to kill while Kirk was dining on fine china in *her* house.

A week ago, Rosi had three friends here whom she could count on. Two of them were now dead. She hoped they had died when they were shot rather than burning to death. The third had left after trying to strangle her.

Rosi could hate Kirk for that. He had no excuse.

She checked her watch again. She had to keep focused.

If she were really lucky, Uncle Richard would pop around and fix everything. But she probably would not be that lucky. The general rule of thumb was that one Guardian did not interfere with another. Rosi was training, but this was hardly a mission that Uncle Richard had sent her on. Somehow, the door opened for or because of her. She had the feeling that Uncle Richard was not going to help. Perhaps this Beatitude Carol, some sort of great-great-uncle could help. If he could be found.

* * *

THE road the skirted the edge of Uncle Richard's estate was a simple path used sometimes by farmers, more recently, soldiers. It was about fifty yards south of Rosi.

Her escort, Harry Thatcher and a Private Hollins from the regular militia, were supposed to be keeping an eye on the road. More than likely they were dozing.

Thatcher was from the area and had a healthy fear of The Castle and the Carols. Rosi might be able to order him into the allegedly haunted woods, but she saw no reason to do so. A watch on the road should suffice. They would see who was coming and going. So far, over the past week, Kirk had stayed in.

That was the important part. Cromwell had a staff in The Castle with Kirk and came by once or twice a day. There were pickets by the gates.

In Rosi's time, the main part of the estate had a wrought iron fence that stretched along the road and for some distance through the woods. She had no idea how much land Uncle Richard actually owned. Now, there was a low wall along the road. High enough to notice, low enough to go over without much trouble. Superstition probably kept the locals off the land.

Rosi stood at the edge of the woods and looked up the long, overgrown lawn towards The Castle. She was used to seeing it well mown. Beatitude Carol had gone off some months previously to fight for the fledgling country and had obviously not arranged for the property to be maintained.

The British had placed several small cannons along the front of The Castle pointing down the lawn. Rosi did not know much about cannons, but Private Benson had told her these would be called guns and would probably be loaded with grapeshot and canister. They would rip apart any force that tried to advance up the lawn. The cannon might even be able to get more than one volley before the few men left would reach them.

Near to the guns were the large stables where the soldiers were quartered. These soldiers would be there to deal with any men who survived the cannon. It would not be wise to try and mount an attack along the lawn.

To the north of The Castle were the gardens.

Rosi recalled how beautiful and mysterious the gardens always seemed to her. She figured that somewhere deep inside Uncle Richard was a romantic streak that she had yet to see manifest, for the gardens, though tended regularly, were intentionally made to look as if they were in a permanent state of disrepair. Whenever Rosi spent time in them she felt as if she was in one of the romance books she like to read.

Approaching from the direction of the gardens would be a shorter route than that of the front lawn. But here again, any force would be exposed for the bushes and trees had been cut down. There were still some trees near the old garden yet not enough to give anyone any cover. And there were a few soldiers encamped there.

At first she considered having one or two men sneak across the garden at night, but from observing on previous nights, they discovered the British burned bonfires near the garden each night.

So, crossing the garden was a sure way of getting shot, Rosi concluded.

There was just no way for Rosi and her men to attack The Castle with a force of any size without being wiped out. Even if they were successful, Kirk would be warned, giving him time to flee. She came to the conclusion that she needed to do was find out what Kirk knew and what he was after as much as she needed to find a way to get the British out of New Richmond. Kirk had to know the possible consequences for fiddling with the past. Why had he done so?

Rosi needed to stop being a soldier for a while and become a spy.

* * *

AFTER the defeat the week previously, Rosi had few illusions as to her skill as a military commander. She was trying to improve the discipline of her men, but was relying on the skill of a few regular non-commissioned officers who had latched on to her command.

In spite of the recent loss, the core of her men accepted her so-called command of the company. This was most likely because of her name and her family's position in the area. The men who had joined her after the battle had little choice but to accept her as well. Rosi wished that someone who clearly outranked her would come by and take over. Until that happened, she was resigned to playing the role.

She was dressed for the part. Her men made sure of this. It seemed as if a day did not pass in which one of them found something to add to her uniform. The watch was one piece. She had an old sword from another officer to replace Zilla's, which had been left behind during the route. Someone had dug up a tri-cornered hat with a large feather. They had even found a pair of riding boots that just about fit her and a riding crop she was learning to slap against the side of her leg to great effect.

She felt a bit like a doll. A macaroni doll.

Doll or no, soldiering had rules. She had to follow them. Her men had to follow them. The enemy had to follow them.

Spying was different animal altogether. If caught the least that could happen was she would be hanged. But spying was what was needed. She had an inkling of an idea, but wasn't quite ready to try it.

Harry had gone into town. When he came back an hour later he refused to go back again.

"They're rounding people up right and left," he said. "I think they're being tortured. I could hear screams, but I couldn't get close enough to know what was going on. The English are tearing the town apart. I think they're looking for something."

What? That was the question.

That would explain why the British had brought a couple of townspeople back to The Castle.

One night, Spartacus had sneaked up fairly close to the old watchtower. The British appeared to be ignoring that, but it was still not practical to go there.

The British did not come close to the edge of the woods often.

Possibly, they were afraid of being shot by snipers, though Rosi doubted it. The Americans had been thoroughly thrashed earlier and she was sure the British did not expect them to return.

Perhaps the British were spooked by the woods themselves. Rosi's men only came because Rosi insisted. The closer they got to The Castle, the antsier they got.

They were good at watching the road. They were even better at sleeping while they watched the road.

Rosi had plenty of time during her watch to sneak along the edge of the woods and do recon.

She also had time to grieve. She had too much time to grieve. Rosi did not remember her mother's death. She had only been a couple of days old at the time. She would probably never get over the death of her father. Then again, she was not completely convinced her father was dead. Of course, he *was*. Rosi knew that. He had been on an airplane that had disappeared in the middle of the Pacific Ocean.

Except in movies, people did not simply show up one day years later and explain that they had been stuck on a deserted island. Uncle Richard had said her father had died, and he would know. Her father's death had been decided long ago by forces Rosi was not allowed to control. Uncle Richard had explained that her father had taken the airplane knowing it would disappear, knowing he had to die for a number of reasons Rosi did not yet understand. Her father had to die so that Rosi would be sent to New Richmond. He had to die, presumably, so that she would be standing in the woods outside The Castle in April of 1780.

"Couldn't you have found a better way to get me here?" Rosi grumbled at her absent uncle, remembering to keep her voice low.

The British might not be sitting around their campfires yelling, but she could hear them talking. Sound traveled well here. Whichever of her ancestors had built the estate was apparently well versed in acoustics and wanted to have fair warning when visitors approached.

This was another reason she preferred her escort to remain by the roads. With only a couple of exceptions, the men would chatter and bicker and there was little she could do to shut them up. The road was a busy one. Even at night it was not unusual for there to be some traffic. If a British soldier heard them there might be enough time for the men to run. If the three of them were caught in the woods, it was highly unlikely that anyone would pause before shooting. That would bring too many soldiers too quickly. If Rosi were caught alone in the woods, chances were that whoever caught her would simply think she was a girl wandering through the woods alone in the middle of the night. Since she had left her weapons behind, she figured that she might have some time to bluff her way out of trouble. She did not want to dwell on the possible consequences, but guessed that, strategically, they were probably better than alerting Cromwell, or worse, Kirk, to her presence.

So, she came to the woods alone, which gave her too much time to think.

She was able to tell herself that her father's plane might have found a place to land, even though it was not true. She could even tell herself that she could possibly find a way to see her father again. Uncle Richard had told her that this was unwise and that he would stop her if he thought she would try. One of the jobs of being a Guardian, he told her frequently, was learning when and where other Guardians had gone to clear up situations and to avoid going there and then and making matters worse. Her father had not been an official Guardian, so had not been expected to keep detailed records of his travels. He had preferred to go on short trips into the future so that he would know publishing trends and stock prices. This had been the source of a bitter disagreement between her father and Uncle Richard some years ago.

No matter how much she tried, she could not rationalize Angie's death. Uncle Richard knew what the score was whenever he went through one of the doorways. Her father had known what would happen to the plane. Rosi knew what happened when she went through a doorway, even if she was not sure what to do.

Angie had simply been in the wrong place at the wrong time. She had been sucked into this time along with Rosi and had done her best to deal with it and help. Angie volunteered to sneak into New Richmond to find out what Kirk was up to. In truth, it had been Rosi's job to fix the damage Kirk had caused. But Angie, with Zilla, had gotten the British to follow her on a wild goose chase. As a result, Angie and Zilla had been trapped in the old farmhouse and they had either been shot or burned to death.

Rosi had seen the charred body. She had recognized both women's dresses. They were dead. Rosi could not rationalize her way out of knowing this.

She could blame Kirk, but she shared some of the responsibility. Angie was dead. Rosi's only real friend was gone. She had never been so alone.

There was no way for Rosi to return home and tell anyone of Angie's death. If she did, would she be able to face Andy, the Sheriff, or Mrs. Kaufman? What would she say? How do you tell someone that their daughter was killed more than two hundred years ago? Would Uncle Richard even let her?

Andy might understand. *Might* being the operative word.

At best, the Kaufmans would have her committed.

At worst?

She knew that the relationship between the locals and the Carol family was fragile. The locals lived with their fears and distrust on the understanding that the Carols protected the town. The Carols also supported the town. They were the chief landowners, the bankers, and the charitable organization. New Richmond got to avoid most of the perils that the outside world faced. The Carols got to live like medieval feudal lords, or rather, like some mad dragons living in the nearby mountain that have yet to demand too much in the way of sacrifice.

Rosi knew that from time to time someone would whip the locals into a fervor that had to be put down. Uncle Richard would not go into details, other than saying that it was not pretty. Even Andy had only hinted at dark times in the local history, and he knew more about local history than anyone but a Carol.

Angie's death might be the virgin sacrifice that broke the camel's back.

As much as Rosi knew that she would have to face up to her responsibilities, she prayed somehow that Uncle Richard would help her through them. On the other hand, she would not be able to tell even Uncle Richard if she were not able to get home. That itself was the real problem.

Kirk had allowed Admiral Cromwell into New Richmond. Kirk had helped the British cut off northern New England from the rest of the rebellious colonies. Kirk had changed too much for this to be a quick fix.

Yet Rosi had to fix it. Somehow, she had to change things back to a point where she had a home to return to. So far, what Rosi had figured out was that she had to get the British out of New Richmond. And she had to get inside The Castle and find out what Kirk was up to.

She thought she had a way to get inside The Castle.

Gingerly, she started back towards the road and her escort. She had been scouting for almost two hours. It was time to go back. Her men would be ready. She was hungry and her arm was killing her.

She had hurt her arm by first falling down a cliff and then being nearly trampled to death by a wounded horse. Rosi discovered that one of the advantages of being a Carol was how quickly she healed. After only a week, she could use her arm fairly good. It would never be as good as new, but at least she could use it. But like with everything, there was a downside, her quick healing caused fear among her men. The word *witchcraft* had even been muttered, but was quickly silenced by Spartacus. Rosie was sure he was not the only one thinking it.

She nudged Private Hollins, who had been dozing, and motioned for him to wake up John. John tended to awaken noisily, so it was better for Hollins to shake him and keep him quiet until he realized where he was.

"Get what you wanted?" John asked, once he had his bearings. He helped Hollins put Rosi's gun belt around her waist. The men enjoyed doing this a bit too much, but Rosi was getting used to it. *A compliment is a compliment*, she told herself.

"Dunno," she grumbled. "Hungry."

"Let's hope there's food," Hollins groused.

"Let's hope," Rosi agreed.

John, who had grown up in the area, took the lead. Hollins, who had grown up in a city and was scared of trees, followed behind Rosi.

CHAPTER 2

ROSI awakened to now familiar sounds.

Men were bellowing at each other, muskets were firing, feet were stomping. Sergeant Major Zablonski was fast turning the odd village into a regular boot camp. The company was comfortably more than fifty men now. A few of the men that had joined their odd group, left as soon as they could.

At night, the town was regularly assaulted by the black fog Rosi had seen so often in the area. This time the fog did not hide the Widows of men lost to the sea, but instead, angry, more violent creatures that tried to force themselves into the village. Some unknown force kept them at bay.

Following the fog came the keening. For a long into the night came what sounded like a woman screaming. The sound was unearthly. As of yet, they could not determine if there was a connection between the fog and the screams.

Their village seemed to exist outside of space and time. That is, it was someplace, but the someplace was nowhere near New Richmond.

Boats, one of the Regulars, had been a sailor and knew something about the night sky. He said that the stars and the moon were in the wrong places.

Rosi knew enough about architecture to be able to narrow the location to someplace in Europe and the time to sometime that resembled what movies represented as being medieval. She kept those two opinions to herself.

It appeared as if their surrounds seemed to change around the village. During the night, they were surrounded by the forest of New Hampshire. During the day it was abandoned and burned out fields. When Rosi glanced around the village all she saw on the outskirts were the charred remains of fields, yet when she stepped across the village border, she was still in New Hampshire.

It was almost impossible to find the village. No could enter unless they were taken there by someone who had been there already. Spooky and bewitching as it made the village sound, at least the British could not find it. This gave the men a feeling of safety.

At night the men hid in the old building inside the village, covering their ears and refusing to look out. During the day Zablonski and the other regulars tried to turn the group of men into a real military unit.

Rosi would leave the village in the evening to do her spying. Her days were spent sleeping, learning to shoot her pistol, and how to command her company. Zablonski actually ran the company, but did not object when Rosi made suggestions. Some he even liked, if not respected. Their biggest problem was trying to reorganize the men.

She had discovered that the men who were the best shots were also the quietest at moving quickly through the woods, and had the best sight. Rosi took the two best men from each company and formed a squad that would take on the job as pathfinders. Before the battle, while everyone was maneuvering for position on the battlefield, they would be in advance of her company and would use their superior range to pick off officers and sergeants. When things started, they could find some high ground behind the company and could continue sniping.

Rosi supposed that this new squad was sort of a combination of snipers, rangers, and skirmishers. She was being generous. Her company would most likely be seen as little more than bushwhacking irregulars. Rosi hoped that the presence of Sergeant-Major Zablonski and the other real militiamen might fool the British into thinking the whole group as a real unit. She knew that irregular units were not infrequently treated like criminals and spies and shot out of hand. Naturally, one of Rosi's goals as captain was to avoid being captured.

While the men were looking, marching, shooting and

sounding like real soldiers Rosi was becoming a better shot, and getting in the hang of being in charge.

If they had the opportunity of working together for six or seven months, or even a year, they would be an elite unit. However, Rosi decided that a week would have to be long enough.

It was time to be proactive.

* * *

"WE have to get in closer," Rosi announced to Zablonski and Spartacus.

"We can't. They have too many men there."

Spartacus had a point.

"We'll figure that out later," Rosi said.

"Can't get no closer," Spartacus insisted. "They have men on the road, on the drive, in the gardens, and in front of The Castle."

Rosi smiled. "It struck me that they didn't put men to the rear."

"The rear?"

"Where they flanked us. They think that we ran away and won't be coming back. Setting up a guard is probably pretty standard, but they won't think that we'll come by the cliffs. We don't have any boats. How could we possible get there?"

"They'd be right, Miss," said Zablonski.

"We go along the cliffs," Rosi explained. "The cliffs only go along for about a mile. We get to the water. We go along the base of the cliffs until we reach the path, or however they actually got up."

The men looked at each other.

"The base of the cliffs?" asked one man, turning pale. "I'd rather stay here and deal with the...." His voice trailed off.

"Miss," started Spartacus. He saw the look she gave him. "Sorry. Captain, its one thing to go and sit in the trees and watch, but are ye strong enough fer that?"

"I guess I'll have to be."

Rosi only asked Spartacus and his platoon to come along with her, but all of the men insisted on joining in. At least as far as the cliffs. No man there was sure about braving the ocean. Rosi figured she would work that part out when they got there.

Shortly after noon the next day, they reached a small beach that was nicely situated by the cliffs. They could not see The Castle, which made everyone feel more comfortable. The only moment of concern was when they were broaching the crest of the last dune before the water's edge.

Spartacus reached over, grabbed Rosi's good arm, and pulled her down. "Hide yerselves," he snapped to the other men. Before Rosi could ask, the older man pointed out to sea.

A British ship was about half a mile off the shore. It took a good quarter of an hour until the ship was out of sight and Spartacus felt secure enough to let the men go.

Tentatively, they approached the water. A few men slipped off their boots and walked near the edge of the surf. When the waves came in, they ran quickly back. Then they followed the water in, only to skip out again just ahead of the foam.

Rosi laughed. "They're acting like they've never seen the ocean."

"What's so funny about that?" Spartacus asked. "Most of us haven't. Not this close up."

"You're kidding! You only live a few miles away. When I was little, Daddy took me to the beach a couple times a year. Everyone goes to the beach."

"Most of us ain't been more than a few miles from home," Spartacus explained. "Perhaps to market or to the city fer something important like Easter."

"How odd. Not even on vacation?"

"We don't have no vacations, captain. We work in the summer. Plough and sow, keep an eye on the land. Hunt for food. Fix the farms. Then there's the harvest. Then's too cold to go traveling. Still got lots to do. Even them as can go places generally don't. The roads'r pretty dangerous. Injuns. Highwaymen."

"Highwaymen?" Rosi almost laughed. Spartacus made it sound like Robin Hood's time.

"Yes, ma'am," Spartacus went on. "Dangerous to go outside places ye know. Get a group together, maybe then. Ye rich enough t'hire escort. No problem then." Spartacus thought for a moment. "No one here ever gave much thought to traveling fer pleasure like rich folk. Don't have the time. Don't have the inclination."

"What do you do? I mean, for fun?"

"Me?" Spartacus shrugged. "I got six children. Got married at seventeen. Wife died with the first kid. Married her cousin a year later when I was nineteen. She were fourteen. Good stock. Healthy girl."

Rosi gulped. She realized that if she actually lived in this time, she would probably be married in a year or two, if not already, and have a kid every year or two. If she did not die in childbirth. "I'm sorry. Where I come from is a lot different. No girl marries at fifteen."

"When do ye?"

"I dunno. About thirty, I guess. Some younger, in their twenties. Guys, too. You know. After college, get a job. Play the field." The men looked confused. Rosi searched for an analogy. "No one buys the first horse they ride." She laughed.

The men did not react as she had hoped. A few grinned, some looked uncomfortable, and the rest were horrified.

"Miss Carol!" Spartacus was scandalized.

"Come on!" Rosi laughed, feeling a bit nervous. "You know how it is."

Apparently they did not.

Oh, crap! Rosi definitely did not like the way everyone was looking at her now. "Tell those men not to drink the water!" she growled. "It'll kill them." Saltwater was not good to drink, she knew, having gotten sick several times when she was little and had swallowed too much. "We'll stay here for a couple of hours."

Boats had already told her that the tide was just starting to go out. "I want a couple of men to go with me. We'll go along the base of the cliff and take the path up. I'm not sure exactly what we'll find up there, but if we can get inside I think I can keep us out of sight. For right now, let's just worry about lunch. Build a fire and cook something. I really don't think anyone will come looking. Those soldiers might fight well, but they're lazy."

Zablonski agreed and set several men to work. The men kept their distance, for the most part. Only Spartacus, Eustace, and Harry sat with her while they ate. Ben seemed angry with her.

"What did I do?" Rosi asked Zablonski when he came by.

The sergeant major sighed. "Miss, the men like ye. It may be one thing for our kind to act like farm animals, but it's different when someone of yer station talks about it."

"But all I did was say how things were where I come from. And what do you mean my *station*?"

"Yer a lady."

"All of the men are behaving like perfect gentlemen. I'm not complaining."

"We're not gentlemen," he said.

"Yes, you are," Rosi responded.

"No, miss. I mean, we're not," he insisted. "We don't pretend to be. T'ain't seemly fer us to pretend to be our betters. T'ain't seemly for our betters to be acting like us."

"What do you mean, betters? We're all the same."

"No, ma'am," Zablonski replied.

Rosi asked Spartacus about that attitude. "Course you ain't the same as us. Nothin' else, yer a Carol. Carols is important people in these parts. Fine folk, by all accounts. Never met Beatitude Carol. He's been over ta England to study. I met Spinster Carol. Nice lady. I remember when she married and when Beatitude were born."

"Who is Spinster Carol?"

"Must be yer great-aunt, ye being Beatitude's niece and all. She was a strange one. Dressed funny. All in black. Use t'wander about the forests all hours, rain or shine. Spoke to people. People as weren't there all the time." He tapped his head knowingly. "She knew things. She knew when one of us was in trouble and she'd help. She was a lady, even if she was a bit daft."

"Why was she called Spinster Carol?"

"She didn't marry until she was well over forty. Lot of people put out when that happened, I heard tell. Some family in Boston expected to take The Castle, but she up and married a cousin from South Carolina or some such place. Richard Carol. Odd fish, beggin' yer pardon him being family to ye and all that. Couldn't stand the cold, they say. Spent one winter here and disappeared. Down south, again, they say. Though...."

"What?" Rosi did not know much about her family, not nearly enough.

"There some as say Spinster Carol done him in. Got with child and then done him in. No one ever saw him leave. When Beatitude came, he were sent off right away ta England. Heard yer relatives in Boston wanted to kill him, take The Castle. He didn't come back until about five year ago, when his ma disappeared herself."

"Where'd she go?"

"Don't know that. No one knows where the Carols go. All's we know is that ye never die. Never heard of no one saw a Carol body. Ye was wonderin' why we follow ye? Everyone knows the Carols are odd fish. Everyone knows the Carols can do things."

"What can we do?"

"Ye should know, ye being the next Carol," Spartacus said.

"The next Carol?"

"The Carol up to The Castle is The Carol. Used ta be Spinster, now 'tis Beatitude."

"I suppose his children will be, or one of them will be."

"Never met the gentleman, myself. Heard he's very rich and very fancy. Them as know tell he's not the marryin' kind. That's why yer here, isn't it?"

Rosi nodded. She was not sure why, but she was sure that a nod was expected.

Spartacus, who had been half holding his breath for the entire conversation, nodded back and sighed.

Rosi stood up deciding she needed some time alone. She

paced back and forth along the beach as she fingered her little St. Christopher, praying that someone would be watching over her.

Motioning Spartacus to Rosi, she had him gather the cleanest clothes he could find and then go with her a short distance away from the rest of the men so he could re-bandage her arm. He sniffed the wound and smiled slightly. She would keep her arm, he assured her as he commented once again on how fast it was healing. Rosi trusted his judgment, but to her way of thinking, it was not healing fast enough.

Though she knew it would hurt, Rosi had him bind it as tight as he could.

As they joined the rest of the men, Rosi removed her sword and then had Harry help her remove her boots. Curiously, the men watched her.

"They'll just drag me down," she explained. No one got it. "The water. Too much weight. Who's coming?"

They stood there awkwardly.

"What's wrong now?" Rosi asked.

Zablonski looked to Spartacus, who shrugged and turned away. The sergeant major stepped forward. "It's the water."

"It's ocean water. Don't drink it, that's all. It isn't acid or anything."

"Beggin' your pardon, Miss. With all due respect, there isn't none of us can swim," Zablonski said.

Jeez! "Just...hold your breath." Rosi would not admit it, but she had not known that trick until she was almost nine.

"Captain," Zablonski said. "We aren't stupid. We know that. It's just that...well...none of us can swim."

"I have to get out there. I have to know what they're doing, and the answer is in The Castle. I'll go alone if no one will come with me," Rosi responded.

The men were embarrassed. They were humiliated at not being able to help their leader. As much as they wanted to go with her, none was willing to brave the sea. They simply could not swim.

Rosi should have thought about that earlier. She should have

known. She had certainly read enough books about the olden
days that pointed out that few people could swim. Even Boats,
who was comfortable enough to splash about in the surf, shook
his head sadly when she asked him. "No, ma'am," was all he said.

What could she do now? She had already said that she was
going to go there along the base of the cliffs. She could not back
out now, not and keep her men.

Rosi looked along the path she would be taking. The tide was
low. There would certainly be enough handholds, she could see
that. Much of the distance could be done scrabbling from rock to
rock, but sooner or later swimming would be necessary.

In for a penny, in for a pound, Rosi thought. That was an apropos
saying, she smiled to herself. "Wait for me. I'll be back sometime
tomorrow. Maybe the next day. When I can."

Zablonski stepped forward. "Some of us will go up to the
tree line. If they capture you, we'll do our best to help."

"Thank you." She took his hand and gave it a squeeze.

She started into the surf.

"I'll go with you!" Someone called out.

Everyone turned to see Will standing by the bottom of the
large dune.

"I'll go with you," Will repeated.

Rosi glanced at Will, who was being slapped on the back by
some of the men. His attention distracted, Rosi pinched her
cheeks just as she went up to him.

"Will."

"Rosi."

They stood there, awkwardly looking at each other.

"Last time I saw you, you tried to kill me," Rosi said.

"I've been thinking a lot," he replied. "I'm sorry."

"That's enough. That's all I need," Rosi said. "Let's go."

Will handed his musket to one of the men and took the pistol
Zablonski held out to him, shoving it in his belt. He stripped off
his jacket and vest. Farming had been good to him, Rosi thought,
looking him up and down, careful not to make it *too* obvious.

Leading the way, Rosi stepped into the surf. It was then that she realized there was something else she had not thought about. It was the middle of April and the water was cold. She took a deep breath and moved on. Soon the water was up to her knees, and she could feel the low waves tugging at her feet as the water drifted back to the ebbing tide.

This is the easy part, Rosi thought, waiting for Will to catch up to her.

* * *

THE men followed Rosi and Will until the ground dropped away, and the two were in the water above their waists. It was not getting any warmer.

"This isn't the brightest idea I've ever had," she said to Will. She smiled back at the men.

"It's an idea," he replied. "That's something."

After about fifty yards, they were able to climb up out of the water and leap from rock to rock for while.

Rosi was the first to miss her footing, falling back and becoming completely submerged. As Will pulled her out, she could hear the men laughing. After she was done coughing up salt water, she stood up on the rock and bowed grandly to them.

Soon, they were around a bend and out of sight of the others.

"This is just about the stupidest idea I've ever had," she said. They were standing on a narrow ledge.

Will laughed softly. "I doubt that."

Rosi smiled and pushed Will gently. It was enough. He lost his balance and with a yell dropped into the sea.

"Now, we're even," she said, sitting down and holding out a hand to help him up.

The low tide allowed them to make some steady and quick progress. As the tide began to rise, they slowed down. Will took point. He had full use of both arms. Rosi's left still could not support her whole weight. After about an hour, it was little more than useless.

By the time the sun was gone, high tide was there in force. Several times, Rosi was almost washed away from the cliff face, only to be saved as waves punched her back against the rock.

Will decided to stay close.

The waxing moon and the stars gave some light. That was a small help.

Rosi could go no further. She found a perch and glued herself to it.

Will was able to go a bit further, but he was forced back shortly.

"We're almost there," he said. "If we can get around this outcropping, it'll be much easier. I could see light from the British campfires."

"I can't." Rosi wedged herself in more tightly. She was tired and wanted to cry.

When the waves were sucked away, they could see that the cliff face kept going down. Low tide was not going to be much easier.

Then at the same moment they both saw the dark hole just under the tidemark.

"It's worth a try," Will said.

Before Rosi could say anything, Will waded over and allowed the water to carry him down. Water gushed out of the hole, giving Will a few seconds to see inside.

He crawled back to her. "It goes all the way through."

"We'll be killed."

"You can't wait." He reached out a hand and held her against the cliff. "We have to try." He turned to go.

Rosi grabbed him with her left hand, biting back the scream that accompanied the pain.

"What is it?" he cried above the noise.

Rosi considered what to say. "To hell with it!" She pulled him to her and pressed her lips to his. After just a moment, they parted. "Just in case!"

Will put one arm around her and they floated, or was it crashed, over to the hole.

"One at a time!" he cried as the water gushed out.

He gave Rosi a push into the hole and began following her in.

Rosi found a fork in the tunnel. "Which way?"

"Left!"

The water forced her to the right.

She screamed as she was dragged along the rock tunnel. The rock disappeared and as the water was sucked out, Rosi fell into a dark place.

She could not feel the walls with her hands. Her feet could not touch the floor. When the water came back in, her head had no problem finding the ceiling. She did just what most people would do in such a situation...she panicked.

Rosi could not see. She was swallowing too much water. She swung her arms around wildly, hoping to hit something that she could hold on to. She was hurled several times against one, or many, of the walls of this little cavern. She was flipped around and spun. Which way was up? Where was the light? "Will! Will!" she screamed.

"Calm down!" Will yelled. "Stop screaming!"

Gasping, coughing, spitting, and choking, Rosi did her best to be quiet. She could barely hear Will over the waves.

"I'm here," he called out. "At the entrance. Can you see me?"

"No!"

"I can't see you, either. Follow my voice! Reach my hand!"

Rosi was tossed up and down a couple more times before her fingers brushed against Will. He grabbed at her hand, but it slipped from his grip when the water dropped, sucking Rosi down.

Rosi felt water pouring down on her, and she was tossed up again.

This time Will got a good grip and began dragging her back up the short tunnel. When they reached the fork, Will was just able to get her around and moving in the right direction when the water shot through. The narrowness of the tunnel created a pressure that gave the water much more power than the waves.

Will and Rosi came out the other side of the tunnel like shot from a cannon. This probably saved their lives, for they cleared the rocks on the other side and landed in empty water. It was rough, but the two were able to right themselves before the tide carried them back against the cliff.

Will got a good foothold first and dragged Rosi up next to him. They hung there trying to catch their breaths.

Rosi retched, vomiting out saltwater.

They were both battered and bruised. Rosi's hands were bleeding and she could feel that her feet and legs had been skinned and cut. She could even taste blood in her mouth. Will was not in much better shape.

They had, however, reached the other side. Rosi looked up and saw the silhouette of The Castle high above them.

"I hope this path has an elevator," she said.

"A what?"

"I'll tell you later. Let's move on."

The going was much easier here. Soon they came to another opening in the cliff face. This time the opening led to a small lagoon like area. The water was calm. There was a chimney through the rock, running all the way up the cliff to the property above. On the far edge of the area there was a small dock carved out of the rock, to which was moored one of the boats the British had used to get here. They would not have to swim back to the beach. Will could row.

Rosi felt like cheering. Will, who would have to do all the rowing, was not quite as thrilled.

Running up the side of the cliff was a series of metal rungs.

"A secret entrance." Rosi laughed. "I'm surprised I didn't know about this." She was really not surprised. There was no reason for her to have known about this place.

"If we could get enough men and some boats—" Will started.

"No. We might be able to slip in, but they would see the boats. There are still ships out there. If we got caught in the open water, they would annihilate us."

They agreed to rest for a few minutes before trying the ladder. Looking around, they saw signs that the British had been here. A broken musket lay on the landing. One of those big soldier hats Rosi had seen in a television show bobbed up and down in the water. A pack sat in the bottom of the boat.

Will searched the sack. Soldiers often carried most of their life possessions in their packs and whoever had left this pack had a rather sad life. Will found a few coins and a full powder horn, which he kept, and a crust of bread, which he shared with Rosi. There was little else other than an old shirt and some strips of cloth. Down at the bottom of the sack, he found a small jar filled with maggots.

"Yuck!" Rosi cringed. "Why would any one have that?"

"For doctoring," Will explained. "Better than a surgeon. Safer."

"How so?"

"If you're wounded, they will eat away any bad skin. Leaves the healthy skin. I've seen it done."

"Disgusting." The thought made Rosi want to retch.

"Better than dying of gangrene."

Thank God twenty first century medicine was so much more civilized, Rosi thought. She was surprised when Will slipped the jar in his pack.

He shrugged when she looked at him.

Rosi had to figure out how to get up the ladder. There was no way she could climb it.

"I saw a movie once," she said.

"A what?"

"Never mind." She had to be careful what she said. Will was somewhat brighter and more curious than most of his friends. "It was about a spy who climbed mountains and he had to find out who the assassin was and kill him."

"Okay. And?" Will was a bit confused. Rosi could not blame him. The movie had confused her as well.

"It has given me an idea," she said. "How long is your rope?"

"Fifty, sixty feet, maybe."

"How high is that?" She pointed at the ladder.

"Don't know." He got up, moved closer and investigated. "A lot higher than that."

"We'll have to do this in stages, then." Rosi's plan was simple.

Will would climb up a ways, loop the rope through the rung, and tie it around his waist. Rosi would already have an end tied around her waist. Will would jump. Rosi would be carried up. Rinse and repeat.

"What and repeat?" Will asked.

"Don't worry about it." She ran her fingers through her hair. She felt disgusting. She had been able to rinse herself in the stream every day. However, not only was she surrounded by men who might *accidentally* wander into her bathing area, the water was frigid. And, there was no soap. If only she had a comb.

Will insisted on climbing all the way up and checking out what was at the top before he helped Rosi up. "There's a ledge about twenty feet from the top." The climb had not been as easy as the young man had thought it would be and it took him some time to catch his breath when he came back down. "We'd better stop to rest there because once we get to the top. We're pretty much in the open for a ways until we reach the shelter of the house. Whatever the case, we should wait until the moon sets before we go."

The last week had been something of an education for Rosi. She always thought that the moon rose when the sun set and vice-versa. She began to realize, with some explanatory help from Spartacus, that the moon rose when it rose and set when it set and sometimes that was in the middle of the day and sometimes it was at night but it was not tied to the sun at all.

That was about all Spartacus had been able to tell her, but she figured out the rest on her own. The rotation of the Earth and the orbit of the moon made the moon go around the Earth, from point A back to point A, in about twenty hours. The Earth's rotation in relationship to the Sun was approximately twenty four hours. Therefore, the two were not in exact sync.

Rosi could practically hear Andy beating his head against the proverbial wall. "Exact figures, Rosi!" he would be screaming. She did not know the exact intervals, and she did not have a calculator, so thank you very much, Andy, and go away for now!

Once she thought about it, she could vaguely remember

Brother Sebastian, her physics teacher last year in New York, talking about orbits and rotation at some point, but all she could remember was that he had a very nice nose.

Because Will was heavier than Rosi, she thought that he would jump and she would rise gently upwards. Sadly, this was not a movie. The rope was not a slick nylon. The rung was not a pulley. Will came down in jerks and Rosi rose, bouncing against the ladder and the rocks and anything else she could bounce against.

Eventually they were able to come up with a way to get Rosi up without too much jostling and without too much acceleration. After several trips, Rosi made it to the small ledge. Will climbed up after her.

"Kirk was here," Rosi said when Will reached her. "On this spot."

"How do you know?"

Rosi held up a cigarette butt.

"What's that?"

"Exactly." Rosi tossed it away and watched it spin down and out of sight.

The ledge was pretty small, and one end wrapped around out of sight forming an alcove that was filled by some sort of bush. They sat there for some minutes to let Will rest.

Rosi was hardly exhausted by the ascent, so she spent her time tossing little pebbles into the void, listening to them hit the water or the landing or the boat, and trying to remember her physics and gravity and acceleration. She had no luck. Brother Sebastian had been wearing jeans that day. So she and Will came up with game where they would drop a pebble and see who could hit the unseen boat below. Will won with seven out of ten to Rosi's four.

Will turned to her. Maybe he was going to kiss her she thought, and moistened her lips hoping she did not look too obvious and realizing that Will probably could not see her all that well. "Did the spy get the assassin?" he asked.

Shoot! "Oh, the spy killed everyone."

"So he got the assassin."

"No," Rosi explained. "The assassin was his best friend and saved his life."

"I see."

"No you don't."

"No. I don't." He started up again.

Rosi sighed and tossed a couple more pebbles and hit the boat twice. In order to brush off her hand, she tossed the rest of her handful of pebbles behind her.

She heard something.

"Will!" she whispered loudly.

"What?"

"Wait!"

She groped around for some more pebbles and threw them behind her. She heard a thud that should not have been there.

"Come back down!"

Will rejoined her. "What is it?"

As an answer, she threw another handful of pebbles into the old bush.

Thud! Thud! Thud!

They looked at each other.

Will took up a small rock and threw it.

Thud!

"Get on the ladder," he said. "I need room."

Will reached through the bush, catching his sleeves and scratching his arms even more. "There's something back here. Feels like a door of some sort."

Kirk had not learned about *all* of the secret entrances, Rosi smiled to herself. "Can you get to it?"

Will could, but he had to rip out much of the bush. "It won't budge. It isn't stuck, it's locked."

"Is there a keyhole?"

Will's hands searched. "Yes. You wouldn't have a key, would you?"

"The universal kind." Rosi pulled out her pistol and handed it to Will.

He pointed it at the lock and pulled the trigger and was greeted by a soft click. "Powder's wet."

Crap! "Wait! Didn't you find some—"

"Good thought!" Will took out the powder horn he had found below and checked it. The powder was fine. The young man was an experienced hunter, so he had little problem reloading the pistol. This time, it fired. The noise was loud. Too loud. In seconds, they could hear two soldiers above them.

Will grabbed Rosi and pulled her to him as the soldiers threw light down the path.

They could hear the two soldiers arguing, but too far away to make out any words. The soldiers, being rather lazy, did not come very far down the path, so Rosi and Will really did not have anything to worry about.

"I think they're gone," Will said, as the light and the noise went away.

Rosi had no problems with Will holding her tightly. She rather liked it. "They might come back," she whispered gently in his ear.

"You think?"

"Definitely."

"Rosi." Will was trying to control his breathing. "Maybe we should try the door."

"I'm in no hurry."

Will swallowed, trying to remain professional. "Captain Carol," he forced out.

The words hit Rosi like a bucket of ice water. Will was right.

It took them a while, but they were able to force the door in enough that they could squeeze through.

CHAPTER 3

WILL lit a taper, so they had some light.

Some was the key word. They could see well enough to avoid walking into the walls. This place would be cool to explore, Rosi decided. But flashlights would be necessary. It looked like they were in some sort of dungeon.

Even though it took them out of their way, Rosi insisted that they check out a couple of the cells. The doors were made of some sort of metal that Rosi could not recognize, but which she was sure had not existed in colonial times. The rooms were oddly shaped with no right angles and walls made of a synthetic material that looked like stone. What was really odd was that the doors appeared to have no locks and opened easily and silently. One door was closed and they could not open it no matter how hard they tried. As Will walked on, not really caring to check out all the stuff Rosi found fascinating, Rosi put her ear to the door. Faintly, oh so faintly, it sounded like there was music playing inside. If only she could hear it just a bit better, she was sure that she would recognize the tune.

"Come on!" Will called softly back.

Rosi cleared her mind. She had things to do here and now. She could investigate later.

After winding around for what seemed like an eternity, they found a staircase that led up to a door. They gently pushed open the door they found and started to close it behind them.

"Stop!" Rosi noticed that the other side of the door looked like a set of shelves. "We might not be able to find our way back." It was clearly a secret door. She saw a small piece of wood and wedged it between the door and the wall.

The room they were in had once been a wine cellar. Rosi had never been here, either, but it was clear that someone had, and recently. There were no bottles left on the racks. The floor was littered with broken glass and was sticky with spilled wine.

One British soldier was lying in a corner.

Will handed the taper to Rosi and approached him cautiously. There was no need for concern. The man was dead. His face was bruised and someone had slit his throat. He had been stripped of anything valuable or useful. Including his boots, Rosi thought sadly as she picked a small sliver of glass from her one of her feet.

The rest of this cellar level was in much the same state of destruction, without any more bodies. The British had taken anything of value and, in what had clearly been a fit of pique, destroyed everything else. There was even some graffiti on the walls. The words were different from the ones she was used to seeing, but the sentiments were the same. Bored and angry youths, lashing out impotently. Harmless rebellion. The language was a lot more scatological and profane than the language youths used in her day, but the idea was the same and the quality of the drawings just as bad.

At the top of the next set of stairs, they heard voices beyond the door. Will blew out the taper and waited. When the voices moved on, he stuck his head around the edge of the door to make sure all was clear.

Rosi and Will made their way onto the first floor of The Castle.

The place was oddly quiet. If Rosi had been quartered here, she would have moved her men inside the building instead of having them set up camp outside. *Very strange*. But she was not British and was not sure how they did things.

In the front hall they noticed quite a few boxes had been packed and carefully stacked.

Rosi motioned Will to follow her up the stairs. The long hallway upstairs was a disaster area. One thing was clear though, the British had not been able to get into many of the rooms on the second floor. Several of the doors had been hacked at with hatchets, beaten with something, and even shot.

Rosi knew that if the doors did not want to open, then they would not open.

Rosi led Will down a hallway to the left side of the house. Praying silently, she placed her hand on the door handle. The door slid open silently.

This room was filled with stuff. There was furniture, paintings, piles of books, all sorts of things. Will was in awe of the veritable treasure trove. There was more wealth in this room than he, his mother, and all their friends would see in a lifetime. Even Rosi was impressed by the paintings and other *objets d'art*.

"This must be what the soldiers have been looking for," Will said.

The soldiers, maybe, Rosi thought. Kirk, though, was after more than just money. The treasure was simply a glittering lure to keep the British here while he figured out what he was after.

Rosi went to one of the windows and peered out.

The soldiers were camped out in front. There were a few fires lit, but most of the men were asleep. Beyond the light from the fires, the shadows of the watch stood bunched together in a few places.

"I don't think they'll be bothering us," Rosi said.

"Why do you say that?" Will wanted to trust her judgment, but was not sure if he could.

"Trust me. Stay away from the windows, though," she added. The building might resist all sorts of abuse, but Rosi feared that it would not be able to withstand a full scale assault.

Having little choice in the matter, Will nodded.

They moved on.

In moments, they were further into The Castle than Rosi had ever been. The hallways ended, and Rosi and Will went through an ever confusing sequence of doors and rooms. Some places were closed to Rosi, so she did not worry about them.

One door led to a long gallery overlooking a large room. In one corner of the room, there were several huddled shapes. One of the shapes moved, and Will pulled Rosi down behind the solid railing and out of sight.

Rosi pulled away and sneaked a look. In the dim light, she could tell these were not soldiers.

She put her wrists together and shook them, signing they are tied up. Will thought for a moment. He nodded understanding.

Rosi tapped her wrist and made a circle in the air. *Later.*

Will shook his head.

Pointing to herself and then to Will she made the sign of them walking, trying to tell him they would leave and return later.

He got that one.

Eventually they found a large wooden door that opened for them and led to a circular stone room. It was the south tower. This was exciting. Rosi ran up the stairs to the top of the tower. From there they could see the harbor, the town, and everything else.

A few fires burned in the town. There was an occasional flash and Rosi thought she heard the sound of shots being fired, but she was not sure.

There was not enough light to see much, but in the morning they would be able to see everything without being seen by anyone. Before going back down, they both looked out to the tree line, wondering if their friends were safe.

They really were not sure what to do. They pretty much had free run of this floor, but decided that the first floor would be far too dangerous.

Rosi knew there was a third floor someplace, presumably over the second floor, she decided pedantically. No access, though.

It was Will who found the little doorway in the hall leading from the tower. He tried to open it, but it was stuck.

"Locked?" Rosi asked.

Will shook his head.

Rosi put her hand to it, and it slid to one side.

In most of the rooms there was a little light, but here there was none. It took Will a moment to light another taper.

"We don't have too many of these," he said.

There was not a room beyond this door. There was not a

hallway. There was a crawlspace.

It was a tight fit, but Will crawled in. Rosi followed.

"We can either go down or across," Will said, stopping.

"Down," Rosi said.

Rosi was fascinated by the crawlspace. Apparently The Caste
was more solidly built than it looked. There were plenty of beams
and support. It was almost as if the builders had supplied ladders
between the walls. Most of the walls were either solid wood or
stone. While Rosi and Will still had to be quiet, they were not in
as much danger of being heard as they would have been had the
walls been made of plaster.

Though the crawlspace was accessible, for whatever reason,
Rosi was noticed spaces just out of the beam of candlelight that
looked as if they had not been used in awhile. The wood was
rough leaving splinters in their hands and feet. And a cloud of
dust filtered through the air almost causing them to cough. They
would have to be careful.

It was Will who noticed the tiny air holes in the walls. Not
only the holes admit tiny shafts of light, but it allowed them to
see into the rooms they were passing.

Most of the rooms were empty, but Rosi was sure it would be
useful sometime.

Will blew out the candle. They waited for their eyes to grow
accustomed to the faint light. The flame made them nervous. For
most every cloud of dust that they stirred threatened to catch fire.
Rosi had witnessed some of the dust particles spark to life,
dancing in a terrifying yet lovely waltz as they drifted and spun
downward, only to disappear into the blackness below.

"There's a passage to the right," Will whispered. "It gets
lighter down there."

"Be careful."

The passage was hewn into rock. Down from there was a
larger passage that ran from a large set of double doors up a small
flight of stairs, past a smaller passage and down another flight of
stairs and around a bend. It felt familiar to Rosi.

Will stepped cautiously out into the passage, motioning for

Rosi to stay where she was.

When Will turned back around to guide Rosi out, he looked confused. He began waving his arms about right in front of Rosi. A look of terror came over his face. He ran up and down the larger passage beating against the stone.

What was he doing? "Will?"

He froze. "Where are you?"

"I'm right where you left me."

"Where's that?"

"You're standing right in front of me."

Will froze. "It's just a stone wall."

"Nonsense!"

"Shh!"

The door at the top of the stairs was opening.

Will pounded on the air in front of Rosi's face.

Just as the door swung fully open, Rosi reached out and grabbed Will. She pulled him in roughly, the two of them falling to the ground.

They froze where they were in a tangled heap as two soldiers walked by.

"I can't stand these stupid reports," one soldier said.

"I can't stand taking orders from some sailor chap," said the other.

"I'm with you, mate. 'im and that boy of 'is. Give me the willies."

"This 'ouse is what give me the willies."

"Only in 'ere for a minute."

"God, I need a drink. You got anything?"

"Yeah. Shh! Don't let that bloody sailor officer see, 'e'll 'ave you flogged." The first soldier took out a small flask and took a drink from it before handing it to his comrade.

"Yeah. Prob'ly 'ave that boy of 'is do it," the second soldier said, taking a drink. "'e's a bloody strange one."

"I don't know what's worse, coming now when it's too bloody quiet or in the day when that boy is playing 'is games."

"I don't want to think of it." He handed the flask back.

They moved down the hall quickly.

Rosi started to untangle herself.

"No!" whispered Will. "They're coming back in just a minute."

It was a full five minutes, Rosi suspected, before the men came hurrying back. They did not linger this time, being anxious to get outside of the building.

Reluctantly, Rosi pulled herself up and moved towards the mouth of the passage.

"What happened out there?" she asked.

"It's just a wall." Will remembered what had happened and his face clouded over.

"You stay here."

"I can't let you go out there alone."

"Don't start any of that macho crap, Will. I know this place. I have to look. I have to know what to do. You have to stay here so you can get me back in. Okay?"

She held up one finger, pointed at him, then pointed at the ground. "Stay!" she mouthed silently.

Will nodded.

When Rosi stepped out into the passage, it was almost as if she felt herself walking through an infinitesimally thin layer of water. When she turned back, she saw that there was merely a stone wall there. There was no passage, no entrance, no sign of Will. Nothing.

She knew exactly where she was. She gave Will a quick wave and walked into her rooms.

There was no one in the upper room. There were a few packs and a couple of boxes, but little else. Rosi stopped at the head of the stairs and took a couple of steps down very slowly.

She looked around to let her eyes adjust. There was someone, Kirk, standing out on the battlement surveying his realm, Rosi thought with a sneer. *He would take my room, the little cockroach.* Rosi smiled. Kirk was smoking a cigarette.

Over by the wall where her bed should have been was where Kirk had put his bedding. There was someone else there, too.

Must be the navy officer the soldiers had been talking about.

"What are you doing out there, boy?" the officer called out.

"I'll be a minute."

"Get back in here now. You have a busy day tomorrow."

"Fine!" Kirk shot back insolently. He flicked his cigarette out in a long arc and watched as it tumbled into the rocks and the sea below. He came inside.

Kirk froze as he passed the steps. His head turned left and right and he started sniffing. Rosi pulled herself as close to the wall as she could.

"You watch your tone with me, boy!" the officer snapped.

"I'll speak like I want to, Beau. I got us in the damn place, didn't I?"

Rosi heard rather than saw the slap. Kirk barely whimpered.

"I said, watch your tone!"

Slap!

"Perhaps I need to teach you another lesson, boy. You're getting too big for your britches."

Both Kirk and Beau laughed.

Slap!

Rosi edged her way up and out.

Near where she thought she had entered the large hallway, she stopped and pushed against the wall.

"Wrong," she heard Will whisper. She saw his arm stick out. It was weird. It was simply a disembodied arm sticking out of solid stone. Must be some trick with lights, she thought. She took Will's arm and let him pull her in. There was a split second, just as her face approached the wall, that she balked. Walking face first into a stone wall could not be good for your looks, she knew. Will, not hearing her internal monologue, kept pulling. She felt the funny sensation again and she was through.

"What do we do now?" he asked.

"We wait until tomorrow. Can you remember how to get back to the second floor?"

"I don't know."

"Well, try."

It took them a while, but they entered the large tower room. From there it was a simple matter to find a room filled with boxes and things. The two were tired and grateful to be someplace relatively safe.

"I wish we could build a fire," Will stated. The temperature had dropped over the last few minutes and it was quite chilly. He went digging around the boxes looking for some sort of blanket.

Rosi pushed the curtains aside and peaked outside. It was the middle of the night and she probably looked like a wreck from all the crawling around in the dust and the dirt.

"Here we are, Rosi." Will produced an old blanket and some sort of tarpaulin that had been used to cover some boxes. "You choose."

The tarpaulin looked warmer. The blanket looked more comfortable. Rosi chose the blanket.

They wrapped themselves up and chose a corner to camp out in.

"We should keep a watch," Will said.

Rosi yawned. "Yeah," she said, putting her head down. "Wake me up in two hours."

Officers had to make decisions, she thought to herself with a smile. This one just got to punish Will for his macho attitudes.

* * *

AT first, when Rosi awakened to see that is was light outside, she was flattered that Will had stayed up all night to let her sleep. *What a sweet boy! He must really like me!* He deserved a big kiss.

Rosi then sat up and saw that Will had also fallen asleep.

"Get up!" she snapped, kicking at him.

There was no food. Will had brought some food in his bag, but it had been soaked in salt water and otherwise crushed by the journey. It was useless. It was worse than useless because it was food but they could not eat it and it reminded them of how hungry they were. There was water in a flask. They each drank some.

A lot of the dirt and grime they had gotten on them last night and the day before had crusted over. Rosi would have adored a nice hot bath right now. Even more, she would have killed for the chance to lower herself down into her nice hot bubbly Jacuzzi, pop open a root beer, munch on some pizza, and watch a good old-fashioned action movie where the good guy does not hurt all over in the morning and the girl never gets bruised or scarred. Will had to help her stand up. Just about every vertebra in her back creaked.

"Christ in a hand basket," Rosi groaned, stretching and yawning.

"What does that mean?"

Rosi had no idea. "I heard it someplace. Or maybe I thought I heard it and didn't really. It's a lot nicer than what I wanted to say, believe me. Ready? Let's see what's going on."

"Any idea where to start?"

Rosi did not have to think very long. When the screaming started, the two quite easily followed the noise to the long gallery.

* * *

WITHIN seconds, Rosi could tell that is was a girl screaming. Someone was giggling. Kirk!

Rosi crawled out onto the gallery. She wanted to look over the rail, but decided not to risk it.

The girl had stopped screaming and was now sobbing, begging Kirk to stop. A couple of other voices pleaded with his as well.

Kirk's only response was to demand a fresh glass of wine. "Not you, you old crone. She can get it for me." Kirk did not sound angry. He did not sound cold. He was simply asking for a glass of wine, as if from a waitress.

It was the casualness to his voice that saved his life, Rosi thought. Had he been raving or snarling or even evil sounding, she probably would have gone after him. Something in his voice, though, scared her. Sent a chill deep into her. She could see on Will's face that he felt the same way.

Rosi could hear the girl stumble across the room. The first

glass fell and shattered on the stone floor.

A man laughed. "Tisn't funny, Beau," Kirk said. "That was a rather nice glass. Girl, try another glass. Bring it to me by the fire and then get back on the table."

"Please," the girl pleaded.

Rosi carefully raised herself and glanced over the rail. Below, an officer, the one Kirk called Beau, was lounging in a large chair. Next to him was a table filled with plates on which food had been heaped so high that it dripped over the edges. There were also pitchers of juice and water, and bottles of wine on the table. Rosi was tempted to give herself up if only to have a couple of minutes at the table.

A young woman stood next to the table, shakily trying to fill a wine goblet without spilling any. Her back was bloody and her blouse torn. Her legs and arms were covered with welts and bruises.

Rosi noticed an older man and woman, a young man, and a child huddled together in near the corner.

Kirk stood by a roaring fire. Several irons were lying half in the flames. Kirk had slipped a glove on and was checking to see how hot they were. Suddenly Kirk froze. He sniffed the air.

Rosi ducked down.

"What is it, boy?" asked someone. Must be Beau, Rosi told herself. Mosley.

"I smell something," Kirk said. "Something familiar." Rosi heard him sniff several times. "Never mind," he said after a few moments.

"Your nose had best come up with something," Mosley said. "Cromwell is getting tired of waiting. Find a way to get into those rooms. Find what Cromwell wants. I like the way you think, boy. And the way you are dealing with this girl. But there are some lessons I have yet to teach you."

"Here's your wine, sir," the girl said.

"Then get back on the table," Kirk said with a yawn in his voice.

"Show some manners, boy," Mosley snapped.

Kirk grumbled.

"What was that, boy?"

"Thank you for the wine," Kirk said politely.

"Please!" the girl sobbed.

"Do be so kind as to get back on the table," Kirk stated again more politely.

"Please!" This time, the girl was joined by other voices. Were they her family?

"Please, get back on the table." Kirk's voice was too calm.

Will reached out and grabbed Rosi. She started. She had not realized that she had been about to stand up.

"You will get back on the table," Kirk went on. "Sally, isn't it?"

"Yes, sir."

"Sally." Kirk said in a singsong voice. "Sally. What a plain name. A plain name for a plain girl. Ha, ha."

Mosley chortled.

"What?" Kirk snarled, fury filling his voice. "Sally? Wasn't that witty? A plain name for a plain girl. I like it when you laugh at my jokes! Laugh! All of you!"‟

They obediently laughed.

"Better." Just like that, the anger and rage were gone. He had no emotional involvement, Rosi could tell. He was simply acting.

"Please tell us what you want to know," a new voice said. From the accent and the fear in the voice, Rosi figured it was Sally's father. "Please let us go."

"Simple," Kirk giggled. "Beatitude has hidden something in one of the upstairs rooms. Tell us which room and how to get inside.

"The Carol sent Sally home almost a year ago," the father sobbed. "She has never been in the rooms upstairs. She only cleans down here. She knows nothing. Don't you think we'd tell ye if we knew?"

"Perhaps," Kirk conceded. "I would like to be sure, though."

Rosi heard him take one of the irons out of the fire.

As much as Rosi wanted to leave the room, she knew she had

to stay as long as she could. She tried to close her ears, but could not. Rosi was sure that she would never forget the pain, the fear, the rage, and the shame of impotent helplessness she could hear in the voices of the girl's family, and that she felt in herself.

Finally, after what seemed an eternity, Sally stopped screaming.

"Is she dead?" Mosley asked.

Rosi prayed the answer would be yes.

"Not quite," Kirk said. He yawned loudly. "I feel like a smoke. C'mon, Beau. Let's take a walk."

Mosley grumbled something that Rosi did not hear. Kirk giggled as they left the room.

Carefully, Rosi raised herself, as did Will. They surveyed the wreckage below.

After a few moments, Rosi and Will left.

* * *

"I'm gonna kill him," Rosi said between shudders. They had crawled back to the room. Neither had spoken for some minutes. Each had been shaking too hard. Rosi had tried to throw up, but there had been nothing in her stomach except a bile that burned her throat.

"A guinea says I get to him first!" Will snarled. "First, we've got to get those people out of there."

"We can't."

"We have to help that girl!" Will insisted.

"No! We have to leave her, whatever happens." Rosi could feel her tears streaming down her cheeks.

"What are you talking about?"

"If we rescue them, the English will know we can get in. They must think they're alone here." Rosi knew she was right. She could tell that Will knew as well, even though the idea offended him.

Making her way to the top of the tower, she looked toward town. Rosi felt Will beside her. The fire had died down. There were quite a few barges in the harbor. Some were pulled up on the shore.

The ship that had gotten stuck on the reef was still there, but most of it was under water. Three British ships were huddled together in the middle of the harbor.

"I think I know how to get the Brits away from town," Rosi said. "I believe I know how to beat them."

"How?"

"We need to get back to the others. I need to talk to them."

***

SHORTLY after dark Rosi and Will made their way back to the cellar and out to the ladder.

Rosi was hungry, scared, angry and weak. Her whole body was shaking. Will had to lower her down the ladder carefully. They got down, got in the boat, and Will rowed them back to the beach.

"We were worried," Spartacus said, lifting Rosi out of the boat.

"Hide the boat. We'll need it," Rosi said. "We're going back to the village."

She sent a squad to go and relieve Zablonski, who had been watching The Castle since Rosi's departure. Both Will and Spartacus tried speaking to her as they made their way back to the village, but Rosi refused to open her mouth. The men had gotten used to the path over the last few days, so they made pretty good time.

Once they arrived, Rosi set a watch and then found as private a part of the stream as she could. Not even bothering to take off her clothes, she sat in the water and let the cold current sweep over her. She grabbed a handful of sand and pebbles and began scrubbing herself all over. She felt filthy, and it was not just dirt.

Holding her breath, she lowered her head under the surface and kept it there until her lungs screamed for air. She did this several times, then tied her hair back and climbed out of the water.

She looked towards the village. They could wait. Daylight

would be the best time to discuss her plan. Rosi needed to be alone. She wandered away and found a hillside to sit on.

"You're going to catch a chill," Will stated as he came into sight. He had made a lot of noise. On purpose, Rosi was sure.

"I don't care," she grumbled.

"But we do."

"Fine." She allowed him to put a blanket over her.

Will sat next to her. "The men have faith in you."

"I'll probably get them all killed."

"They know that. But they're with you. We're with you. I'm with you."

"You won't be. I'm sending you away tomorrow."

"But, Rosi—"

"I'm sending you away. I need you to do something. I owe that to Zilla."

"That wasn't your fault."

"Don't you understand, Will? This is all my fault. I'm not sure how to explain it, but it is." Rosi was crying and it made her feel so young.

"No. I guess I don't understand."

They sat quietly for a minute.

"Where will you send me?"

"I'll tell you tomorrow."

"Rosi—"

"I'm your captain, Will. I order. You obey."

Will looked offended. He stood up straight and saluted. "Aye, captain." He started off, but came back and squatted next to her.

"Captain."

"Yes, Will."

"Just in case." He put his hands on her cheeks and kissed her.

When he stood up and turned to leave, Rosi stuck out a foot and tripped him. She grabbed his shoulder, turned him onto his back, and sat on him.

She laughed. "I'm going to show you how we kiss where I come from."

And she did.

Later, Rosi lay with her head on Will's lap and contemplated her boots. They were much too big and made her feet look big. She needed a new pair. Or maybe some nice sandals to show off what remained of her feet. Every inch of her body hurt. Eventually, someone would make her put on one of those horrid dresses and she would end up looking as frumpy as Angie had.

Poor Angie. What was Rosi going to tell her parents? If, that is, she could get home. That was the million dollar question.

No. Deal with Kirk first. Then worry about getting back.

Will was asleep, snoring softly.

Good idea.

Rosi pulled the blanket over her. Her clothes were still soaking wet, but the blanket gave her some warmth. She rolled over onto her side and took Will's hand.

Sleep came quickly.

CHAPTER 4

ANDY and Dan felt like they had been walking for days, which might actually have been the case. Both of them noticed that instead of moving steadily from east to west in roughly a straight line, the sun seemed to be moving in odd little circles and zigzags. Then the sun would set and the moon would do much the same sort of dance in the night sky. This happened several times. The two young men were confused.

They had been surprised, though pleased, to learn that the Ful'puli spoke English. Very good English. Better than maybe they should have.

"Retrograde motion," Dan suggested, trying to show off for the young Fula'puli woman.

"Epicycles," Andy countered, annoyingly.

The path they were on confused them. They had been told to stay on the path and only to leave with one of the Fula'puli. This made going to the bathroom really awkward. Each step seemed to take them much further in relationship to the world off the path than it did on the path, like walking on a moving sidewalk.

They stopped fairly often to eat and drink. The Indians did not seem to be in much of a hurry. They did not seem to be very talkative. Dan tried several times to engage the girl, H'Cab in conversation but did little else than waste his breath. Through bits of conversation they realized the she was, in fact, a princess. When they did stop, Dan and Andy looked back and saw that there was no path behind them. When they first noticed this, they each wanted to say something, but ended up merely shrugging. There was no point in trying to come up with an explanation.

From time to time, they would cross right through a village or farmstead, which had been built on the path. When this happened, one of the Indians would make sure to grab the hand of one of the boys. Dan began to see this coming and made sure to be near H'Cab as they walked through.

"Safer this way," H'Cab explained after noticing Dan's actions.

One time, when they were stopped on what appeared to be a road, a British company walked right through them. Men and horses crossed so close that either of the boys could have reached out and touched them. No one seemed to notice the small group. But their presence was somehow perceived in the unconscious, for man and beast shied to one side or the other when they came close, as if avoiding an uncomfortable spot without thinking about it.

At one point, after a day or six months, depending on how you looked at it, H'Cab produced costumes for Dan and Andy.

"Are we going to a ball?" Dan asked.

"We are going to meet a friend," H'Cab answered. "It would be best to dress like the others."

Dan thought he looked rather dashing in his outfit. The Indians had found them some pretty decent clothes, but they were quite itchy.

"You want I should go and get you satin and silk?" H'Cab asked sarcastically.

Dan would have preferred that, but did not think it would do to ask.

The pants were funny, being those knee britches that girls sometimes liked to wear, but the boots were great and the jacket and vest showed off his athletic physique quite nicely. He was sure that H'Cab noticed, so he made sure to stand up straight and show some leg.

He looked over at Andy. The poor kid should get out and do some exercise and play some sports. He wore shoes and long white hose. He did not fill out the jacket very well. And he wore the frilly neck thing. Dan had drawn the line at that. Andy looked like a young Ebenezer Scrooge or perhaps Ichabod Crane.

Andy liked the outfit. He really felt a part of the time now. Angie would like it. Andy usually hated the way he looked, but

Angie always told him how handsome he was and what nice legs he had, even his lame one. When she was around to remind him, he sometimes actually believed it. Andy sighed. Dan still looked better than he did.

They looked at each other and laughed. "You look ridiculous," they said in the same breath. This made them laugh even harder.

"All right you two," H'Cab broke in. "You both look fine. We're not going to a society ball. Move it!"

Soon, the small group turned off the path. Both Andy and Dan were careful when they stepped off the path, worried that they would fall over something.

They were near a river. Next to the river was an encampment.

"Colonial militia," said Andy.

"You think?" Dan replied, looking around.

"It's military and clearly not British."

The Fula'puli were leaving them behind, so the two hurried to keep up. The Indians stopped near a tent in what appeared to be the center of the camp. Dan and Andy were told to wait, while the H'Cab and her brother went inside, along with two other of the Fula'puli.

Dan and Andy sat and looked around. There were quite a few men around. Most carried weapons of some sort, and there were guns neatly stacked in those little Christmas tree formations where they leaned against each other.

Dan looked around. "There are a lot of women here."

"Don't you ever not think about girls?" Andy asked.

"No. But I'm surprised to see so many women."

Andy smiled. "Armies at this time were often accompanied by women and children. The families of the soldiers. A lot of people must have been displaced by the war. Where else can they go?"

A woman brought them over some food, which they ate hungrily. They both held out their bowls for more, which got them nothing other than an amused smile. The Fula'puli men who had stayed outside waved away the food.

There were quite a few horses and wagons around the camp.
"Cavalry?" Dan asked.

"More likely raiders. It wasn't uncommon for small groups to form around a specific leader. Often these bands stayed in a particular area. Sometimes they were paid by their leader. It happened in all the armies of the time. The government could only afford so many soldiers. This gave wealthy people an opportunity to have more control and authority than they might have had if they had simply bought a commission in the regular army. It gave them a lot more freedom. Remember, the easiest way to become a captain of a ship is to own the ship and name yourself captain. This situation often made it difficult for army commanders to plan strategy."

"Doesn't sound very efficient."

"It wasn't. But it could be effective," Andy pointed out.

"What if you were an incompetent captain?"

"Then you either sank or got promoted. Or died."

Dan thought about this. "I wish we could buy commissions in our army."

"It resulted in a lot of bad officers."

"Like the Duke of Wellington?" Dan smirked.

"There were some successes, but ultimately it was a bad idea, especially as armies became larger and more permanent."

"Perhaps, but if my father could buy me a commission—"

"Dan, money can not do everything."

"Spoken like someone who never had any money!" Dan snapped back. "I never thought I'd make much of a junior officer. But I'd be a great general. Like Montgomery."

"Montgomery was lucky. He didn't so much win his battles but failed to lose them. He was a plodding general more concerned with his place in history than the reasons for the war."

"Who would you prefer, Andy?"

"Patton."

"A vainglorious butcher!" Dan exclaimed.

"Bite your tongue. An effective leader and brilliant strategist," Andy retorted.

"More concerned with headlines than the lives of his men."

Andy and Dan were getting heated, but their conversation was cut short when the flaps of the tent opened and H'Cab looked out. "Could the two of you give it a rest and come inside?"

They followed her in.

Even though the day was bright and sunny, inside the tent was rather dim and gloomy. There was little furniture inside, just a cot and a folding desk. A young man stood near the desk talking to H'Cab's brother, whose name was H'Ketor. The other two men were named A'N'As and Pra'Yam and they spoke even less than H'Ketor. The young man, who looked to be about twenty, was dressed like a dandy. His vest was trimmed in gold and his jacket and pants were bright, almost electric, green. His boots were polished and seemed to shine. A hat with a large plumed feather lay on the cot.

H'Cab motioned for Dan and Andy to wait.

The young man finished his soft conversation with H'Ketor, fished out a watch that was attached to one of the many chains that ran across the front of his vest and noted the time. Turning to the two young men, he smiled broadly, showing off a lot of clean white teeth. "And who might you two be?"

"Dan Meadows, sir." Dan was always respectful to those in authority.

"Andy. Andrew Montrose."

"I know your family, Mr. Montrose." The man stepped forward and shook both their hands. "I don't know your family, Mr. Meadows, but no matter. One can't know everyone, can one? I am Beatitude Carol."

"Beatitude Carol," Andy said suddenly.

"Mater was a religious woman and wished for me to glorify God."

"Do you?" Dan asked.

"On occasion, I'm sure."

"THE Beatitude Carol?" Andy persisted.

"I've yet to meet another. I think I would remember. Yes.

Yes, I would remember. I must be THE Beatitude Carol."

"You see," Andy began. "I've read about you in the history books and…."

Beatitude's jovial expression was replaced by a stern look that told Andy to be quiet. He then turned to an aide who sat on a small stool to one side and motioned him out of the tent. "You should be careful of what you say, when you say it, and around whom you say it," Beatitude said severely, his face turning ominous and shadowed with potential malice. Then his happy face returned. "I hope the history books will be kind. Who sent you here?"

"Sent us here?" Andy asked.

Dan piped in. "No one sent us here, sir."

Beatitude stepped up to them and looked at them carefully. He looked into their eyes and even checked their teeth. Dan felt like he was at the vet's. Then the man actually sniffed at them.

"No one sent us, sir," Andy said. "We came on our own."

"Possible," Beatitude said, frowning. "But unlikely."

"But true," Dan argued. "We were at a friend's house—"

"The Castle," Andy explained.

"Yeah," Dan went on. "The Castle—"

Andy interrupted. "It's really a friend of mine."

"Rosi's a friend of mine, too."

"But she is more a friend of mine. You were merely there to see if she was all right and to make a pass at her," Andy said.

"But that doesn't mean that she's not a friend of mine. It seems to indicate that my relationship is stronger with her than yours is."

"But, if I may point out, you don't have a relationship with Rosi yet."

"You're splitting hairs." Dan scowled.

"And you're getting ahead of yourself. I was at a friend's house, and you came later. She wasn't even there then."

Beatitude looked over to H'Cab. "Are they always like this?"

"You'd best stop them while it's still possible," she answered.

"Quiet, you two." Beatitude spoke softly, but there was a

tenor to his voice that made them stop talking and look at him. "I don't really care. You were at The Castle?" He pointed to Andy to answer.

"Yes, Angie, Angela Kaufman, my girlfriend, was sleeping over with Rosi Carol and they saw something or had some sort of nightmare."

"Clearly," Dan said. "Given when and where we are, we can stipulate that they saw something."

"True, but we have yet to establish that it was an external vision or an internal vision."

"One can assume that if they both saw the same thing, the vision was external and physical."

"Should I shoot them?" Beatitude wondered out loud.

"I don't think it would work," H'Cab said, sadly.

"Boys!" Beatitude said. "Shut up!"

"Sorry, sir," they both said simultaneously.

"Rosi Carol?" he asked. "One at a time. Mr. Montrose. And Mr. Meadows, do not speak until you're spoken to."

Dan opened his mouth to reply, but a look from Beatitude shut it.

"Mr. Montrose."

"Yes?"

"Rosi Carol?"

"Yes."

"Rositsa Carol?"

"Yes."

Beatitude thought for a moment. He turned to H'Cab. "Did you know this?"

"No. Sorry, I could have saved you the bother, but I thought it prudent not to ask too many questions."

"Is she ready?" Beatitude asked. "Rositsa Carol."

H'Cab shook her head. "I don't think so. She sent no sign that she was involved, but there are problems."

Beatitude nodded. "I smelled some confusion in the air."

"Beatitude," Andy broke in. "How did we get here?"

"You don't need to know."

"But you will agree that we have the right to know."

"I will not," Beatitude said firmly.

"You see," Andy went on. "From the history books I read, you—"

"Don't tell me anything. If I need to know, I will ask. You were at Rositsa Carol's."

"Yes. And a door opened and we were brought here."

"What happened to Rositsa and...." Beatitude thought for a moment. "Angela?"

"Oh, they went through the door right after Kirk did."

"Kirk's my brother," said Dan, not wanting to be forgotten.

"Your brother's here?"

"Yes, sir. He's at The Castle now. With the British?"

"And the two girls?"

Dan looked at Andy, who shrugged. "We haven't seen either of them," Dan said.

"We were unable to find them," H'Cab said. "We came across these two instead."

"You did the right thing," Beatitude said. "However, they don't belong here with me." He paced back and forth for a minute. "You should take them back. Find Rositsa Carol, if you can, and leave them with her. They're her problem."

"And if I can't find her?"

"I'll be there in a few days."

"I don't think you're supposed to be in New Richmond," H'Cab said.

"Neither is Cromwell," Beatitude pointed out. "I have no choice. I have to go back. Perhaps I can hinder Cromwell, even beat him. It will take me some time to get there. Plenty of time to let the girl show her stuff. If she's as good as we've been led to believe, then she'll be able to figure it out."

"I hope you're right."

"So do I. Get these boys out of here and keep an eye on them." Beatitude nodded to Dan and Andy and walked out.

"What do we do now?" Dan asked H'Cab.

"Weren't you listening?" she said. "We will take you to your friend. We go now."

"Why don't you take us home?" Dan asked.

"Perhaps later. Now to your friend."

* * *

AGAIN, Dan and Kirk were led to the path and started another odd journey. According to the sun, they continued to head south and west, away from New Richmond. Then they headed north. Then south again. Andy began to feel dizzy after trying to keep track of their journey.

"Don't worry," H'Cab said. "We are taking you where you need to go."

A'N'As and Pra'Yam left them and ran ahead. They did not come back.

The small group walked and broke and slept and ate and walked some more. Was it a few hours or a year? Andy stopped trying to figure out how long it was, and Dan got tired of slapping his Rolex to see if it would start again. Finally, they stepped off the path and found themselves near a stream. It was dark, but showed signs of a coming dawn.

They followed the stream for while, stopping, on H'Cab's insistence, to wash up.

"Are the girls okay?" Andy asked.

"I do not know," H'Cab answered. "But A'N'As has left a sign that she is here."

"I didn't see any sign," Dan said.

"Did you look for one?"

"No."

At that moment A'N'As came into sight. He nodded to his princess.

"Let us go on," H'Cab said. "We are almost there."

They went up a hill, where they found a couple of men who had apparently fallen asleep on watch. These men were quite surprised to find themselves awakened by strangers.

"What do you want?" one of them asked.

H'Cab nodded to Dan to reply. "We're looking for Rosi

Carol."

"Captain Carol's in the village," one of the sleepy men replied.

"Captain Carol?"

"Ayuh," the other one replied, nodding.

H'Cab grabbed Dan and Andy's hands and led them across a cold stream. The two were stunned to see a village appear right before their eyes once they stepped onto the far bank. It was an old village that looked like it was falling down, but it was filled with men.

There were quite a lot of men in the strange village. Most of them were just waking up. There were a couple of small fires burning and Dan and Andy could smell breakfast being prepared.

Two men walked up to the small group. "Who are you?" one of them asked.

The boys introduced themselves.

"Who are your friends?" he asked, eying the Indians suspiciously.

H'Cab spoke up. "We can answer for ourselves, Sergeant Major Zablonski."

"Fine. Who are you?"

"We are who we are. You need know naught else."

Zablonski and the other man were not pleased with this answer, but they could get nothing else from any of the Indians.

Dan and Andy explained that they were here looking for Rosi.

"Looking for Captain Carol?" Zablonski exclaimed. "She's around here someplace. You seen her, Spartacus?"

"Ain't seen her since last night," said a man who looked older than the rest. Dan was surprised to note that it looked like he was smoking his hand. "Went over t'creek t'bathe. Then was talking with young Will."

"There you are," Zablonski said, as if that actually answered anything. "She'll be back by and by. Sit down and eat if you like."

They were handed some food. Again, the Fula'puli refused. They were all being eyed suspiciously by the men there. Dan and

Andy explained that they were Rosi's friends, and that mollified a few of them, but the others were not quite so trusting.

Then Dan saw Rosi coming. She was a sight for sore eyes! And she was with some guy!

And she was holding his hand!

* * *

ROSI and the guy, smiling at each other, were clearly oblivious to everyone else. Dan just knew that they had been out all night.

She was not any different. Rosi was just like all the other girls Dan had met and heard stories about.

When Rosi saw them, she shrieked happily. She reached Andy first and threw one arm around him, kissing him on the cheek. When she reached Dan, she acted a little shy as she took his hand.

"Hi," she said softly, sweetly.

What game is she playing? "Yeah," Dan threw back as coldly as he could.

Rosi was momentarily confused by Dan's reaction to seeing her, but she had other things on her mind.

"Where's Angie?" Andy looked around. "Angie!"

The men standing around quickly found things to do that took them elsewhere.

This was what had been distracting Rosi from the moment she had seen Dan and Andy. She was happy to see them, of course. But now Andy had the right to know. And there was no way to soft coat this. She took his hand, led him to the riverbank, and sat down with him. Dan followed and stood behind the two.

After she broke the news to Andy that Angie had been killed, Andy and Rosi held on to each other and cried for a long time.

Even Dan was upset. Presently, he came over to the two of them and sat down next to Andy.

After a while, Rosi told Andy and Dan what had been going on. She glossed over the Kirk bits as best she could for Dan's sake, but she could not hide everything. She was surprised that Dan was not surprised.

"I'll deal with him when I get to him," Dan said tightly.

When Andy told of his and Dan's adventures, Dan scowled throughout and refused to be brought into the conversation.

Dan kept his eye on this Will fellow. Will did not like Dan much, either. So the two of them spent much of the morning glaring at each other.

It was midmorning by the time Rosi and Andy were able to pull themselves together.

* * *

ROSI nodded to Zablonski who turned and bellowed out several sharp orders. Most of the men continued about their business, but the sergeants and several of the older men came over to a makeshift table Rosi now sat at of the head of.

"I want everyone to listen," Rosi announced. "I need as much input as possible."

Rosi felt very professional. She even had a long stick to use as a pointer in case she had to draw designs in the dirt. She stayed standing and paced back and forth in front of the men.

She began. "We need to get the British out of New Richmond. As long as they are there, they are safe from sea attack and can protect themselves easily from land attack. That is, as I understand it. Am I right?"

The men nodded and mumbled their agreement.

"We could flank them from the cliffs, like they did to us," Robin suggested.

Rosi nodded, acknowledging his contribution. "We don't have the boats. Even if we could get enough boats to get a large number of men there, we would probably be seen by the navy. Even if we could get past the navy, we hardly have enough men. We would be overrun in no time. No, we have to get the British out of New Richmond so that they can be met by a larger force and beaten. You're wondering how. We know why the British are here. Cromwell expects to find something at The Castle. If we can get Cromwell to think that we have what he's looking for, he will come after us. Even if he does leave a garrison force in New

Richmond, most of his men will come after us."

"How do we get Cromwell to think we have what he wants?" Ben asked.

"That's a good question, Ben. There are places in The Castle that his men cannot get to. If we can make it look like we have gotten into those rooms and cleared them out."

"How do we make it look like that?" one of the newer regulars named Lenny asked.

"Simply by going in there and stripping The Castle bare. If we can create a diversion that will draw the soldiers from The Castle for a short period of time, an hour or so, we go there with as many wagons as we can beg, borrow, or steal, and make sure the British know we did it. They will chase us."

"They will eventually catch us," Robin pointed out.

"There is one of our problems. Here are our problems in order. Can we get a number of horse drawn wagons? How do we create a diversion that will get the soldiers away from The Castle? As you all know, the British will eventually catch us. So, where do we go? How do we get help? Ideas?"

Andy raised his hand. "I have an idea. The old riverbed. Is it dry this year?"

"Ain't been more'n a creek for years," Spartacus said. A couple of the other men nodded.

"There's a place I know," Andy went on. "Even when there's only a stream it can actually get pretty deep, and forms lake and there's a small island."

"I know where ye's talking about," said Spartacus. "There's a sharp bend there."

"Yes, that's the one. We sometimes go skinny dipping there." Andy turned bright red. Then he remembered that Angie was dead. "Used to," he said, as his eyes filled with tears.

Rosi went to him and put her hand on his shoulder. "Thank you. Spartacus, how far is that place from The Castle?"

"Don't rightly know. I'd have to check it out but can't be more'n ten miles."

"Excellent. I want you to take five men with you and find the most direct route there from The Castle. Remember, I want a route that they can follow us on. You leave those five men there. They will start to prepare it for us. That is where we will stop. Will, I need you to ride and find General Alcott. If he and his men have regrouped, they can meet us there, as soon as they can. Now, we need a diversion and we need one soon. Gentlemen, Cromwell and his people are destroying the town. They are torturing the inhabitants. There is no telling if and when they will find out how to get what they are looking for. I will give us two full days to get what we need. What's the third day?"

"The nineteenth," someone said.

"We go on the nineteenth, early morning," she decided. "Will, that means we will be at the bend in the old riverbed sometime in the afternoon. Sergeant major! Make sure there is always one platoon here to train. I want a constant watch on The Castle. I want to know if there is any major change in the enemy's disposition. I want the rest of the men out, scouring the area for any material we might need. Wagons, mules, food, guns, whatever they can find. If people don't give you what you need, take it and leave a receipt. I will answer for it."

Zablonski snapped a smart salute and started conferring with the other sergeants. Soon, men were running back and forth, bellowing orders, and squads were forming.

In moments, Rosi stood alone at the table. Dan watched her. She looked particularly vulnerable. She also looked a lot more hesitant than she had sounded just a minute before. All the men were busy. Even Andy was arguing with the pipe-handed man as the two of them drew maps in the dirt. Dan scowled. His bad mood had increased when Andy came up with the idea of the bend on the old riverbed. Dan would have thought of that eventually.

Having arranged the mission, Rosi walked with Will to where his horse and two men were waiting. She blushed deeply when he gave her a quick kiss before he started to crawl up on the horse.

Dan did not see Rosi come up to him, but felt her gentle touch on his arm.

"I know things seem really odd," she said softly. He had to lean in to hear her and enjoyed the way her hair brushed against his cheek. "I'll try to make sense of it. I really will, Dan. But for now I simply need your help and support."

Dan understood. He could see that Rosi had gone through a lot these last few days. He and Andy had been through enough, but they had not been in the middle of combat and had not seen any of their friends die. Andy would have been a mess. Rosi must be a wreck. "Of course," he murmured softly enough to make her lean in even closer. "Anything you need."

"Captain!" It was that other guy. He had dragged some sorry excuse for a horse along.

Dan fumed when Rosi rushed over to Will, threw her arm around his neck, and kissed his cheek. Watching the sweet little scene, Dan laughed. "How pathetic. And look at him. He'll be lucky if he doesn't fall off the horse and break his neck."

Will turned on Dan. "You think you can do better?"

"I've been riding since I was three. We ride real horses, not old nags like this."

"You got a problem with me?" Will stepped in.

"Yeah, punk."

Rosi squeezed between them. "Guys! Will, please! Dan, what are you doing?"

Will muttered something that Rosi could not hear and stepped away. Dan scowled and started off.

"Dan?" Rosi started after him. "What's wrong?"

"Nothing." *Like you don't know.*

"If it's nothing, then there's no reason for this little performance. Will has an important mission to do and it's dangerous."

"Oh, yeah, I've heard that old line. You fell for that crap!"

"I'm just saying give Will a break."

"And I'm not good enough for a dangerous mission?" Dan said.

"That's not what I said."

"It sure sounds like what you were saying. Look, you're going about this all wrong. You should be trying to find us a way home."

"I am!"

"Nonsense." Dan snorted. "You're playing Joan of Arc for your boyfriend here. That fruit Beatitude made it clear you were the reason we were here."

"So it's my fault, huh?"

"Looks like it. He seems to think so. H'Cab seems to think so."

"So you're listening to that little—" Rosi did not like these Fula'Puli. She had tried several times since they showed up with Dan and Andy to speak with them, to thank them for bringing the two safely to her. Each time she tried, they pointedly avoided her. Rosi really could have used their help. Perhaps they could tell her more about Beatitude, since they clearly had some sort of connection with him.

"Leave her out of this!" Dan snapped back.

Rosi was fuming. "So it's my fault that Kirk helped the British take New Richmond? I'm trying to fix that."

"You're supposed to fix the whole world, huh?" Dan sounded incredulous. "Beatitude said he was coming here. He has real soldiers. They'll know what to do."

"Everyone here is a real soldier." Rosi waved at the men around. "And they've accepted my plan. If you don't like it, then fine. You can wait here. You'll be safe."

"Are you saying I'm a coward?" Dan could not believe his ears. "I'm trying to be reasonable."

"Dan, I'm trying to do the best I can."

"Why don't you let men who know what they're doing take command?"

Rosi could not believe she had just heard that. "Why you...sexist, ignorant, stuck up, yahoo!"

"Are you gonna smack me?" Dan mocked. "Go ahead! Or are you gonna cry, now?"

Will, who had done his best not to get involved, stepped in now. "Leave her alone."

"Or what? You want a piece of me?"

The two grappled. Will was taller, but Dan wrestled. In moments, the two were rolling on the ground, scratching and tearing at each other. Some of the men came and pulled the two apart.

Rosi turned to Will. "You'd better go."

"Yeah, tell him to run!" Dan snarled. "He got what he wanted from you. How many of the other men did as well?"

"Dan, shut up!" This time, she did smack him.

There was a stunned silence from the whole company.

Rosi reached for Dan's hand. "Dan, please."

But he was gone, storming into the woods.

Rosi gave Will a distracted good-bye, then she went looking for Andy. When she saw him sitting by himself, seemingly lost in thought, Rosi realized that Andy probably needed to be alone far more than she needed comfort.

She went back to her command table and scribbled distractedly on bits of paper and drew in the dust. The men went about their business. They seemed to think that she needed to be alone as well.

* * *

ROSI was pleased to learn that If-Christ-Had-Not-Died-For-Thee-Thou-Hast-Been-Damned Essex would be remaining behind. He had proved to be a fine shot and spent the bulk of the day teaching Rosi how to load and fire her pistol.

It was a complicated and time consuming process. First, she had to pour a charge of powder down the barrel. She had to take the ball and shove it into the barrel and ram it down with the rod. Then there was the wadding.

Putting the rod back in its proper place seemed to be of the utmost importance. The first time Rosi tried, she put the rod on the ground next to her and Essex just about had a fit.

"There's a place for it!" he almost shrieked.

"But the little rings are too small and take so much time," Rosi replied.

"The rod goes back there," he insisted. "What if you have to move? You won't remember everything. Put it back where it belongs."

Rosi primed the flash pan with powder.

Essex told her to aim at a tree about twenty five yards away and pull the trigger.

There was a brief flash when the flint hit the lock, creating a spark that caught the powder in the flash pan. This caused the powder in the barrel to catch and explode. The explosion, having no other direction in which to go, went down the barrel, forcing the ball out at a very high speed. The ball did not hit the tree, but it flew in the tree's general direction.

Rosi was disappointed. She had seen plenty of movies and television shows where people shot pistols and it had always looked so easy.

Essex reassured her that she was doing well. "These little things are not very accurate. They're not as accurate as a musket and not nearly as accurate as a rifle."

"Then we should all have rifles," Rosi suggested.

"We don't have any rifles. Too expensive and slow. Don't expect to hit a target, just get the ball in the right area at the right height and hope it hits something. If nothing else, it will make the enemy duck."

"You mean, you give the officers weapons that aren't as good as the men's weapons?"

"I guess I never really thought about it like that, but sounds about right. Most officers are better shots than you are. They've had more practice."

Rosi laughed. "I guess I will pray that our men are good shots."

"Better to hope the English are bad shots," Essex said.

"Why?"

"English soldiers are taught to shoot at the officers first."

That was a sobering thought.

The battle at The Castle was a surprisingly distant memory. It had only been a few days ago, Rosi knew. But so much had happened. She did not even have much time to think about Angie. She had often been annoyed watching television or reading books where people seemed to let personal tragedy wash off them like water from a duck's back. Now she would have to rethink her attitude.

Essex practiced with Rosi, making sure she had the hang of loading the little weapon. It was awkward to load. Her left arm was getting better, but she could not do the fine work with her fingers. The arm was strong enough to hold the pistol while Rosi did everything else slowly and carefully with her right arm. Firing the pistol was a different story. The kick was so strong that Rosi's arm felt like it was being wrenched out of its socket each time she fired.

However, Rosi found the experience fun. She was actually giddy and shrieked and laughed like a little girl the first time she actually loaded and fired the gun herself.

Even though Rosi's squad did not have a lot of men, they did have a surfeit of weapons. Each time someone had fallen during the battle, someone else had taken their weapons and ammunition. Rosi had two pistols, her sword, which Spartacus had promised to teach her how to use, and a long bayonet shoved in her boot.

Andy and Dan were each given a musket and taught to shoot. Andy was knocked to the ground the first few times he shot. Furthermore, his shots went wild. Dan seemed to have a pretty good grasp on what was going on and after the first couple of shots, was hitting his tree consistently.

"It pulls to the right," Dan told H'Cab, who was coaching him, to explain why he had missed the first couple of times.

Who was this H'Cab woman? Rosi wanted to know. Rosi was the captain. This woman should ask her for instructions, shouldn't she? Rosi did not like the look of her one bit. And she took too much interest in Dan, showing him how to shoot a musket. Men were supposed to do that. This girl should be off with a papoose in a teepee sewing moccasins and cooking.

Rosi knew that thinking such things was not worthy of her.

Couldn't this Indian woman dress more like Zilla had dressed? That would be more seemly. Less threatening.

Rosi tried to shake such thoughts out of her head. She could tell why Dan fired better than Andy. Andy held the musket in his hands. The recoil slammed it against his shoulder. The H'Ketor fellow was trying to tell Andy this, but he could not get it. Dan held the weapon firmly against his shoulder. He would be bruised by the end of his lesson, but not too much.

It was fairly late that night, just as most of the men were dropping off to sleep, that the plan for the diversion was come upon. It was Dan who had the bright idea.

When he explained it to Rosi and several others, they all knew that it might work. All they needed were some small watertight barrels, a lot of rocks and gunpowder, rope, a timed fuse, and some strong adhesive.

Andy came up with the adhesive and the waterproofing. "Tar," he said. "Pitch."

The timed fuse, and a way to light it, was a bit more difficult. Dan's plan was good, but whoever carried it out would neither be able to take fire with them nor use flint. This was a tough problem.

Sometime just after four in the morning, Rosi awakened from an unsettling dream she could not remember, with the answer to the fire problem. She dove for her bag and dug into it. There, wrapped up exactly as she had left it so many days ago, though slightly crushed and tossed about, were the things that Rosi had taken from the silent boys. There were a couple of packs of cigarettes, matches, a lighter, and a large re-sealable baggy filled with what appeared to be dried grass. Suddenly, Rosi realized what it was. So, apparently, did Dan who sat there watching her.

"It's not mine," Rosi said.

"Sure."

Never mind, she thought. *I can deal with this later.* She took the *grass* out of the baggy and started to throw it into the low fire. Then stopped. Not the best of ideas, she decided. She tossed it into the woods.

"I saw this in a movie," she explained to Dan. "How to make a timed fuse. How long does it take for a cigarette to burn down?"

"I dunno." Dan was a jock and was not supposed know things like that, which was not completely true, but he was not about to tell Rosi about anything like that. "Ten minutes or so."

"That sounds about right. Look, you light the cigarette. Then, you place it in the pack of matches." Rosi took an unlit cigarette and put it in the matches, closing the flap of the matchbook. "The cigarette will burn down and set the matches on fire. This will light the fuse, which can be as long as you like, depending on how much fuse we can get. Then, boom! Your bomb goes off."

Dan had to concede that Rosi had a good idea. "And the baggy?"

"Keeps everything dry," Rosi pointed out.

"And if it doesn't work?" They had both agreed that they only had enough for two tries, not enough for practicing.

"Then someone lights the fuse by hand and prays he can get out in time."

Once the day started and people were up and about, men started coming back with supplies and even one wagon. Rosi sent some back out with a new shopping list.

By late the next day, Rosi and Andy were still terrible shots. Dan was among the best in the company.

Most of the men had returned. Spartacus had come back alone, having left his men to get the battlefield ready. He would stay with Rosi.

Zablonski left with half the horses and more men. He would prepare the defenses and wait for Rosi.

Soon, there was enough equipment to set Dan's plan in motion. Dan and Andy had already made two adequate bombs.

Now all they needed were two men who could swim.

Essex, reluctantly, admitted to being able to swim. Not well, but he could swim.

To Rosi's horror, the only other person in the group who could swim, and probably the best swimmer, was Dan.

"Will you do it?" Rosi asked gently.

"Of course I'll do it!" he snapped. *I'll probably get blown up doing it*, he thought. *But that will show you, won't it?*

PART II

Opening Moves

CHAPTER 5

DAN and Essex left shortly after dark with the two bombs, four small empty barrels, all liberally smeared with pitch, and a barrel half filled with the stuff strapped to a not particularly happy horse that did not know how lucky he was to be making a nice, safe journey into town rather than the much more dangerous ride the other horses would be making in just over twenty four hours.

Just before Dan and Essex left, Andy went and spoke to him briefly and shook his hand.

Rosi was surprised to see the two so chummy with each other. She supposed that a lot had happened in the time they had been here.

Rosi watched Dan and Essex go down the path and turn out of sight. With a sigh, she turned and looked for Andy to talk to. He was not there.

"Where's Andy?" she asked no one in particular.

"He was over there with the Indians," Harry said, pointing. Nobody was there.

Rosi looked around the village. There was no sign of Andy or the Indians. They had vanished like a puff of smoke on a breezy day.

Rosi went into one of the old fallen houses and cried softly to herself. Angie and Zilla were dead. Will was gone. Dan hated her and where he was going, he might be dead soon, too. Now Andy had disappeared.

Before Spartacus rode off the second time, he had said some very complimentary things to Rosi about how she was coming along as a leader. Rosi had smiled at that. When everyone was asleep these nights in the village, Rosi had carefully practiced a confident swagger. She wished her voice were lower and more commanding. She tried to scowl when she gave orders so that the men would not wink at her. If anything, she had felt like more of a mascot, a revolutionary doll, than a leader. In just a day she would be taking these men out of the village and it would stop being a game.

Rosi searched her mind for movies and shows that would tell her what to do. Not surprisingly, she realized she knew very little about tactics and a lot about posing. The men had accepted her plan. It was a good plan, if everything went according to plan. But what if things did not work out? What if Will could not find General Alcott? What if the British caught Rosi's band before it reached the river bed?. If. If. If. If Rosi kept on coming up with *if* situations that would result in defeat, despair, humiliation, death, the collapse of Western Civilization, she would surely go mad!

Her arm hurt.

She was hungry.

She wanted a drink.

Rosi was surrounded by forty some men who would gladly do anything she wanted, who would happily die for her, and she was as alone as she had ever been.

* * *

DAN did not really have much to say to Essex on their journey to New Richmond.

Essex did not really have much to say to him, either.

They did establish that Dan would never be able to remember Essex's first name.

They also established that Essex did not really know how to swim. He knew how to tread water for a few minutes, and he knew how to dog paddle.

"Why did you say you could swim?" Dan asked.

"I kinda thought no one else could swim," Essex explained. "So I'd look brave when I volunteered. Will you have time to teach me?"

Dan had no idea, and said as much. "The trick is not to panic. Try not to make too much noise. Oh, and if I grab you, let me control you. I was a lifeguard one summer, so I know what I'm doing."

Essex was not particularly reassured.

Dan did not particularly care. He was having second thoughts about this whole plan of his. Well, not so much about the plan, the plan was a good one, but about his involvement in it.

He had half a mind to talk Essex into just walking on, straight past New Richmond. Essex was very straight laced and would probably argue, but he seemed so brow beaten that he would be easy to bully into making a run for it. Dan gave this careful consideration for about three minutes.

No, he would stick around and do his part of the plan. Someone had to do something about the mess Kirk had made of everything.

Sure, Rosi would try and she was pretty bright and all, but she was young. All those locals were treating her like a princess and she was certainly letting it all go to her head. They were also, it seemed, taking advantage of her. That Will guy certainly was. Dan was very angry about that. But he would deal with that later, when he had more time and he could get Rosi away from the others.

What was Dan doing getting caught up in all of this? Rosi was a kid next to H'Cab, who treated him with respect.

He had thought a lot about Rosi over the summer. He had written several letters that he had then thrown away. Thank God he had.

"Who are you talking to?" asked Essex.

"Huh?"

"You were saying something."

"Oh, sorry. Just talking to myself." God, that was stupid!

The thing to worry about now was how to get out of this place alive.

Remember, he made a mental note. *Do not blow yourself up.*

He wondered how many people in similar situations forgot to take those simple, patently obvious precautions and ended up, well, dead.

They eventually arrived in the town. It was clearly New

Richmond, Dan saw, but so much smaller and even more boring. In Dan's experience, most towns were boring at three in the morning.

Two sleepy soldiers stepped into the road and motioned for them to stop.

This, Dan knew, was the moment of truth.

"Deliveries for the…the…." Essex started.

"Dancing Cavalier!" Dan spoke up. The fool had forgotten the cover story!

The soldiers visibly brightened. "Perhaps we should 'ave a taste. Just to be sure."

Dan smiled. "If you like vinegar," he said. "Help yourself."

Both soldiers scowled as they waved them through.

"Sorry," Essex whispered after they looked back and seen that the soldiers were once again relaxing by their fire.

"Yeah. Don't worry about it."

The Dancing Cavalier was almost quiet when they arrived. A couple of the British were passed out in the front and one or two still chatted with some of the bargirls.

Young Captain Sam was not too happy to see them when he came out from his office. Nevertheless, he ushered them inside and shoved them into chairs.

"I'm not expecting a delivery." He loomed over them and looked decidedly dangerous.

"Rosi Carol sent us," Dan spurted out. He was surprised to see Young Captain Sam there, even though he'd been told what to expect. How could the same man look older now than he would later?

"Rosi Carol?" Young Captain Sam asked.

"Yeah."

"Prove it."

Rosi had sent a short note to Young Captain Sam. She had given it to Essex, but Dan had insisted on carrying it. He pulled out the slip of paper and handed it to Young Captain Sam.

Young Captain Sam read it quickly. "What do you need?"

Dan quickly explained the plan.

Young Captain Sam smiled. "Ye are brave, lads. Stupid, but brave."

"You don't think the plan will work?"

"Is not my place to think about such things. Ye'll be wanting the cellar, to be sure."

Young Captain Sam got up and went to the door. He carefully looked out. "Follow me," he said.

Dan was sure he would never be able to remember how they actually got to the cellar. The way was winding and confusing, much too far to be inside this building. They went up and down and left and right and all around. Furthermore, Young Captain Sam had refused to help the two carry the barrels. *Not my place to interfere* was all he had said. After what seemed like an impossible distance, Young Captain Sam opened a door to a large room filled with barrels. He pointed to a trap door.

"When will you go?" he asked.

"Tonight," Dan said. "Just after midnight."

"I'll bring ye food and drink. Try not to make too much noise."

Dan wanted to ask some questions, but Young Captain Sam was gone and the door was locked. There was a lantern in the room that gave some light. They would not need much.

Throughout the course of the day, Dan and Essex went over the plan a hundred times. They checked out the bombs a hundred times. They were even able, once it got later, to heat up the pitch they were going to use as adhesive.

Dan even tried to explain to Essex how to swim. "The trick is learning how to hold your breath," he explained.

Then, on the floor, he showed Essex a few strokes. Essex tried, but proved useless as a swimmer. At least, on a wooden floor, he looked hopeless.

"We'll have the empty barrels to float on," Dan said. "So actual swimming won't be necessary. If you get in trouble, try to float on your back and I'll pull you out. I was third place at State's last year. I'll never win a Gold Medal, but I can drag you to shore if I have to."

They napped a fair amount. They ate whatever Young Captain Sam brought them. The food was undercooked, Dan thought. But it was food. The beer was flat and watery, but it was the weakest stuff the inn had.

"Ye don't want to be drinking the water." Young Captain Sam laughed.

The beer gave the two young men some Dutch courage.

Just about midnight, Dan lifted the trap door. He was not prepared for the stench.

"What's down there?" he wondered aloud. "Dead bodies?"

Young Captain Sam, who had come to see them off, laughed. "It be best ye do not know," he said. He helped to lower the barrels.

Each of the bombs was lashed to two empty barrels. Dan was pleased to see that they floated nicely. He was very unhappy when he lowered himself down. His bare feet did not like the feel of the muck on the bottom. Essex was none too happy either.

Dan was able to keep the contents of his stomach inside.

Essex was not.

Young Captain Sam handed down the lantern. "There'll be a hook on one of the pylons. Leave it there when ye get close to open and blow it out."

The trap door closed. Dan and Essex were left alone with the rats and the sludge.

They did not have to wade for too long, the bottom dropped out. Fortunately, they were able to use the barrels to keep them above water. About twenty feet from the edge of the boardwalk, Dan hooked the handle of the lantern over a nail in a pylon and blew the flame out. He could barely see Essex.

"Hold on to both bombs," he said.

"Why?"

"I'm going ahead for a moment."

Dan swam to the edge of the open water and looked around. He could see the ships a few hundred yards out. They were dimly silhouetted by a sky that was only marginally less dark than the shapes of the ships.

There was some noise from above. Dan could hear voices rather clearly as several soldiers chatted aimlessly about their girls and mothers.

The voices were directly above Dan. He waved for Essex to be still.

"What is it?"

"Shh!" Dan listened. "They'll be able to see us."

"What do we do?"

"We stay quiet."

A shout came from the direction of the Dancing Cavalier. "Free ale!"

They could hear the soldiers running towards the inn.

Dan grabbed Essex by the arm. "Now, we go. Be as quiet as possible," he whispered.

For the first half of the journey, Dan was sure they would be seen from the town. For the second half, he was sure they would be seen from one or another of the ships. He led Essex on a bit of a wide arc to come in between the ships from the seaward side.

"They'll think that no one will come that way," he explained to his partner.

Dan picked the two largest ships as his targets. As they swam up closer to the first ship, Dan could hear men on the decks.

Too late to back off now, he decided.

They used the pitch to stick the loaded barrels to the side of the first ship. It didn't stick as well as they thought it might, but Dan jury-rigged one of the empty barrels under the loaded one, and the barrel and the pitch combined held the bomb in place. It wouldn't last long, but it would last long enough.

The first bomb took them about half an hour to set up. The second one took them less time.

Dan turned to Essex and helped him get a good grip on the two remaining barrels. He pushed the barrels and the man a couple of dozen yards away from the ships.

"Wait here," Dan said. "Be as still as you can. I'll go and set the fuses." His hands were covered with pitch and he spent some time scraping them off as best he could. Still, they were sticky and black. He hoped that would not interfere with anything.

Carefully, Dan swam back to the first boat and pushed the fuse into the barrel. A plug had been cut to help him. Then he tied the fuse to the pack of matches. He almost coughed when he lit the cigarette. God, it would be stupid to be caught at this moment. They would hang him, wouldn't they?

Probably.

The thought made him queasy. His hands shaking, he shoved the cigarette into the matches, carefully attached it to the barrel.

The second bomb was harder. Dan was not as nervous, which made the water feel colder. Then he did not dry his hands carefully enough, so the first cigarette disintegrated. So did the second and the third. The fourth was his last one, so he treaded water as long as he could using only his legs and blew on his hands until they were sort of dry. After several tries, he was able to light the cigarette and slip it in place.

"Should be a few minutes," he told Essex, swimming up next to him.

Essex almost jumped out of his skin when Dan appeared out of the gloom and spoke to him. "Back to the inn?" he asked.

Dan had another idea. They would swim out into the harbor. Once, if, the explosion happened, they would be able to see where most of the men were and swim in the other direction. Dan had the idea of swimming in the direction of The Castle, but decided that would be too difficult with Essex. It would have been pretty hard on his own, for the ships were on the other side of the harbor.

If the plan worked, then he and Essex would wait until the soldiers left the town and then either swim back to the inn, or, better yet, walk back nice and dry.

"How much longer?" Essex asked.

They were about a hundred yards from the ships. Soldiers were wandering around the boardwalk. Best not to try to get back now, Dan thought, confirming his plan. "Just a couple of minutes." He looked at his watch. The crystal was filthy and Dan couldn't tell what time it was, even with the glow-in-the-dark hands. "Nuts!"

The water was getting really cold.

"Anytime now," Dan whispered, pulling Essex closer to him so that they would not drift too far apart.

"Should be about now," he said a few minutes later.

"There must be a problem," Dan decided an eternity later.

"What do we do?" Essex asked, shaking violently in the now very cold water. Dan was sure that the British would hear Essex's splashes.

Dan knew what had to be done. He did not like it, but he knew what had to be done.

"Wait here," he said.

"Where are you going?"

"Back."

"Are you crazy?"

"Yeah."

Dan swam a few strokes back, took a good solid bearing on the direction, and dove under the water.

All those years of swimming at The Cape paid off. Dan surfaced about twenty yards from the second ship. He slowly crawled forward.

At last, in the gloom, he could see the shape of the bomb against the side of the ship.

Then he saw the matches catch and flare up.

"Oh, crap!" Dan turned, took a deep breath, and dove under the water, kicking to give himself as much depth and distance as he could.

He did not so much hear the first explosion as feel the force of it ram into him like a brick wall hitting a sports car.

He spun around in circles. The air was forced from his lungs.

Then the second explosion sent a shock wave through the water that knocked him the other way.

He felt the second explosion, and then nothing else.

Essex ducked down when the first explosion went off. Since nothing hit him, he did not try hiding from the second explosion a few seconds later.

"Dan!" he called out in a loud whisper that he himself barely heard. "Dan!"

Then came the other explosions as the fires set off the powder on the ships.

Dan and Andy had planned the bombs well, and Dan and Essex had set them perfectly.

"Dan!" Essex didn't even bother trying to whisper now. "Dan!"

CHAPTER 6

ROSI stood with Spartacus at the edge of the trees, to either side stood the better part of two platoons. They fidgeted, but for the most part, stayed fairly quiet.

She checked her watch. It was about two-thirty.

It was the waiting that was killing her.

She nodded to Spartacus and then slipped back and made her way down the line, stopping to clap each man on the shoulder and to whisper something encouraging.

She could never think of anything really encouraging to say, but she tried. The men seemed to like her around so she smiled as brightly as she could and tried to sparkle. Perhaps that might allow them to forget, if only for a moment, that their guns were not primed.

The guns were loaded. They were not primed. This plan of hers hinged on the British doing exactly what Rosi thought they might do and not having any inkling that there was any danger. Any accidental shots would certainly warn the enemy, who would then bring its superior numbers, equipment, tactics, training, and experience into play.

To help in the deception, Rosi had ordered a halt to any harassment. The men were not happy about this, but that was just tough.

In about half an hour, the wagons should be reaching their starting position, right around the bend of the road, about a quarter of a mile from the main entrance to the estate. They should be safe. Unless someone should send a messenger or otherwise go anywhere near the wagons. Men could hide. Three large wagons and horses could not.

Had it been raining, things would have been easier for the men with the wagons.

Had it been raining, things would have been very uncomfortable for Rosi and her two platoons hiding along the edge of the forest.

Had it been raining, things would have been impossible for Dan.

And Essex, too, she forced herself to remember. He was going into danger as well.

"I'll be back in a few minutes," she whispered to Spartacus.

The older man nodded.

"I'm taking Ben with me," she said.

"Thank you."

Ben, the youngest member of the company, was so nervous that his teeth were chattering. That might have been partly the cold. Even though the sky was clear, it was pretty chilly. Rosi was half afraid that their breath would give them away. She was sure that if Ben's teeth were not stopped, the British soldiers billeted in the stables would certainly hear them.

She made some noise as she approached Ben, so he would not start or yell or anything. She motioned for him to follow her.

She had spent enough time over the last week in these woods at night that she was able to make it to the road without following the drive. This allowed them to avoid the sentry, though they would have a good look at the three men in a few minutes.

"What is it, captain?" Ben asked.

"Not so loud," she said automatically. Good God, these people had no volume control. She supposed that it had something to do with living in the outdoors. People who grew up in cities learned to speak quietly. Their neighbors were feet away. Out here, the neighbors might be miles away. Even in *her* New Richmond, the modern one, you could practically fit a tenement apartment building between houses, even in the poorer sections of town. On the other hand, most of these people fed themselves by hunting. Certainly they had to learn to move around silently so as not to scare away next week's dinner. And she had no doubt that the British would be as skittish as rabbits.

"I need you to stay by the road and let me know when the wagons arrive," she explained.

"Don't you think the sentries will hear me?" Ben asked.

Rosi sighed. "I want you to come and warn me. Come back the way I just brought you."

Ben looked down the hill and through the trees to where there was a low fire.

Rosi could see that the three men were sitting, leaning back. They looked asleep.

"It would be easier if I came back that way," Ben suggested, looking hopefully at Rosi. He might be younger than Rosi, but he was already taller.

Rosi wondered fleetingly if historical generals were taller than their soldiers. It would certainly make giving orders easier. She felt awkward trying to boss around men she had to strain her neck to see. They probably were taller back in the day. It made some sense. Officers were aristocrats and had access to medicine and food. Regular soldiers were not and did not.

"What was that?" Rosi had drifted off and missed what Ben was saying.

He had drawn his knife and was moving towards the sleeping men.

"Stop!" Rosi hissed.

Ben either ignored her or did not hear her.

"Stop!" She ran up and stepped in front of him.

"Let me go." Ben shoved his way past her.

"Now is not the time," she said.

"They are the enemy," Ben insisted. "Now is the time. That's why we're here."

"There'll be plenty of time for killing later. Now is not it." She grabbed his arm and would not let him shake her off. "What if one of them woke up? What if one of them yelled?"

"I'm quiet. They won't hear me."

"They could."

"They've killed your friends. They've killed my friends. They've burned my home. They have to pay."

"They will." Rosi was scurrying to keep up with the younger man. They were getting perilously close to the sentries, now. "Even if they don't wake up, they will be seen when the others come by."

"We'll hide them."

"Then they will be missed. The plan only works if all the parts work. There's no contingency plan. Stop!" Rosi was sure that her last words were too loud.

Oh, the Hell with it, she thought. She had been training as well these last few days. She dodged in front of Ben and threw him over her hip.

He fell heavily. Certainly someone would hear the "oof!" as the air was knocked out of him.

Rosi grabbed the long, wicked looking knife and sat on Ben's back.

"Be quiet!" she hissed.

"Wat's that?" One of the sentries called out.

"Wat's wat?" another one asked.

Rosi glanced up and saw that two of the men were standing. The third snorted in his sleep and curled up into a ball.

"'Erd somethin'."

"Wat?"

"I don' know. Somethin'."

"Wait 'til ye know wat, then wake me, fool." The second man tossed a log on the small fire, then sat down and wrapped his great coat around his shoulders. He grumbled something Rosi did not understand.

"I'm goin' t'look anyways," the first man groused.

The sentry took a brand from the fire and started walking around the area, staying in the light from the fire, Rosi noted. He waved the brand around and peered into the gloom.

This probably saved them, Rosi thought. The flame from the brand and the fire would wreak havoc on his night vision.

Ben struggled to get up.

Rosi placed the edge of the big knife against the back of Ben's neck. "Shh!"

"'Oo's there!" The sentry called.

The sentry was now on the far side of the light, so Rosi relaxed a little. She kept the blade pressed against the young man's skin, though.

Presently, the sentry tossed the brand back in the fire and explained to his sleeping comrades that it would probably have been their dinner had the others bothered to help. He leaned back against a tree near the fire and drew deeply from a flask.

Rosi thought back to her lessons on the triangle trade and old Hornblower books and decided he was drinking rum. That would, and did, put him to sleep in good order.

Rosi stood up cautiously and backed away from Ben.

He scrabbled to his feet and glared at her.

"I coulda done it."

"Obey the damn orders, soldier!" Rosi snarled. "Follow me!"

The bend was about a quarter of a mile from the sentry. Moving quietly, they made it in about ten minutes.

"Stay here!" she ordered Ben. "Do as I say. When the wagons arrive, come to me and let me know. Quietly. No killing."

She turned to walk away.

"Would you have done it?" Ben asked before she had made it more than a few steps. "Would you have killed me?"

Rosi tossed the knife to the ground at Ben's feet. "When the wagons arrive, come and tell me."

* * *

BACK in the line next to Spartacus, Rosi wondered about the lack of a contingency plan. She had not wanted to worry too much about what to do if her plan failed. Was this wise? Her ego assured her the plan was flawless. Her brain told her that she was no more a soldier than any of these men, perhaps even less of one. Had she given these men an out, a plan of escape, then they probably would take it. Hell, she probably would take it.

She had to get Kirk and the British out of The Castle and, somehow, out of New Richmond. These men could not assault The Castle. If they did, the soldiers inside would cut them down.

Or those from the town would.

If the plan failed, the men knew enough to run. Rosi hoped. They would most likely return to the village. If any got caught, though, Kirk would find out about the village and would bring the British in. They would win, too.

So, there was no real safe place for them. If the plan failed, full flight from the region was the only answer. Who would follow her? Few, if any. Most would go back to trying to fight an organized enemy by themselves. Most would be captured or killed in a week. Probably both.

If the plan failed, that would be the end of Dan, as well. Most likely, he would be caught and shot. Would the locals hide him? For how long? Could Rosi stay hidden long enough for Dan to come and find her?

Most likely, if Dan got away, then he would go to Boston or New York. He would realize that he was stuck here and now. Like Kirk, he was smart enough to do well. Rosi hoped he was smart enough to keep a low profile, make some money, buy a house, stay quiet.

Most likely, though, Dan would be killed. His chances of surviving were pretty slim, even if he succeeded. If the explosion did not kill him, the cold water would. And Dan would certainly stay with Essex as long as possible, increasing the likelihood of hypothermia.

His death would be *her* fault.

Rosi could rationalize that Angie's death was not her fault, even though she felt the guilt. She was sure that Angie and Zilla died by accident. However rough these soldiers were, she had a feeling they generally did not make war on women. There were rules to this sort of thing. Dan was not a woman. Dan was following *her* plan. *She* was the leader. The responsibility was *hers*.

Kirk was her responsibility as well.

What was she supposed to do about him?

It was possible that they might find Kirk at The Castle. There was no real need for him to leave.

She could not possibly leave him with her soldiers. He was

clever enough that he might be able to talk his way out of trouble. Even if he could not turn them to his side, he could talk. These men were a superstitious lot. They knew something was odd about Rosi. They knew that there was a connection, of sorts, between her and Kirk. If he told them the truth, they might simply hang on to both of them until someone with more authority came along. If it was this Beatitude Carol all might be all right. Then again, Beatitude Carol might not be all that understanding, especially if he saw what had been done to his house. Most likely, they would hand the two of them over to someone else who would probably not be very understanding at all.

So, if Kirk were found here, she had to do something, to make a decision.

She could not possibly leave Kirk here and now. He had already shown what he was willing to do. She was under no illusion that she could persuade him to keep his mouth shut.

Could she take him home?

Time travel had a peculiar effect on people. The first few times she had done it, her mind had rejected what had happened. She had simply forgotten the details. It was as if she had been dreaming a particularly vivid dream that drifted from her consciousness as soon as she woke up. She remembered that she had dreamed, but could not remember the details.

Before she figured out what was going on, she had spent only a few hours on her journeys. Once she was aware of what she was doing and consciously participated in the events, she had total recall.

Kirk would probably remember what had happened. Particularly because he appeared to be able to sense the doors and know what was going on. Uncle Richard had told her that while the ability was inherited, it was by no means confined to the narrow Carol gene pool. There were others with the gift. Kirk clearly had it, to some degree.

Dan and Andy were involved enough, and traumatized enough, that they would most likely recall the events clearly. Did

Rosi have to worry about them when they got back? Probably not.

Even if Dan and Andy could be persuaded to keep their mouths shut when they got home, could Kirk?

He might be hauled off to an asylum and locked away if he started blabbering about tears in the fabric of time and space. More likely, he would talk and eventually someone would listen. Even Uncle Richard knew that there were certainly people around the town who could figure out what was going on were they to spend the time digging around. Someone was bound to put two and two together and reach four.

The relationship between the townspeople and her family was tenuous enough.

The Carols did not need the scrutiny.

There were cells below The Castle. Could Rosi lock him up and throw away the key? How was that done? Did she have the authority? Did she have the right? Was she judge and jury?

The simplest way to solve the Kirk problem was to shoot him. People died in battle. Dan did not need to know that she had pulled the trigger. He would probably suspect. Should she allow what was, honestly, a school-girl crush to influence a decision as important as this? Probably not, but she was going to anyway.

If Kirk happened to get shot and killed by someone else, that would be perfect. But if Rosi was going to not only be judge and jury, but executioner as well, then she could not, could not, could not delegate responsibility.

She would have to pull the trigger.

Could she?

Kirk was not stupid. Once he saw Rosi, he would understand her options. He could, and most likely would, make her problem harder by simply doing nothing.

Could Rosi pull the trigger and kill him in cold blood?

She had no doubt that Uncle Richard could. But would he do so to help Rosi? If Uncle Richard were going to help her, would he not already be here?

If her plan failed, then the problem was moot.

If her plan failed.

Before she had time to worry about the quality of her plan, she sensed several of the men moving.

"What is it?" she asked Spartacus.

"Someone's coming?"

"British."

"Hope not," he said. "I'll be right back."

He ran silently into the dark. They could be quiet when they wanted to be, Rosi thought.

Not even a minute passed when Spartacus came back. He had Ben with him.

"Beggin' your pardon, Captain," Ben whispered, plainly put out by their confrontation earlier. "Harry and the wagons have arrived."

Rosi allowed herself to sigh in relief. *Well*, she thought. *That's something.*

She looked at her watch. 3:15.

* * *

THE extra fifteen minutes just about drained Rosi. She had no doubt that the others felt the same.

Was it possible for twenty men to hold their breaths for fifteen minutes?

They heard the first explosion.

They did not have to wait long for the second explosion. It was a doozy!

All hell broke loose. The night sky flashed with the huge explosion that Rosi and her men felt. To her, it sounded like an explosion straight from Hollywood.

Within seconds, British were rushing from the gardens and the stables. They were followed by those inside The Castle. Everyone rushed for the cliffs.

Rosi would have given a lot to see what they saw. Even now, the explosions were continuing.

Dan had done it!

Please be OK. Please be OK. Please be OK. Rosi kept repeating to herself. *Essex, too!* she shouted in her head, feeling guilty for not including him at first.

Then the yelling began. Officers yelled. Sergeants yelled. Men yelled. Squads were formed. Horses were saddled.

They were organized and moving even more quickly than Rosi had anticipated.

"Boats!" Rosi called out, making sure not to be too loud.

"Captain." He crawled over to her. Sergeant Major Zablonski had insisted that the 4th platoon go with her as well as the 2nd. "Boats is a good man," Zablonski had said. "Experienced and will keep to himself." Frankly, Rosi barely understood a word the man said. Even as simple a word as captain came out sounding something like *kah'un*. She was not about to say anything.

"Take." She thought for a moment and looked down the line. "Ben and two other men. If the sentries stay behind, take care of them. Then signal the wagons."

Four men drifted into the dark.

Within minutes, the British started moving off. Down the drive they went, quickly and efficiently.

Rosi certainly did not want to fight these professional soldiers. Next to them, even her experienced men looked sloppy.

She was relieved to see Kirk riding off with the officers.

"Spartacus!" Rosi said a couple of minutes later. "Send some scouts ahead. They didn't take everyone."

Spartacus nodded. "I know what to do, Captain."

The British had indeed left a few men behind, but they were distracted by the scene in the harbor. They were dispatched quietly and with only a few shots fired. The ruckus below covered any noise her men made. Rosi had asked the men to kill as few men as possible. When she made her way up the drive, she saw the a few British had been trussed up and were being frog-marched towards The Castle. They would eventually be closed up in one of the second-floor rooms.

Rosi wanted to go to her tower and check out the town, but Spartacus stopped her.

"Some of the British hid in their when they realized we was coming," her sergeant said. "I'll have their bodies removed."

Rosi was happy to learn that her force had lost no one.

She went to the edge of the cliffs to look down at the town.

One of the ships was burning brightly. Rosi could not see all that well, but it looked as if some men were trying to fight the fire. Some men were simply trying to leave the ship.

The second ship was mostly under water. Her masts and sails were burning. While Rosi and the men watched, there was a flash of light under the water, and then a big eruption.

"Got the powder room!" Spartacus whooped.

Somehow, Dan and Essex had also gotten several buildings on the water front.

The British would certainly have their hands full tonight.

"Take the surviving prisoners, tie them up, and put them in the stables," Rosi told Spartacus, hoping there were surviving prisoners. She knew that any survivors would most likely be shooting at her and her men later on in the day, but she had given explicit orders that there would be as little bloodshed as possible during this phase of the plan.

Rosi called out to the rest of the men, who followed her into The Castle.

"Those doors are locked, Captain," one man told Rosi. "We couldn't open them last week. Nor could the Brits."

Rosi smiled. "They'll open now."

She ran up the stairs and placed a hand against the first door she reached. It swung open. "Jam it open, clean it out, and move onto the next. If you can carry it, take it."

Several men cheered and rushed into the first room.

Rosi went down the hall opening doors, letting men in. She was about to open the final door when Hollins caught her attention.

"You'd better come with me, Captain," he said somberly. "Downstairs."

Rosi knew from the look in his eyes what he had seen. "Let's go."

As she went down the stairs, the rest of the men rushed up. They were looting The Castle. The Castle had protected the Carols for hundreds of years. Now Rosi was letting angry men pillage its wealth and so much of its power.

Pity, she though. *Had to be done.* "Make sure you drop some things," she called out to a couple of men who were carefully maneuvering a large grandfather clock across a landing. "We need to make sure they know we were here and that we cleaned the place out."

The men cheered and tossed the clock over the railing with a warning yell. It landed with a crash and a series of funny springy noises. Someone below swore good-naturedly.

Rosi sighed. The clock was a particularly nice Comtoise that would have stood in the dining room and would have been wound by Uncle Richard almost every day before breakfast. It still could not keep time, no clock in The Castle could, but it had been quite pretty.

Hollins led Rosi to the long gallery Kirk had been using. There, one of the men had already untied Sally, who was being held closely by her mother.

"Stay away!" the father cried. He stood in front of his family, tears running down his cheeks.

"You have to stay here," Rosi said.

"We have to go home!" the man stated with a sob.

Rosi explained that they could not. Nor could they come with her men. "We have no way to take care of her."

"Then I'll come with you," the man insisted. "I'll kill some of those sons—"

"No!" Rosi snapped. "You stay here with your family."

Several men gently carried Sally up the stairs. Everyone had heard the story from Rosi and Will. Each man they passed stopped and stood silently for a moment. A couple actually reached out and softly touched the girl's hand.

Rosi left them in the furthest room. She supplied them with as much food as two men could carry. She handed the father a pistol, a bag of shot, and a horn of powder. "We should be back in a couple of days," Rosi said. "But just in case."

She shut the door behind her as she left.

Hollins was still with her. "That little gun won't do much against the British if they find them here."

"It's not for him to use on the British," Rosi said.

Shouting encouragement to her men, she ran down the stairs and went to her rooms. There, she found boxes of papers. She did not even bother to find out what there papers were. She simply grabbed a box and carried it up to the first wagon, which was almost full. Then she had Ben and Harry go down and get the rest of the boxes.

A squad of men was sent to burn the camp.

Rosi went to check on the watch. The two men in the watchtower were almost asleep. They would not be sleeping any time soon after the flow of obscenities Rosi leveled at them when she found them dozing.

She took a moment to glance out at the town below. The fire on the first ship was almost out. A few men were still on the smoldering masts. The second ship would soon be settling into the mud. A third ship was burning, but was being maneuvered away from the others. Even at this distance, Rosi could tell that the sailors were in control of that fire. The buildings burning along the waterfront still gave off enough light for Rosi to see people milling about. She imagined that she saw Kirk in the crowd, but really, she could not see well enough at that distance.

Rosi heard something break as she was walking up to the first wagon. Probably a priceless Ming vase, she thought. She saw a black shoulder bag on the ground. There was a recognizable sticker on the back. It was her computer bag. When she lifted it up, she realized that her laptop was inside.

She handed the bag to Ben, who was sitting in the first wagon. "This is mine," she said. "Keep it safe."

"Take it down to the road and wait for us," Rosi said to the driver and his escort. There weren't many horses, so the men were wedged in among the booty. "Go to the bend, but don't go around it." She slapped the horse closest to her on the butt and had to jump out of the way of the wagon wheel. She stumbled and fell. That always worked in the movies.

The men laughed, and two helped her up.

Maybe she watched too many movies, she thought.

Can you watch too many movies?

The second wagon was almost full. They had three wagons, so things would be happening pretty shortly.

Rosi would be in the second wagon. She had been offered a horse, but the monsters scared her. Spartacus had tried to show her how to ride one day but she could swear the beast had tried to bite her. No, she would go in the wagon.

Sitting in the wagon in the middle of an exposed road made Rosi nervous. Waiting the eternity it took for the third wagon to be prepared made her more nervous.

At last, the last wagon came down the drive and turned onto the road. There was a moment of terror when the wagon driver took the turn too sharply and the men had to jump out to make sure it did not tip over.

It did not.

Just about the time the sun began to rise over The Castle bluff, the watch from the tower came running up to Rosi.

"They're coming!"

CHAPTER 7

AFTER the warning, Rosi knew it would only be a matter of time before everything started. A short matter of time.

It was five minutes or so before the British rounded the far bend and came into sight. It felt as if it had been a very long five minutes. She probably glanced at her watch more during that time than she had the rest of the night. Rosi realized she was probably making the men nervous. Certainly, the look Hollins gave her suggested as much.

She made some effort to look like she was winding it, then shoved it deep into her vest pocket. *Forget about it,* she though. *It doesn't matter.*

Finally, the British did come into sight.

The British did not see the wagons at first. The sun was rising, but it was fairly murky under the trees. About the time the first soldiers were turning onto the drive, they saw the wagons.

Well, not exactly. First the soldiers noticed the three men Boats and Ben had taken care of.

Then they heard the shots from Rosi's snipers that dropped two men in front of them.

Then they noticed the wagons.

It was probably this sequence of events that saved Rosi's plan. The British moved forward with momentum. They might reach the wagons through inertia by the time Rosi's men got them moving. A few bullets whizzing through their ranks altered the direction of their movements.

The soldiers reacted swiftly. A man was sent back towards town and the rest began their pursuit by about the time the wagons started moving.

This surprised Rosi. She somehow expected the wagons to take off like cars, going from zero to sixty in two-point-five seconds. Well, may zero to ten.

It felt more zero to five or maybe zero to two.

She saw two of her snipers in the trees next to the wagons. They were waiting for their mates to reach them. Then they fired.

None of the British fell, but they slowed down and ducked.

It gave the wagons a few seconds.

Six snipers jumped into the third wagon and began hurriedly reloading their weapons. These men had rifles and had better range than the usual muskets.

Rosi knew enough about tactics to realize that if the British forced a battle right now, her men would be annihilated. The snipers helped to keep the enemy further back.

She sent Ben running for the third wagon, to send two snipers to the front. Rosi refused to explain every order to each man, but she did explain to Spartacus.

"If we reach a tight enough bend or rough enough terrain, they can jump down and get in two, maybe three shots before we are too far ahead for them to catch up with us," Rosi explained. "The men in the third wagon can then run up to the first and take a short rest."

All they had to do was slow the pursuers down a little bit.

* * *

ROSI was most surprised, and annoyed, at how slowly the chase progressed.

She had seen lots of old cowboy movies in which there was some sort of long chase scene. The Indians galloped and whooped and fired arrows from horseback, and the settlers flew across the dusty plain in their Conestoga wagons. The women folk drove the wagons at break-neck speed, while the men folk shot at the Indians.

In these movies, more often than not, the U. S. Cavalry showed up at the last minute and wiped out the Indians. Rosi felt that this scenario would be her preferred choice to the alternative of being a massacre or mass scalping.

Actually, Rosi had a pretty good idea what her fate would be were she captured by Indians *or* redcoats. Worrying about her hair, unwashed and frayed as it was, might well be the superficial concern of a vain and shallow girl, but it was certainly more palatable a mental image than being carried off to the British camp as a prize…or worse, as a gift to Kirk.

She reached back and felt her hair, as if to make sure it was still there. She smiled at Hollins and scratched her head, hoping it was just an itch and not evidence of tenants.

This chase was not being done by wagons bouncing through the dust.

None of the drivers was about to go that fast or furious.

"Captain," the driver of the first wagon told her when she ran up to confer with him. "Cain't go too fast'r this wagon'll fall'part. T'weren't made t'go fast. Goin' fast's'I'can."

Rosi thanked the driver and stepped off the moving wagon and waited for the second one to come by. Hollins reached down and lifted her up.

She was not exactly sure how far they had to go. She and Andy had guessed that the distance was ten to fifteen miles. She knew there was a pretty big difference between ten and fifteen miles, but it had never really occurred to her to worry about that. To her, it was maybe a ten to fifteen minute difference if she were on her scooter. But if she were going to go *that* far, she would probably go with someone else who had a car. Since she was not driving, all she cared about was not being late. In her day, Route 1A was only about five minutes from downtown New Richmond. The highway did *conveniently* arc along *behind* the low hills that marked the edge of Carol domain. Even I-95 was only a few minutes further away. It simply never struck Rosi that going any place in the area took any real time.

As for her men, they thought that both ten and fifteen miles were great distances. Most of them had never been further from the area than Portsmouth, if that far, and that was not even twenty miles away. As she had found out just a few days ago, several had never seen the ocean, though they probably lived in earshot of it. A fifteen-mile journey inland to an old dry riverbed was probably not something any of them had experienced. It would be going out into the middle of nowhere. The old riverbed was even fairly out of the way in Rosi's day. Though if you were really quiet in the middle of the night, you could hear the trucks go by on the bridge a bit further on. Naturally, no one went out to the old riverbed to be quiet. Everyone went there to make noise in one way or another.

This was some distance. Rosi hoped that they would make it by nightfall. There actually was a faster way to get where they were going, but the rutted, windy, root-covered excuse for a road kept the British from catching up.

For the most part, the sides of the road were too steep for the few horsemen Rosi could see to flank the short wagon train.

Once or twice in the morning, the horsemen found an area where they could pull away from the traffic jam of British. However, this put them in range of the men from all three wagons, so they would yell and fire and whoop and ride back to the safety of distance.

* * *

"WHAT'S going on?" Rosi asked, sitting up. "Why isn't the rear wagon moving?"

"I dunno, captain," Hollins replied.

"Would you mind going and finding out?" Rosi was not sure if her men lacked initiative or simply were used to being told what to do. Probably both.

Hollins returned to the wagon a few moments later. The front right wheel had come loose from the axle somehow. "Maybe we should leave the wagon," he suggested, helping Rosi down. "We don't have time to fix it."

Rosi did not answer. She ran back to the broken-down wagon and glanced over the back.

Fortunately, the wagon had just crested a fairly steep hill, and the hill was part of a sharp blind turn.

The British were now only few dozen yards behind. Rosi could see a couple of them poking their heads around the bend, only to duck back when the men on the wagon started firing at them.

Rosi pointed up to where the mountain they were on sloped up from the inside of the turn. "Send some men up there."

"But, captain," Spartacus, who was in charge of the third wagon, said. "We won't be able to do any damage to them from there."

"Perhaps," Rosi responded. "But if they are up there, they can do a great deal of damage to us."

Spartacus shrugged and sent Bartlett and two other men to the top of the hill.

"We can't leave the wagon," Rosi explained. "This might be the slowest chase in history, but it is a chase. They have us in sight and can reasonably expect to catch us. All we have to do is keep them out of range but in sight and they will follow us. That's the plan. If we leave the wagon, it might slow them down too much. It will certainly slow down the main body." She pointed down the hill to where the road twisted back into sight.

There was a much larger body of redcoats moving along steadily. They were in no hurry. The advance guard would eventually catch up to the group of rebels. Once the rebels were contained, they could be systematically wiped out. It would not even take the British very long, Rosi realized.

The company needed to keep moving.

The British needed to follow. If they stopped, or if it looked too obviously like Rosi was letting them keep up, then the plan would fail.

There was no reason for Cromwell, or Mosley, to order the entire garrison after the three wagons. If Rosi had indeed taken whatever it was they were looking for, then it was an understandable reaction. If the British realized that this was a trap, then enough men could return to New Richmond and The Castle to defend it and still field enough men to decimate this small force.

The plan had seemed like a fairly decent one when Rosi had thought of it. Nobody had had any real objections. When she thought about it, Rosi realized that most of the men in the company were used to being told what to do. They might not be in the army, but they worked on farms or lived with their parents or wives and had never had to make important decisions. Certainly not life and death decisions. The real soldiers were not officers. Zablonski, Hollins, and Boats, trained men, understood how to follow orders. They concerned themselves with being able to make the men do what had to be done. She trusted them implicitly to be able to know how to deal with most situations that needed to be handled on the spot in the middle of battle. Would they understand the bigger picture? Would they care?

Dan was hurt and angry with her, Rosi knew. His pride was wounded. He was so hostile when the plan was being discussed that no one would have paid him any attention if he had proved cold fusion. He was a natural leader. Everyone liked him, even that little Indian tramp. He was bright and knew the area. His insight could have been useful.

Andy was also bright. He was so broken up by the news about Angie that Rosi was surprised he had been any help at all. In the end, he had come up with the location where the trap should be sprung. That was something.

Rosi realized she was like many leaders. She wanted someone who could tell her what she should do, but there was no one. It was Rosi's job to make the plan and carry it out.

She could not spend time trying to second-guess the plan. It was too late. The plan would succeed if everyone did exactly what they were supposed to do.

If Beatitude or the New Hampshire 4th failed to show up, then the British would most likely win the battle. They might win anyway.

If Kirk and Cromwell continued to think that the means to control the time portals was an object, like a key, than most likely they would continue to follow Rosi's company. If they realized it was a person, they could bide their time. A person would have to return to New Richmond to fix things.

Several shots brought Rosi back to the here and now.

She ducked behind the wagon.

Hollins laughed. "That was up there," he said, pointing up the hill. "They musta had the same idea you had, captain."

"Who got there first?" Rosi wondered.

Hollins went around the horse and yelled something up the hill. "Look up, captain," he called over to Rosi.

She looked up. Bartlett was standing up the slope thirty feet or so waving.

She waved back.

"Keep them from coming around the bend in force," Rosi said. "And shift the men around."

The men on the third wagon had been doing most of the fighting so far today. Rosi had planned on the men firing by wagons much like they would fire by ranks. It never struck her that the people in the front would have very few chances to engage the enemy.

"And tell the men in front to get out and move about. Stretch their legs. Eat some lunch." She had the feeling that their pursuers would not be doing much while they all waited for the wheel to be fixed.

How odd for her little chase scene to be bogged down because someone had to change a flat.

* * *

IT seemed as if it took forever to fix the wheel. The overall result was simply that the timetable was completely screwed. That is to say, the plan was further off schedule than it had already been.

Rosi had estimated that the whole journey would take about three hours. From the landmarks that she sort of recognized, she guessed they were about a third of the way. They should reach where they were going sometime around sundown. As long as there were no more flat tires.

What would Patton do?

They had reached a straightaway. They should be able to put some distance between them and the British.

The British had been keeping their cavalry well to the back.

Horses made good targets, Hollins had pointed out.

So did Rosi, she discovered. Whenever she came back to check on the rear wagon, the British intensified their fire.

There was no real danger. The British never got close enough, or in large enough numbers, to be anything more than a nuisance, but they could be a nuisance.

"If you need us," Spartacus said, having returned to the rear wagon. "We'll send someone back to talk with you."

The rear wagon was pock marked by shot. Everyone who had spent any time on it was cut by splinters. Thank God nothing worse had happened.

Rosi had the feeling that her men had done little more damage, though the sharpshooters were keeping a running, albeit low, tally.

When they reached the straightaway, several men had run forward and cleared the road. It was almost a quarter of a mile long and fairly wide. This allowed the wagons to pick up some speed.

It was when they were all but through this stretch that they ran into the Preacher.

Rosi wondered if this was the same Preacher Angie had run into in New Richmond.

The Preacher was in a small carriage, but was taking up enough space in the road that no one could pass.

When asked to move, he had simply refused. He would move for no sinner, no rebel against God's Anointed King.

When several men went to his carriage and physically tried to move it, the Preacher laid about him with a horsewhip, driving the men away. As he swung, he sang, in a loud and lusty voice. "Kings are by God appointed, and damned are they that dare resist, or touch the Lord's anointed."

When the redcoats first entered the straight stretch and saw the jam ahead, they stopped. Perhaps, Rosi thought, they were afraid of a trap. It did not take them long to be disabused of this notion.

For the moment, they were not moving forward, but were

conferring and trying to come up with some sort of plan.

Rosi jumped from her wagon and made her way to the front.

"What's the problem here?" she demanded to know.

"He won't move." One of the men, Shelly, said. He was resting in the first wagon after a bullet grazed his arm. The wound wasn't serious, but he had almost fainted when he saw the blood. He was self-medicating, using Beatitude's brandy. He was on his second bottle.

"I got that much."

Rosi stepped towards the carriage and stopped when the Preacher slashed his whip at her. The tongue flicked mere inches from her face. She felt a small punch of wind accompany the snap.

"Who is this harridan you follow!" The Preacher bellowed.

"It makes no difference who I am!" Rosi snapped back.

"Which of you men does she belong to?" he asked.

"They belong to me," Rosi said. "Not the other way around."

"You share yourself among these men?" the Preacher shrieked. "Are you men to be led astray from the glories of Salvation by this wanton slut. Will you take her diseases with you to Judgment?"

He raised his whip again.

Rosi pulled out her pistol and leveled it at the man. "Move your arm," she said. "And I'll put a bullet in your face."

"You would shoot a man of God? Is this what you men have come to, slavishly following this Jezebel? Behind you are the King's men. Tried and true, they have protected you from the dangers of the savages and the wilderness. They are your brethren. You should not be fighting them. You should be embracing them."

"We are at war with them," Rosi said to the man. She turned to Hollins. "Go see what the British are doing." she whispered hurriedly.

Hollins ran to the rear.

"You, however, follow your lust and let this Eve corrupt you," the Preacher continued. "War? How can you be at war against your King?"

"We're fighting for our rights," Rosi said, knowing that the answer was fairly lame.

"Rights? You have no rights but those that come from God."

"Then we are fighting for our God-given rights."

"Who are you to decide what God has in mind for you? You are subject to God's laws and to God's rulers. The King, whether a vile child like you approves or not, is Anointed by God. If you men resist his word, then you deny God's power and glory. *Whosoever therefore resisteth the power, resisteth the ordinance of God, and they that resist shall receive to themselves damnation.*"

"Jesus," Rosi muttered, too loudly.

"Blasphemy! Men, these soldiers, these servants of God's will, mean you no harm. They only are a threat to those who would pervert His Will and the will of His Anointed ruler."

Hollins came into Rosi's line of vision. "They're forming squads. They will be approaching any moment," he whispered to Rosi.

"Render unto Caesar that which is Caesar's," the Preacher was saying. "Hand over this Judas to the King's men and let them punish her for her evil. Let this rebellion end. There can be no good from it. King George is the greatest monarch in the world. Who are you, pitiful insects to a man, to strive with him? Let scum like this slattern wage her war. Go home to your families. Go home to your wives. Go home to your children. Go home to your farms. Go home to your lives. For the sake of your souls leave off this ill-advised adventure. I will speak to these soldiers. As they are God-fearing men, they will understand you have been led astray by a floozy and her loathsome charms. What promises has she made? What services has she given that compare with the Glory and Salvation of God? If you follow her, in the end, there will only be despair, disease, and death to you and those you love. This great land will be burnt and pillaged as God and His armies of saints ride forth from the heavens in aid of His Anointed King."

"Hear, hear!" shouted one of the wounded men who had

been resting with the help of Beatitude Carol's wine. He then belched loudly.

Most of the men laughed at this interruption. Not all. Rosi could see in their faces that no one was convinced by the Preacher's arguments. Some though, were frightened by his zeal.

Passion was far more dangerous than reason, Rosi thought. The Preacher only needed one or two men to go over, and the rest might well follow.

"Duck!" Hollins snapped.

At the same moment, Rosi heard someone some distance to the rear, yell. "Fire!"

She and all her men hunched down. A spray of lead bounced on the road behind them. Quite a few shots thudded into the wagons.

"They'll be close soon enough," Rosi said to Hollins. "Return fire!" she called out. "Don't worry about hitting them. Just keep them back."

She heard sporadic fire from her men.

They ducked again as another volley stirred up the dust around them and chewed away at the wagons.

The sharpshooters, spurred on by Spartacus, ran to the rear and started sending more accurate shots into the steadily approaching wall of redcoats. This was not what Rosi had planned on.

"Get out of the way, old man," Rosi called up to the Preacher. "You'll get shot."

The Preacher sat up straight and held a Bible above his head in both hands.

"The LORD *is* my strength and my shield," the man yelled, raising his eyes to the heavens. "My heart trusted in him, and I am helped. Therefore my heart greatly rejoiceth, and with my song will I praise him. He will protect me for I obey him and love him and his Justice. Throw down your weapons and embrace the Goodness and Will of our Lord."

What would Patton do? Rosi asked herself, as the Preacher started singing at the top of his lungs.

She had a brief vision of plugging the annoying man, but rejected the idea. She had to be better than that if she wanted to keep her men.

"Do something, captain!" Hollins pleaded, as they all ducked once more.

The next volley, or the one after that, would start to do real damage.

Rosi kept an eye on the singing Preacher and motioned for Hollins and Spartacus to get the men off the road. Humming "Onward Christian Soldiers" just to be on the safe side, she scurried along the side of the road until she stood next to the carriage. She aimed her pistol and, knowing what Patton would do, shot the Preacher's mule in the ass.

The mule reared up and took off like a bat out of Hell, straight towards the British.

The Preacher was tossed into the back of the carriage.

Rosi was knocked over, and almost slid down into the ravine by the side of the road. She would have disappeared over the edge, except that Spartacus grabbed her and tossed her unceremoniously into the second wagon as it sped by.

She pulled herself up and watched as the carriage plowed into the ranks of British. It was kind of like bowling, she thought.

* * *

BY mid-afternoon, Rosi could see the riverbed not too far off in the distance.

This area looked almost the same as it did in her day, but without so many trees.

If the road followed the same path that it would in two centuries, then it would follow the old river bed for a few miles until it crossed the river using a nice, modern bridge. Soon, they would be able to see malls and shops and churches and all the trappings of modern civilization. For a moment, Rosi forgot when she was and was looking forward to seeing the sights of her own time. A stray shot whipping through the trees brought her back to 1780.

Rosi sighed.

As the road approached the river, it straightened out. Not good.

The ground to the left, or the west, or towards the river began to become less impassable. Not good.

A fairly large troop of cavalry was moving along, a hundred yards or so to the west, hoping, no doubt, to cut off Rosi's retreat.

She gave a whistle and signaled to the men in the front two wagons to be prepared. It was a wasted effort. The men were already readying their weapons. They were prepared to fight.

She saw a number of puffs of smoke moments before she heard the shots. Then she saw the men.

A group of rebels had hidden in a copse of trees and had opened up on the cavalry.

A few British fell. Rosi did not count. The rest fired back and returned to the main body.

Several of the men from the trees rushed out and grabbed what horses they could. One of them mounted a horse and rode straight for the wagons. After a few seconds, Rosi recognized Sergeant Major Zablonski.

"Sergeant Major!" Rosi called out, trying to sound cheerful. "I am happy to see you." She was, to a degree.

Rosi was not truly happy about anything at the moment. What she had thought would be two or three hours of fast and furious riding had turned into almost nine hours of constant bumping, rocking, and ducking. About an hour earlier, she had tried to eat. Someone had assured her that she was eating mutton liberated from the British camp, but she had her doubts. She had been handed a bottle. Someone assured her that it was filled with wine. She had her doubts about that, too. No one had come up with a name for whatever was in the bottle. The food gave her an image of something that barked.

The quality of the food and drink was made moot when her wagon began a very fast charge down a steep slope made more from roots and holes than dirt. If she were stuck here, she would make sure to invent concrete and asphalt for the roads. In any case, once the thrill of the ride down ended, Rosi indecorously threw up her lunch.

Fortunately for her ego, she was not the only one.

Unfortunately, she was the only one who threw up over the side.

Briefly, she transferred to the front wagon. There, not only had several of the men been sick, but the rest were taking medicinal advice from the now soused Shelley who was teaching everyone a new song.

"Miss," Zablonski said, pulling his horse next to the wagaon. "I realize you are not fond of these beasts, but if you would like—"

"Happily!" she cried, holding out her arms.

Laughing, Hollins placed her in front of the Sergeant Major, who rode off.

"They'll follow," Zablonski said. "Won't be long, now."

"Didn't know you rode horses," Rosi said, trying to avoid biting her tongue.

"We do all sorts of things where I come from, Miss."

Rosi had never asked where he came from. His name was Polish, to be sure, but he did not sound it. She thought it would be rude to ask.

"A company of redcoats have reached the ferry," Zablonski explained. "That's what the scouts said." The ferry was where the bridge would be in Rosi's day. "It'll take them a couple of hours to pick up and join their friends."

"Any word from the 4th or Beatitude?"

"None yet, Miss. But still's early. Sun's on the way down. 'll be dark in a coupla hours. Got plenty work t'do, but plenty time."

Zablonski skillfully, Rosi thought, turned the horse off the main road and down a narrower path that led to the riverbed.

Rosi could hear water. She could hear a lot of water.

A head of her was a large open area of flat marshy land. Just below her, the two banks came close together. A rather large stream of water which ran along the riverbed formed a nice, rough series of rapids as the stream ran towards the sea, entering the ocean just below where the country club would someday be.

At the far end of the open area was where the beach would be at the bottom of a fairly steep bank. The beach was across the stream. On this side, was open land. Most of it would be too soggy for the British to use for cannon or horse. If it all worked out, they would have to approach by foot.

If it all worked out, someone would come and help within a day.

If not, the British numbers would most likely prevail.

For the first time in hours Rosi felt as if it might all work out. The British had sent half their force to the old ferry. They would most likely try and combine forces prior to rushing Rosi's position.

That gave Rosi and her men time. That is what they wanted most of all.

"Who are those people?" Rosi asked, pointing to the people moving around the beach.

"Picked up some strays," Zablonski sighed. "Mostly women and children. But beggin' your pardon, Miss, never expected to have a woman officer. Might be all right to have them around if we need them. Musket's a musket."

"How very forward thinking of you, Sergeant Major." Rosi laughed. She could grow to like this gruff man. They were approaching the stream, so Rosi told him to let her down. She wanted to drink and wash away the dust. She could walk the rest of the way.

"Wagons'll be here soon," he said.

The first wagon was cresting the bank. Rosi heard a couple of shots. "Think they'll make it."

"Yes, Miss." Zablonski nodded and rode on.

The water was delicious, Rosi thought. She dunked her head into it.

It was cold, too! She gasped as she pulled it out.

It had not been that cold a few weeks ago when they all came out to skinny dip!

Of course, that had been late July.

And it had proven cold enough then, Rosi giggled. *Mind out of the gutter!* She told herself.

Grinning at her private joke, she sloshed across the water and to the beach.

The women had been busy. Two earthen walls were already well on their way to being finished.

Rosi sat on a large rock and pulled her boots off. They could dry for a minute, and she could wiggle her toes.

Angie came over and sat down next to Rosi, taking her hand. "When they told me all about this lame plan, I figured it was yours and that you'd need someone sensible around to help."

"Well, it was the best I could come up...Angie! Jesus!"

CHAPTER 8

ROSI and Angie threw themselves into each other's arms. They hugged. They kissed. They cried.

"Zilla's here as well," Angie was able to force through her sobs.

Rosi glanced over to see Zilla standing with a group of children, instructing them on how to dig a hole.

Slit trench, Rosi reminded herself as she dragged Angie over to the older woman.

Zilla stood sternly glaring at the boys, who were clearly having more fun digging the trench than they should be.

"I see you, child," Zilla said to Rosi without turning her head. "You boys been told how to dig that ditch! Now you be getting to work or I will come down there and show you what I can do with the shovel."

One of the older boys muttered something under his breath. Rosi could not hear him, but could gather the gist of what he said by the laughs of his mates.

Zilla stormed over to the boy. "Do you have somethin' to say to me?"

"No, Miz Zilla." The boy smirked.

"Jimmy Parker! I know your ma and da. Do you want me to be telling them what you have been saying?"

"No, Miz Zilla." The boy grinned at his friends.

"I know what you've been up to in barn when your da's at market. Should I tell him? Your ma? Should I tell Miss Bet Sykes who you been making eyes at?"

Jimmy Parker quailed. "No, Miz Zilla!"

Zilla grabbed him by the shirt and dragged him out of the trench. "You are an unnatural child, Jimmy Parker! Now you get over and fetch this young lady's boots. You clean them and polish them! And use your spit, boy. I want her to see her pretty face in the leather."

She sent the boy scurrying to the rock with a well-placed kick to the rear. The other boys hooted after him until Zilla turned on them and roared.

They quickly returned to digging.

Zilla turned to Rosi. "I agree with the little girl, child. When I heard this plan I knew it had to come from you. I'm not sure why we are diggin' holes for our men to fight in. It seems like a scatterbrained idea. They'll be in holes soon enough. We do not need to be digging them now," she said soberly. She took a soiled cloth and wiped her hands. "Now you come here and embrace old Zilla!"

The three women were in each other's arms before the sentence was finished. Tears fell afresh. They laughed and sobbed.

It was Zilla who broke the embrace.

"Child, you will be busy soon enough. You go and soak your feet and rest for a few minutes." She turned to Angie. "Go and get your friend some food. As much as you can carry. She looks like she hasn't eaten in a month. Go now! Shoo! And don't be eating any of it!"

Angie ran off laughing.

"Child, I promise that the little girl did not cook the food, though can she put it away. You sit down and rest. I felt I was doing the right thing when I had those boys put you in charge, but I did worry. But any woman who can convince Angus to let you stay in charge has what it takes."

"Angus?"

"Angus, lass!" Zilla laughed and glanced over at Sergeant Major Zablonski. "He's a stubborn man that one."

"And you're a fine woman, Miss Zilla," Zablonski said, coming over.

Rosi could tell by the way the two of them looked at each other that they had discovered electricity. She had a mental image of the two of them tied to kites and flying over Philadelphia. She giggled.

"Angus?" Rosi asked the man, who blushed under his bushy beard.

"I was christened Przemyslaw, Miss." He smiled.

"Learn to answer to Angus, Sergeant Major," Rosi said.

Zablonski nodded. "It's better than most. Now you rest for a while as Miz Zilla says. We have everything under control."

Rosi considered the battle that would be coming and nodded. "Let the women and children work as long as they can. Let the men rest for a while. They deserve it. Rest and food."

Zablonski nodded agreement.

"And," she added, "put some sharpshooters on those—those...."

"Hills, Miss?"

"Yeah." The formations looked more like rock chimneys, but Rosi did not want to get into a debate over that. Especially since she was not sure.

They were in an area where the old river, probably hundreds of years ago, widened into what must have been a fairly large pool. Dotted around the pool had been a series of islands. When the river dried up, or shrank, the island formations remained. They did not look like hills to Rosi, but more like those stone formations she had seen out west a few years ago when her father had taken her to a week at a dude ranch. Rosi had not liked horses then, either, but her father had insisted she spend each morning taking riding lessons from an ancient cowboy who kind of looked like Walter Huston in that movie with Humphrey Bogart. Daddy's instructor was a grad student named Lucinda.

Neither of them learned how to ride a horse that week.

Realization rushed into Rosi's consciousness. *Daddy!* She almost screamed aloud. "Uh. Sergeant Major. Get some sharpshooters on those hills and harass the enemy. The wagons will be here any moment. We need to give them time to get over the stream."

Zablonski nodded and moved off.

Angie reappeared with a wooden bowl full of food and some

sort of wooden spatula. "They don't have any forks or spoons of any sort. I don't know if this is because they don't use them or they didn't think to bring any."

Rosi dug into the food enthusiastically. It was green, had red and orange chunks in it, and had a gravy vaguely reminiscent of chicken. It was certainly better than the last week's fare of carbonized squirrel.

Angie talked while Rosi ate. "You wouldn't believe how many people are around, just wandering in the woods. This war has displaced them. Not just the fighting, but allegiances as well. I know you don't think that they care for the whole philosophy of the war, and they probably don't, but they are just as involved. Most of these women's husbands have gone off to fight. Many have never come back. They don't even know if they're dead. Planting season is coming soon. Some have been chased off their land by landlords who are loyal to the British.

"They've been forming small groups. Zilla and I having been gathering them together. We had a regular shantytown over by the ferry. We'd still be there except your Sergeant Major showed up yesterday. Did you see the way he and Zilla were looking at each other? Anyway, he told us to come with him. Most of us did. Not all. Some are still there, and the British came this afternoon. I hope they got away. There are a lot of women and children, men too, out there wandering around the woods. It's getting warmer, but things will be a mess when their food starts running out and they have no homes to go back to. The British having been burning down farms of rebels all week. Asking a lot of questions, too." Angie paused for a breath. "Rosi?"

"Yes," Rosi answered through a mouthful of stew. She was listening to her friend, but could not help glancing up when she heard some shots fired by the small path.

The wagons were slogging their way through the marsh.

Zablonski had either reacted very quickly or anticipated her order, for there were already men placed on the tops of the *hills* who were firing at the British on the far bank. The shots were probably ineffective. Most likely, they did not even reach the far bank. They would, however, slow the enemy down.

"Rosi," Angie went on. "Most of the questions were about you."

Rosi sighed. "I know."

"And we heard rumors that you'd been caught and killed. I knew that couldn't be true. I knew it!"

Rosi felt bad. Once she had realized that the bodies in Zilla's house were human, she had simply assumed they were Angie and Zilla. She had not bothered to determine anything further. Okay, so the men had told her the bodies were Angie and Zilla's, but Rosi should have had some faith. Rosi never for a second really believed that *she* would be killed, but it had only taken her a second to conclude that Angie was dead.

"We ran forever," Angie was saying. "It felt like weeks. The guys found us a mule for a few hours before it gave out and died. They even carried us some. You can't run in these shoes, they're terrible. One time we hid in some hay while the British rested in the barn. One guy was sitting on the hay just a few feet away from me. It was that Conner fellow. He's the only one not interested in catching you. He wants me." Angie swallowed. "He'll be out there, won't he?"

"He'll be fighting a battle, not after you," Rosi responded.

"You know," Angie said. "Those British, they hate Kirk. He better find them a way to get you or to make that Admiral happy, or he'll be cut loose. If that were the case, I'd rather be us caught by the British than Kirk. I heard the things they were saying they wanted to do with him. Rosi. It was me. It was me. I was the one who got too tired. I couldn't go on. I couldn't take another step. I knew the Brits were only a few minutes behind us, but I had to stop. I was so tired I was crying. So the guys, they swapped clothes with us so the dogs would follow them. We all thought that the Brits would simply rough them up a bit when they caught them. Beat them up and send them on their way. We didn't think. I didn't think. What a horrible way to go!" She was weeping now, as was Rosi. "Rosi. Rosi!"

"What is it, Angie." Rosi held her friend.

"I never even learned their names! If I did, I didn't remember them. I didn't even know their names!"

The two girls held on to each other for some minutes.

Rosi filled Angie in as best she could. She did not know exactly where Andy had gone to, but they were glad that he was safe. Angie was also the only person Rosi could talk with about how worried she was about Dan and Will.

They were still sniffing and wiping their eyes when Jimmy Parker came and handed Rosi her boots.

"Sorry, they're not dry," he said, trembling.

"Don't worry, Jimmy." Rosi laughed. "I'll tell Zilla you did fine. Now, tell me. Where are you children stationed?"

"I'm not with the children." Jimmy Parker looked offended. "I'm a runner," he said proudly.

Rosi looked at Angie, who explained that some of the older boys had volunteered to act as messengers and carry ammo and water. It sounded like a dangerous job.

Rosi smiled and put a hand on Jimmy Parker's shoulder. "Just stay out of the line of fire then, Gunga Din."

Jimmy just looked confused.

"But first," Rosi added. "Take Angie here, Miss Kaufman, up to the camp on the bank."

"I am not going to be sent to sit with the old women!" Angie roared.

"You will go where I send you!" Rosi snapped back.

"My place is here with you."

"Angie." Rosi's took her friend's hands. "I lost you once. I'm not going to lose you again."

"I'm not going to make it that easy for you. I want to help. Little Jimmy here gets to help." Jimmy scowled at the adjective. "I can carry powder just as well as some kids."

Rosi sighed. "Sergeant major!" she barked.

"Miss?" Zablonski appeared suddenly.

"Have someone take Angie, Miss Kaufman, up to the camp. She is to organize some sort of hospital. She can commandeer any and all supplies that she can find. Angie, that is certainly more important than carrying gunpowder back and forth. You'll probably end up having to fight anyway. Sergeant major, has anyone heard from the general? Beatitude?"

"Not yet, miss."

"See, Angie? We'll probably have to retreat up the bank. Keep the wounded comfortable. Cover our retreat."

Zablonski growled an order and Spartacus came and led the protesting Angie away.

Rosi pulled on her boots, before turning to the waiting sergeant major. "Do you think we have time to get me to the top of that hill? I want to look around."

She pointed to the furthest of the three tall formations. It was about two hundred yards away and slightly to the north.

The British were beginning to come down the far bank. They were milling about. Soon, they would enter their formations.

Rosi guessed that about now, the officers were trying to determine out what Rosi's company was doing on the far beach. They were probably clapping themselves on the back. The company had no easy retreat. If it was forced to retreat up the bank, it could only do so if it were routed.

Rosi understood this. She was burning her bridges. She was burning the bridges for well over a hundred men, not to mention the women and children.

The British knew this as well. This meant that they could take their time.

Any time the British took meant Rosi's company had more time to dig in, and reinforcements had more time to show up.

"We'll get you there," Zablonski promised. "There and back again."

He lifted Rosi onto his horse and mounted behind her. Four other men, sharpshooters, came on another horse and a mule.

* * *

ROSI had a great view of the battlefield. The air was clear. The sun was beginning to set, but that would only really affect the enemy. They would not be able to see to attack.

The forest along her side of the river had grown right up to the edge, so there was little danger the British could approach them with enough of a force to pose a real threat from that direction.

She probably would not even bother sending scouts too deep into the forest. It was dark. It was foreboding. There was a blackness deep inside the trees that made her uncomfortable.

This battle might be between the British and her outnumbered and outgunned company, but there were other forces involved. They seemed to be pushing the trees towards the edge to hem in the battle.

Rosi was too far away to tell what these forces were. Was her mess encroaching on the territory of another Guardian? Were the Widows here to watch the deaths of their sons and lovers?

Although the sun was bright, there was a slight mist slowly rising all around.

Someone, something was watching.

She had not thought about it during the day, but it struck her that the only living things she had seen all day had been people and beasts of burden. No startled rabbits had scurried through the growth. There had been no birds. Nothing.

The hill she was standing on was to the northwest of the beach. It was higher than the other two hills, which lay to the west. She was even higher than both banks. This had most likely been an island at some point. She wondered about it as a strategic point. It gave her a good view of the whole area, but gave no one much of a view of the beach. The other two hills blocked that.

Both she and Zablonski doubted that the British would bring cannon. It was too hard to bring them along the path and too far along the road to the ferry.

If she had cannon, she thought, she could put them on this hill and cover much of the valley. It would be almost impossible to get them this high, if they could drag them through the marsh below.

Cannon would not do the British any good here. There was no line of sight to any part of the beach other than the northern tip. If they tried to lob shot over the two lower hills, they could only attack the steep incline that was the riverbank.

She would have to keep sharpshooters on the other two hills, if only to keep the British from putting theirs up there.

Rosi really did not need to keep anyone here at all. Her few minutes had already told her what she needed to know.

The British foot soldiers had made camp on the southern spit of hard ground nearest to the beach. The stream was fastest there. Too fast to be forded with any ease.

The British cavalry was sweeping north along the marsh to where the ancient river had narrowed again. The stream was fairly deep there.

The British would most likely attack, if they attacked, between the two western hills, or to the north of the middle one.

Another reason to keep men on the hills was to keep an eye on what the British were doing. The hills kept prying eyes from seeing her defenses, but the blind spots went both ways.

On her beach, she could see only a little of the activity, but she knew it was going according to plan.

The first line of defense was a series of slit trenches and low earthen works.

Those manning them would fall back to the wagons, which had been spread out and tipped over forty feet or so back from the water's edge.

The third line of defense was the royal Governor's carriage of state. Someone had stolen it and it had ended up in the woods not too far away. Zablonski had come across it when he was fetching Angie, Zilla, and the other women. Low dirt walls were being put up on either side of it. This carriage was designated as Rosi's command post.

The fourth line of defense was the top of the bank, where Angie was trying to set up a hospital to the north. Rosi could see her friend up there.

The British would most likely not attack this day. They only had a few hours of sunlight and dusk left.

The moon would not rise until the wee hours of the morning.

Around three, Rosi thought.

If she were the British officer, she would wait until morning. Rosi's men would have the sun in their eyes. It should not take the British too long to take the hills. Then, they could force the rebels to keep their heads low as the British maneuvered however they liked. Rosi would be forced to pull back to the second line of defense to avoid sharpshooters. This would allow the British to wade across the stream with impunity.

A night attack would suit Rosi just fine. The darkness would make the defenders' odds better. Or at least less bad.

If the British thought Rosi might escape this self-sprung trap, then they would have to make a full effort to catch her. Certainly, if Kirk and his protector, she had heard his name was Mosley, had any say in the matter, the attack would happen soon. They would be impatient.

Rosi's heart rose a bit when she saw some horsemen appear to the north. But it sank again when she saw that the British rode to greet them, not fight them.

The British reinforcements had arrived.

Nuts.

A few shots rang out.

Rosi looked to the south.

A few British soldiers had wandered too close to the southernmost hill and had been fired on. They were comfortably out of range and were yelling something at the sharpshooters. They were probably laughing at them. Rosi had told her men to fire too soon and too often. She wanted the British to have a false sense of security.

"Duck, captain," said one of the men with her. It was Bartlett.

"What is it?" she asked.

He did not bother asking. He took a couple of steps forward, aimed and fired.

Rosi crawled forward enough to see that a British horseman had ridden fairly close to her hill.

His horse reared up at the near miss and the man was thrown

into the muck.

He stood and made a gesture at them. It was a very colorful gesture, one that Rosi made a mental note to use once she got home.

As the man chased after his horse, Rosi turned to her men. "Time to go, I think."

They agreed.

She stopped Bartlett. "Thanks. Do you think that you could get down and back to our lines on foot if they tried to take this hill?"

"And take two or three of them down before I left, Captain." He grinned.

"One or two would be fine." Rosi smiled back, showing teeth that had cost her father a mint to make perfect.

Bartlett blushed.

Men were so easy!

"Keep one man with you. Stay until it gets too dark to see the edge of the marsh and then come back."

Bartlett snapped a decent salute and grabbed the man next to him.

Rosi waved down to Zablonski and then slid down the hill.

* * *

"MY biggest worry is the lack of a moon," Rosi said to Spartacus and Zablonski a short while later. She had inspected the various lines of defense as well as the top of the riverbank, where she survived a barrage of invective from Angie Rosi had not thought her friend capable of.

"As long as she stays out of the line of fire," Rosi told Zilla, who tried to explain Angie's anger.

Rosi did not anticipate going up the bank too often. The way up, and down, was by rope. She probably could have climbed without the rope except that her arm was getting tired and sore. She realized it was healing faster than most of the men around were comfortable with, but it was too slow for her. Climbing the rope would have been hard enough. Rosi had the advantage of dozens of men who were perfectly willing to raise her up and lower her down. She was beginning to get used to the preferential treatment and knew, deep down inside, that if she had much more of it, she would certainly start taking advantage of these men. She had to watch herself. One thing she could do is not have them pull her up the steep slope whenever she wanted to talk with Angie. It helped that Angie was not speaking to her.

From the top of the bank, Rosi could see the battlefield from another perspective.

"If we can't see them, Miss," Zablonski offered. "Then they can't see us."

"You are right. But it will not be that dark." Rosi pointed to a man on the far side of the marsh who was watching the company. "They know where we are."

"We know where they are," Spartacus pointed out.

"But they will be moving. We won't. We can't move the trenches. Even if we move the wagons, we can't move them too far." Rosi sighed. "I'd like to put a forward line between the two hills."

"I can find you the men," Zablonski said.

"Not too many," Rosi said. "Crossing the stream will take time. The British will most likely move as many men forward as they can before moon rise. They'll be moving through marshy ground, so they might make noise, but we won't be able to see them. It won't be too hard for them to take those hills if they want to. Once the moon comes up, they will be able to strafe us. Shoot us from above."

"Yes, miss," Zablonski said. "If they attack us."

"You said that they might not," Spartacus reminded her.

"I said that I hope that they do." Rosi thought for a moment. "Spartacus…sorry, Sergeant, have some of the boys ready to bank those fires. They don't give out much light, but anyone on those hills will be able to make out all of us. And they'll be close enough to shoot us. If we lose the hills, those fires go out. Angie and Zilla's fires, too. Tell Angie to sterilize anything that needs it now. And get her as much water as you can. She will need it."

"Are you sure you don't want to tell her?" Spartacus asked wryly.

Rosi grinned back. "Not on your life." She smiled. "Now, sergeant major, you need to find me a way to get light out to that marsh."

"Won't do no good, miss," Zablonski said. "If we can light the area, they'll just stay back."

Rosi nodded. "I have no objection to that."

A yell came from one of the hills. "Captain!"

"What is it, Zeb?" Zablonski roared.

Quite a few of the men were moving toward the stream.

"White flag!" the sharpshooter yelled.

Several men cheered. Others joined in.

"Quiet down, lads!" Zablonski yelled over the noise. "Get back to your positions. Now!" He turned to Rosi as the men started going back. "Parley," he said.

"Parley?"

"Yes, miss."

"Parley." Rosi thought for a moment. "Excellent idea. We will meet with them in ten minutes. Someone find me a dry piece of cloth, a comb, and a bucket of water!"

PART III

Endgame

CHAPTER 9

"CLOSER in!" Zablonski bellowed at the English officer.

"Come, man!" the officer yelled back. "We'll be in range of your rifles!"

"And we'll be in range of yours!" Rosi shouted back. "C'mon, Kirk! Don't be a jerk! It isn't that dark! I can see those men behind you."

Rosi could not hear Kirk, but she could see him giggle.

He leaned over and said something to the officer, apparently Mosley. Mosley turned and snapped something behind him. The men lurking behind drifted back.

"Is that far enough?" the officer yelled out. "Or would you like them to move further?"

"'bout two miles further would be fine," Zablonski called back with a laugh.

The officer made a gesture that Rosi felt was even more obscene than the one the other officer had made earlier, though he did not seem particularly angry. She would have to remember this gesture as well.

"What is the girl doing here?" Mosley called out when they got closer.

Kirk whispered something to Mosley, who laughed.

Again, Rosi could not hear what was said, but this time she understood the gesture.

She lunged forward. "Kirk, you—"

"Miss!" Zablonski snapped, dodging in front of her.

Rosi kept moving until she ran into the sergeant major, which stopped her in her tracks. It felt like running into a brick wall.

"Keep the child back." Mosley laughed. "Or send her back to her parents."

Rosi snarled.

"They are trying to make you lose your temper, miss," Zablonski said.

Spartacus stepped to Rosi's side. "Don't let them get to you, Captain."

"You, Kirk!" Rosi barked. "You and I need to talk."

"There's no talking, girl," Mosley said. He seemed to be in a chipper mood. "I have the duty to inform you all that you are under arrest for sedition, taking up arms against His Majesty's forces, murder, and what not."

"That doesn't sound very formal," Rosi pointed out.

"It isn't, girl," Mosley replied. He turned to Zablonski. "There shan't be a trial. We aren't cruel masters. If you surrender now, I will recommend to the admiral that you be treated as leniently as possible. Your officers will be hanged, but I don't see why your men can't go home after flogging and the token nose removal."

Zablonski did not answer. He simply stood at attention.

Mosley patiently waited for him to respond. "What is it, man?" Mosley said. "The terms are fair. A few scars on your back are preferable to a bullet to the head."

Zablonski did not answer.

Mosley turned to Spartacus. "Do you speak for this rabble?"

Rosi was tired of this. "I speak for the company, lieutenant."

Mosley smirked. "Is that all you do for these men?"

Zablonski's hand tightened on Rosi's shoulder.

Rosi sighed. "Whether or not you approve of my command, it is mine."

"And you hold your commission from the Governor of New Hampshire? The colony's legislature? From that rabble in Philadelphia?"

"I hold my commission from the men themselves."

"What an intriguing proposition. Most uncivilized."

"It's the way a democracy works."

Mosley laughed. "Why would any rational person want a democracy?"

"Beau!" Kirk stepped in. "Focus on the issue at hand."

"Very well." Mosley bowed mockingly. "Commander?"

"Captain," Rosi said.

"Captain. Look at your men. They are trapped. Even if they wanted to flee, where would they go? If they try to climb that bank, it will collapse. A few will make it, to be sure, but no more than a score or so. There can be no escape to the north, south, or east. My men will cut them down. The rapids to the south are too strong and would kill most of your men. The stream to the north is too deep. I assume that few of your men can swim. If they try to cross the marsh, they will be outnumbered. You have no rational option other than surrender. My protégé has assured me that you have valuable information that my admiral is in need of. Perhaps if you do, your life can be spared. What do you say?"

Rosi looked away from Mosley. She saw that Kirk was not listening. His attention was far away. "Kirk!" He did not respond. "Kirk!

"What?" he scowled.

"You, me, over there. In sight, but I need to talk with you."

Mosley stepped forward, as did Zablonski and Spartacus. "You can say anything you want in from of us," the officer said.

Rosi kept her eyes locked on to Kirk's. "It's okay, Beau," Kirk said. He smiled. "I supposed she wants to tell me how much she likes me."

"In your dreams, creep," Rosi said through gritted teeth. "Twenty paces over there."

* * *

KIRK led the way over to a small clustering of rocks a short distance away. To get there, they had to walk through some marsh about six inches deep.

"This swamp is going to ruin my stockings, Rosi Carol," Kirk sneered. "They are silk and quite expensive, I assume."

By now, they had reached the rocks. Rosi stopped herself from throttling the boy. "Are you out of your mind, you idiot?"

"I only have so much clothing."

"Shut up. You know what I'm talking about." Rosi glanced

over at Mosley, who was watching them intently. "Does that man read lips?"

Kirk shrugged.

Rosi angled herself, just to be sure. "What the Hell are you up to?" she snapped.

"What am I supposed to do? You sent me here."

"I had nothing to do with that," Rosi said, not really sure if she were telling the truth.

"We were in your house, your room." Kirk angled himself so that he was not looking at Mosley either. "There's something in The Castle that can do this. That can send people through time. Do you realize how valuable that is?"

"Yes." Rosi did, probably more than Kirk. "That's why they built a castle to protect it. You could have found ways to return home that were less temporally invasive."

"Home? Home?" Kirk snorted. "Why would I want to go there? I can be rich and powerful here. These guys have no idea what's going to happen in the next hundred years."

"Yeah," Rosi cut in. "But if you make changes, you won't have any idea either."

"I know how to make a steam engine. I could figure out a cotton gin. I could develop the airplane a century early. I might not be able to make a computer, but I know enough to be the richest man alive. Where's the downside?"

"The downside," Rosi said. "Is that you are playing with forces you can't possibly understand. You are playing with millions, billions of lives. England is supposed to lose the Revolutionary War. That is the way history works."

"Why?"

"What?"

"Why?" Kirk repeated. "Why does England have to lose? For the advancement of some abstract idea like democracy?"

"There is nothing abstract about the good that American democracy has done for the world." Rosi thought for a moment. "We put an end to slavery."

"At the cost of hundreds of thousands of lives," Kirk said.

"And forty years after England did, peacefully. England let women vote earlier than America did. These limeys might like a little pomp and circumstance, but they seem to do democracy quite nicely. If Great Britain still controls the Americas, imagine the excesses of American imperialism that might be avoided. Imagine the greater role Great Britain could have to avoid so many of the atrocities. Me? I just want to get rich, buy Cuba, and surround myself with women. You seem to want to save the world. Why not let the British have the resources to stop Hitler before Czechoslovakia."

"That's not the way it works, Kirk."

"It could be. Are you saying that your family has had the means to travel in time hidden away in The Castle all these years and has not interfered at all?"

"We only try to fix problems that need—"

"Come on!" Kirk laughed. "Tell me, how did your family get so rich? Don't tell me that your uncle is a legitimate antiques dealer. Where does he get his goods? Does he steal them? Does he buy them? That strikes me as interference. Did you know that your Uncle has never paid a cent in taxes? No one in your family has? Legally your family does not even exist. I had my dad's assistant look you up. When you moved to New Richmond, you disappeared from the records. A week later, your birth certificate disappeared. Are you aware that New Richmond appears on almost no maps. Online references are deleted within days, if not hours. It exists, but barely. And you are telling me that you are all altruists? I've been in your house. I've seen the photo albums. Your uncle hobnobbing with Picasso. Dancing with Mata Hari. I've seen pictures of you."

Kirk looked at Rosi, who must have shown surprise on her face.

"You haven't seen those, yet. Yes, I think they are of you in a few years." Kirk smirked. "I took a couple home with me. I liked them *very much*."

Ew!

Kirk leaned in. "Trust me, you have all interfered."

"If we have, it would be to preserve the time-space continuum."

"Oh, yeah." Kirk laughed. "The time-space continuum. I saw the movie." Kirk pulled a photograph out of an inside pocket. He looked at it carefully. Rosi leaned over to see, but Kirk would not let her. "Well, we must be doing something right. You are still here."

He started to put it away, but took another look at the picture before slipping it into his pocket. He leered at Rosi. "So am I." He giggled and jumped out of the way when Rosi lunged for him.

"It's all right, Beau," he called out. "We're just playing!"

Rosi willed herself to act calmly. "You are playing with—"

"I know, I know." Kirk yawned. "Forces beyond my control. Blah, blah, blah. You sound like a broken record."

"I can help you," Rosi said.

"You'll help me to wealth and power?" Kirk laughed. "I accept."

"No. I don't mean that. I mean if you help me set things right here. You know. Kick the British out. United States of America. Democracy. I can help you."

Kirk tapped the pocket with the picture in it. "Clearly, you are going to help me at some point." He giggled.

She hated that giggle.

"You will be hunted down," she said, trying to ignore him. "You'll be caught. I am far from the only one who'll get involved. If you help me, I'll do what I can to help you. To convince them that they should be lenient with you."

"You're lying," Kirk said. He waved away her objections. "Don't bother trying to convince me otherwise. If there were others who were going to stop me, they would most likely have done so by now. They might have let you try. After last week, though, they would have sent someone else."

"I can handle this," Rosi protested.

"If I'm as dangerous as you say," Kirk went on, all but ignoring her. "Someone would be here. If there really is someone else. I figure that they have decided that I am your problem. You sent me here. Don't say you didn't!" he snapped when she opened her mouth. "You somehow activated the time machine and sent me here. You will not help me."

"Look, Kirk," Rosi said, trying to sound sweet. "We just want to...."

"Little coy miss might work on them. It might work on my worthless brother. It won't work on me." He tapped his pocket. "I know. I also know you plan on killing me. Don't even bother denying it. Will I be shot? Will you have one of your men shoot me, or will you do it yourself?"

"If I need to I will," Rosi said, unsure of herself.

"Can you do it?" Kirk asked. He was far too calm for Rosi. "Can you look me in the eyes, place a pistol barrel to my forehead, and pull the trigger? Can you? You have a pistol. Is it loaded? Shoot me. Shoot me now."

Kirk reached out and pulled Rosi's pistol from her waistband. He put it in her hand and placed the barrel against his head. "Go ahead." He held up a hand towards Mosley. "It's all right, Beau!" he called out. "If she pulls the trigger, you let her walk back to her lines! Do you hear me, Beau? If she shoots me, you let her go back! Promise me that!"

It was an eternity before Mosley returned a hesitant *yes*.

"Word of honor, Beau!"

"On my honor!" the man called back.

Kirk smiled. "There you are. They'll most likely catch you and torture you in the night, but he will let you go for now. That whole word of honor nonsense. Funny, no? So, Rosi Carol. Here you are. I tried to kill you on the launch. I have no idea how you got out of the water alive. There was something else down there. I saw it. Not clearly, but I saw it. It was magnificent. And it went for you. And then it and you were gone. And then you came back. Everyone was so concerned, but they were stupid. You weren't bleeding. Your legs had healed. You weren't even in the water, were you? So, I tried to kill you. I would have done so. Now you can kill me. Just pull the trigger. Do you need help?"

Rosi hated him.

"Let me cock the gun for you." Kirk reached out pushed the hammer back.

The soldiers on both sides were watching the exchange. Even if they could not hear the conversation, they could see enough.

Rosi could hear some of her men encouraging her to pull the trigger. Some of the British even were calling for her to kill Kirk. One man placed a wager on it.

"You're mad," Rosi said, realizing that it must be true.

"So? Would that make a difference?" Kirk asked. "You can't let me go, can you? If you let me stay here, I will change history. If you take me back, I'm too much of a danger. I might talk. I won't whisper in a darkened room at Halloween. I'll scream as loudly as I can."

"Time machines?" Rosi forced a laugh. "Who would believe you?"

Kirk sighed. "Perhaps you are right."

"Perhaps?"

"Okay," Kirk conceded. "*Probably* you are right."

"So it might be a good idea," Rosi suggested. "Simply to take you back and let you decide if you want to get locked up."

"Eventually, someone will come. Eventually attention will be directed at your family. My parents aren't townies. They won't be mollified by old wives' tales and sleight-of-hand. They have influence outside of New Richmond. If they insist that people start looking, someone will. Can you people stand up to that sort of scrutiny? You've survived because you've been able to convince everyone to look the other way."

Kirk had a point, Rosi knew. Her palm was sweating. She needed to wipe it. Her finger itched to pull the trigger.

"Will you lock me up?" Kirk asked. "Will you tell Dan? Will you tell my mother, who does love me, that her little boy will spend the rest of his life in a room and never see the light of day again? Can you seal that door with me behind it? Is that your justice? Can you sentence me to that sort of life when it is your fault I'm here? You certainly can't give me to the authorities. What law have I broken?"

"If I don't stop you, billions of lives will be lost." Rosi was on firmer footing here.

"Whose lives? Point to one man or woman who will die because of me. How can I kill someone who does not exist? I challenge you, Rosi Carol."

Rosi thought for a moment. Surely the soldiers had told them about the fire. He could not know anything else. "Angie. Men following your orders killed Angie. You are responsible for that."

"Perhaps," Kirk mused. "They were however, told to not kill or even hurt anyone. Furthermore, I did not order them to do anything. I am a civilian, without any authority. Anyway, my friends have these little things known as telescopes. Last time I looked, Angie was sitting with you in the stream. So, that is a moot point. You can't name any one person I killed."

"Treason," Rosi suggested.

"Against whom?" Kirk asked.

"I'll think of something," Rosi said. "I know what is right. I don't have to prove anything to anyone. I have obligations. I have responsibilities. I have to do what is right. If I have to do some unpleasant things, I try do what is right."

"Who decides what is right?"

"I do," Rosi said. "It's my job."

Kirk laughed.

"What's so funny?"

"You are, Rosi. You are so funny you are obscene. You have a position. You're the new sheriff in town, I tell you what."

"Guardian."

"Guardian. That sounds ever so much nicer. And your job is to preserve the time line."

"Yes." He was quick, Rosi thought.

"You think that you have the right to kill someone to preserve the time line, for the greater good?"

"Yes. If I have to. Or imprison you. Or somehow remove you from the timeline."

"Who gives you that right?"

"I'm a Guardian." Somehow, this did not sound right to Rosi.

"Who made you a Guardian? Were you elected, or did some watery tart throw a sword at you?"

"This isn't funny, Kirk."

"No it is not, Rosi Carol. There does not seem to be much I can do. I have to win, don't I. Otherwise, I'm pretty much screwed. I get no defense. No trial. No jury. You simply pronounce me guilty and punish me. If you want to be my judge and jury, then I dare you to be my executioner. I ask only that you take my body home and let my parents cry over my corpse. Tell them what you will."

Rosi wanted to pull the trigger. Her fingers ached to squeeze. Her ears cried out for the retort. Her eyes begged to see his head explode.

Kirk had to be punished. But did she have to be the one to do it?

"Someday," Kirk said. "You will show me the machine and we will ride it to the ends of time together. I know that. You will not shoot me."

"I hate you," Rosi said.

"Perhaps." Kirk giggled. "But you also are obsessed with me. You have spent this whole day thinking about me."

"Thinking about how to stop you."

"I'm easy to stop. Just shoot me. But...." Kirk gestured out, beyond the men. "That won't be so easy to stop."

"What won't be?"

"You can't even take your eyes off me now." He laughed. "Look out there. Do you see it? Do you see the darkness that pursues us, guides us, pushes us, hems us in? It has been following us since this morning, but it has been hovering outside The Castle for days. I have stood on the balcony and seen it, just out of the corner of my eye, just a hint of black that won't let me look directly at it. There are people inside. They are calling me, just too soft to hear, so loud it is deafening. Why do they call me, Rosi Carol? Why do they keep me awake with their screams? What do they want from me? Who is it among them that reaches out to touch me? Why do they hate you so? I can't tell what they are saying, but they hate you. You have hurt them, given them pain. They beg me, I am sure, for vengeance. You speak of the lives I have destroyed. Are these the souls you have ripped untimely from their lives' un-begun journeys? Who speaks for your victims, Rosi Carol? Who protects the children born from my new history? Who comforts their mothers throughout eternity? Who consoles their fathers? Who are you to decide what souls are saved and which are cast into limbo?

"Perhaps mine is the history that should be, and you are she who brings about centuries of war and hatred. Perhaps you are the one who should be stopped. Should I take the gun from your hand and place it against your forehead? Do you want to feel the cold steel? Do you want to smell the powder? Do you want to see the final flash before the endless darkness? Or should I lock you in your precious dungeons. Perhaps you are she who pounds against the walls in the night and screams for mercy, screams for death. Look at the darkness, Rosi Carol. Can you see it? Can you see it? I can see it almost. I know it's there. They can't. My men cannot. Your men. Cannot. Can you?"

Beyond the men, Rosi could see a blackness so deep and endless that it almost blinded her. It strained against itself, ready to engulf the riverbed. Far inside the depth moved figures, straining to leave.

"Leave them alone, Kirk," Rosi said. "They will not help you. They are far too dangerous."

"Who are they?"

Rosi did not know why she answered, but she did. "They are the Widows. The daughters and mothers and lovers of the lost. They are so filled with anger, all they want to do is destroy. Your fight is with me, Kirk."

"I will win."

"Perhaps."

"I will get the truth from you." He giggled.

"I've seen your handiwork."

"You were watching?" he seemed actually proud. "I knew I smelled something. I thought it was burning flesh. Well, perhaps these Widows will help me. They must be victims of Guardian justice. Perhaps they are your victims, Rosi Carol. How many souls will be cast into the darkness before someone stops you, Rosi Carol?"

"That's not fair!" Rosi growled.

"Will I be a victim?"

"I wouldn't be surprised."

"Will Dan be a victim?"

"Watch it, Kirk."

"Angie and Andy?"

"I said watch it."

"Will your uncle?"

"I'm warning you." Rosi was seeing red.

"Was your father?"

"You son—"

"Was your mommy a victim? Did you kill your mommy, Rosi Carol?"

And Rosi pulled the trigger.

* * *

THE click was deafening.

There was not another sound to be heard.

Rosi stood there dumbly staring at Kirk.

"You pulled the trigger," he said quietly.

"Yes," she replied weakly.

"Not because of the lives I've destroyed," he said.

"No."

"Not because of the damage I've done."

"No." She wanted to cry.

"But." Kirk reached up and gently took the pistol from Rosi's hand. "Because you did not like what I said about your mother." He leaned in very close to her. "Well, I guess we learned something today," he whispered harshly. His breath was hot and moist on her ear.

She closed her eyes. She was sweating. She could feel her pulse racing so fast her heart was about to leap from her blouse.

She tried to hold her breath to keep from breathing too hard.

Kirk placed the barrel against Rosi's stomach and slid it firmly into her waistband, before pulling away. "If it ain't primed, it will never fire." He giggled. "There's a lesson for you!" He spun on one foot and walked back to the British lines.

Rosi waited until he was almost to the soldiers. She turned and forced herself to walk back to the three men who were waiting nearby.

Mosley had a smirk on his face, but Zablonski and Spartacus were concerned.

"Well, captain?" Mosley could barely keep from laughing. "Are you surrendering?"

"Go to Hell, lieutenant!" Rosi snapped. "Come along, sergeant major. We need to get ourselves ready."

"A bit of advice!" Mosley called after them. "We will attack at sunrise! Make your peace with God, because you will be seeing him then!"

"I owe you a guinea, sergeant," Zablonski said to Spartacus as they walked back.

"I wish I owed you, sergeant major," Spartacus replied. "That boy is evil. Even Mosley said it. He said that the world would be a better place if the boy were put down."

"We'd best get to work," Zablonski said. "Miss, some of the younger boys are working on a way to get light out there in the marsh. If we can keep fire going out there, then we can keep snipers on those chimneys longer.

"They won't be attacking until morning," Spartacus said. "I don't think he was lying."

"He wasn't," Rosi interrupted. "There is no reason for them to attack before sunrise. It is eminently to their advantage. Unless, of course, our reinforcements are imminent. That means that we pray they do attack earlier and that we can stay alive long enough for help to arrive.

CHAPTER 10

THERE were still a few hours until sunset. Rosi wished she had a chart. The men seemed to have a good idea of what the sun was going to do. Rosi did as well. She knew it would set sometime in the evening. She figured it would be early evening, but unless she saw it written down, she would not be able to anticipate it within an hour or so.

Rosi had all the available men move as far up as they could. A few of the enemy had wandered within range of the snipers and been sent scurrying back to their lines. One even had to be helped by his friends. They waited until he was out of sniper range to help him.

Given the depth and current of the stream and the width of the marsh, Rosi's men were able to establish a thin line that ran from the east bank just south of the southern-most spire, along the base of the spire and across to the northern spire.

To the north, the line had to make a sudden jag to the deep part of the stream. The riverbed narrowed there somewhat and the British commander had pushed his men as close to the northern spire as he could, going so far as to use several empty wagons to keep his men shielded. They could not do much, but they could harass Rosi's men if they moved too far forward.

Rosi noticed that a lot of junk had been accumulated by her men and by the camp followers. The four sturdiest wagons formed her second line of defense and her command post. There were, in addition, several dogcarts and handcarts that had made their way to the gathering. The women and boys had gathered together a fair amount of wood from the edge of the forest. There was also a potpourri of other goods and equipment, much of which had been stolen from The Castle. This did not resemble a refugee camp but more of a gathering of Gypsies. Poor gypsies who were about to be slaughtered, but gypsies nonetheless.

Rosi had two fire pits dug into the higher ground behind her command headquarters. She wanted to minimize the light given off by the fire so that the British could not use it to help them target her men. But she needed fire. Her men would need warm food and water. Rocks could be heated up to keep feet warm. Several boys had fashioned primitive bows and arrows and thought to set the arrows on fire later in the night to set fire to some of the dryer swamp grass. Rosi also had a fire pit dug on the top of the bank to help sterilize what little medical equipment there was. The general consensus was that everyone was happy that the women were around to take care of the wounded. They were perfectly willing to let Angie try out her strange notions. They were ecstatic that there were no doctors around. Doctors, Rosi was told, tended to have a very simple approach to treating wounds in this sort of situation…amputation.

She also had bonfires prepared at three spots along the extended front line. Bartlett complained about the effect on his night vision. Zablonski and Spartacus, surprisingly, agreed with him.

"He might be unpleasant," Zablonski pointed out. "But if he can't see the enemy, he can't shoot him."

Rosi explained that she would put the bonfires as far out in front as she could, but she wanted the light to keep the British as far back as possible. "The men will be stationed far enough behind the bonfires that the British will need to come fairly close to attack. Their night vision will be screwed up as well. And we'll be able to see them as silhouettes. Easier to shoot. Before we light the bonfires the snipers will fall back to the western spires. The other one is too exposed."

The men nodded, but did not seem convinced. Then Rosi came up with a brilliant idea. Or rather, she remembered a television show she had seen and borrowed from it. "Eye patches," she announced gaily, explaining that those would help the men retain their night vision in one eye. The men grumbled a bit at this odd idea, until Boats said something unintelligible, but clearly supportive. Soon, the snipers and quite a few of the men in the hastily dug ditches near the piles of wood were sporting makeshift eye patches.

They all looked funnily piratical, which made her laugh. Fortunately, they seemed to get the joke and laughed as well.

* * *

AS evening came, both sides settled. The late afternoon had been filled with the sounds of men digging in and preparing for battle. Foraging parties from both sides had run into each other, clashed, and then returned to safety of the camps and the main bodies. The stories told by Rosi's men were vicious and heroic. If their reports were to be believed, the whole British army had been massacred.

Rosi learned, when she investigated one such incident, that the reality was that the men had yelled a lot and fired off their muskets wildly. Rosi had gone down stream as far as she safely could to check out the alleged battlefield. Quite a lot of grass had been trampled. A couple of saplings had been shot. There was no sign of any dead or wounded from either side.

The enemy seemed to have had the same impulse to investigate. A red-coated officer stood at the far side of the small depression that had been the site of the encounter. It was not Mosley. At least, Rosi did not think it was. She could not be sure as the man was too far away for her to be sure who he was. She did not see Kirk. Had Kirk been there, Rosi had no doubt he would have tried to capture her. As it was, the officer laughed when he apparently realized they were both there for the same reason. Doffing his hat, he bowed grandly, and with a laugh rode off.

The last moments of sunlight were punctuated by a few gunshots from snipers intended, no doubt, to make the British keep their distance.

As the sun set, Rosi saw fires dot the landscape to the East. The enemy did not really make any attempt at hiding the pinpricks of light. Those soldiers would be kept as warm as they could be as long as they could be.

Rosi did notice there were few fires near to the outer range of the snipers. The men did not want to be seen. The officers did not want movement to be seen. Rosi thought the British would make sure the fires continued to burn brightly even when they were attacking. They would not want her to suspect anything. Zablonski and Spartacus both agreed when she mentioned it to them. That made her feel somewhat better.

Just as the sun plopped down on the far side of the rise to the East, Rosi ordered the bonfires lit. Within minutes, each was a raging inferno. The last time she had seen a bonfire as bright as these had been in the middle of August, so long ago. Some lame party by the stream.

When the northern bonfire burst into full flame, she realized just how perfect her timing was, as the light revealed quite a few of the enemy just thirty or forty feet from the burning piles. The British men leaped to their feet and ran back to their lines as fast as they could.

A few of her men fired after them, but no damage was done.

* * *

ROSI took the time to make her rounds. She wanted to make sure the men were comfortable. On her instructions, the women on the high bank had been cooking for hours. Those women and the older boys were constantly moving back and forth carrying warm food and warm water. Rosi allowed only a hint of spirits in the water. Her men needed to be in good shape. Battle would come, sooner or later.

She had thought to do a Henry V and listen anonymously to her men. This was not going to happen. But she did make sure that each group of men was visited. She covered her own misgivings and fear so the men would think she was confidant. It helped that the night was cool. Rosi wrapped herself in a large blanket. She was not that cold, but the blanket not only warmed her, but hid any shivering she might do.

The bonfires were the brightest areas. Even fifty or so feet from them, they gave off heat. They gave off a lot of light. This meant that the men could be seen without a lot of trouble. Anyone close enough to shoot at them would be seen as well. And shot. The men up front were cheerful, but they kept quiet as well. Spartacus was in command of the forward bonfires. His corporals, Rosi hoped, would show a lot of initiative when the time came. Both Spartacus and Zablonski insisted that they would.

By the stream, there was a series of manned slit trenches. Rosi was hoping that the British had not seen these being dug and would not anticipate them. When the front inevitably fell back, easily outnumbered by the British, it would retreat across the stream. The men in the slit trenches would delay the British as long as they could and then slip across the stream themselves.

The men on the spires had promised that they would come down when it looked like the front had to retreat. Rosi doubted they would, though. Most likely, those men would fire as long as they had light. Once they could no longer fire, they were harmless and, therefore, probably fairly safe. Certainly no one could shoot them unless the men on the tops were stupid enough to allow themselves to be seen. It would be hard to dislodge them without a real effort. If the British won the battle, there would be little or no reason to stay in the area. Why would they worry about a handful of riflemen? It probably would not be worth keeping enough men around to starve the snipers out.

The men in the trenches were the least comfortable of all of them. They were not allowed fire of any sort. They were given warm food, more gruel really, and drink. Rosi set up a system of rotating the men from the front to the slit trenches regularly, a couple at a time. She did not want her men crossing the stream too often, as they would get wet and then cold. Boats was in command of the trenches. He was also in charge of the one boat they had, a small rowboat, which spent most of the evening moving back and forth. Rosi took it several times herself, with Zablonski and her entourage of runners.

The men back on the far side of the stream were in better

shape. There were slit trenches there as well, but only the sentries stayed that far forward. The men assigned to the West bank were able to huddle behind the wagons. The fires there were in pits and gave off little light. Eustace kept the few men there quiet, and awake.

Robin was in command of a small group of men who would act as a flying squad to shore up weakened sections of the line.

Back and forth Rosi went, from the front lines to the command wagon. She felt like she must be the only person ever to gain weight in the middle of a battle. Each time she stopped to speak with any men, they urged food and drink on her. Back by the command wagon, Harry Thatcher always had food waiting for her. After a couple of times, she and her sergeant major could not look each other in the eyes for fear of laughing and offending someone.

Her little forays did seem to cheer the men up, though.

* * *

THE first attack was launched just about midnight.

Rosi was far behind the lines checking on the command wagon when the first shots were fired.

At first, neither she nor Zablonski thought much about the sounds. The night had been punctuated with occasional pops as both sides nervously shot at shadows and imagined foes.

This time, the popping continued. It sounded rather like fireworks shows Rosi had seen all through her life. But when Sergeant-major Zablonski leaped to the top of the command wagon, Rosi started to hear other noises. Yells, mostly. This was not fireworks!

Rosi jumped to her feet and held out her hand so her sergeant major could help her up.

The British had attacked to the south. The bonfire was the lowest there and the moon was all but out of sight.

The battle unfolded almost in slow motion, Rosi thought. Or, rather, it was as if she was looking at it under a strobe light.

The action around the bonfire she could see just fine. She

was only two hundred feet or so from it. The British had opted to attack along the edges of the light rather than right through it. That made sense.

Beyond the light of the bonfire was dark. The flashes from the weapons gave Rosi and Zablonski snapshot, split-second visions of the fight. A small wave of British seemed to rise from the ground in stop motion and burst against the wall of men just this side of the bonfire. The snipers on the southern spire shot down into the mess. Rosi could only hope that they knew what they were doing.

The southern flank was Rosi's weakest area. The marsh had pushed the bonfire back almost to the stream, so they was no second line of defense on that side of the water.

Rosi could see silhouetted forms of the men on this side of the stream readying themselves. There was some movement and firing to the center and to the north.

"Not to worry about, Miss," Zablonski said. "This attack is to the south. It's just to make us nervous, y'see. If they wanted to push us back to the stream there, they have the numbers. They're hoping we'll realize we're exposed there and move our men about."

"We should get over there," Rosi decided. She started to descend from the wagon.

"Nay, Miss." The sergeant major gently grabbed her arm and held on. "Nothing we can do. 't'will be over by the time we got there."

"We can tell Robin's to take his—"

"Too late, Miss." Zablonski pointed into the darkness.

Rosi tried to look where he was pointing. There was nothing to see. What little light that the moon gave off was hidden behind some ominous looking clouds that had appeared a short while ago. Any night vision Rosi had was ruined by the flashes of battle. One flash revealed enough and told the story to her. Robin was leading his small squad of horsemen along the far edge of the stream. In just a few moments, they would counter attack along the northern flank of this wave of men.

Once it happened, Rosi saw a series of flashes and heard dozens of pops. Men screamed. Horses whinnied. There was a large explosion. The bonfire rose off the ground and spread out in a large circle.

And then it was over.

There were a few scattered shots, but not enough to give Rosi any idea of the results.

A few men cried out in pain, or whimpered.

The coals from the bonfire glowed red, but gave off no real light.

There was no discernable movement.

"Did we win?" Rosi asked after a few moments.

Sergeant Major Zablonski put two fingers in his mouth and sent out a piercing series of whistles. After a moment, a different series of whistles came back. "For now, Miss," he said. He clambered down and then held out his arms for Rosi.

She jumped down, feeling safe. "Get Angie!" she snapped at one of the runners. "Move it, boy!" she snarled when he did not hop fast enough. "The men can rest back here, Sergeant major, but they are not on vacation."

"Yes, Miss." He laughed. One boy was lolling on a pile of dirt. Zablonski gave him a kick that sent him rolling into one of the trenches. The others laughed, but jumped up and started pretending to be busy.

Rosi started off for the stream. "Get some stretchers up here!" she called back. "There are bound to be some wounded." She prayed there would not be too many.

"Grenadiers," Zablonski explained, when the two reached the stream. "They blew up the bonfire. Now they can move in closer."

Grenadiers?

"They made a mistake," Rosi said "They should have blown up the bonfire before the attack. Our guys would have been blinded. They could have rolled up the entire section."

"We was lucky they made that mistake," Zablonski said.

"We won't be that lucky again."

Just then, the small boat came ashore, pulled, rather than rowed, by a couple of Robin's flying squad. There were four men in the boat. Each of them men had been wounded, though not too seriously, two in the shoulders, one leg, one arm. They were out of the fight. Rosi hoped that Angie's first aid would help prevent gangrene and amputation. The man shot in the leg was a redcoat. One of the other men helped him stand up and they all made their way back, led by a couple of the runners.

Rosi noticed that they were not making a lot of noise. Give them a few minutes, she thought. When they get to the top of the bank and into Angie and Zilla's capable hands, the screaming will start.

When Rosi and Zablonski reached the other side of the stream, they were led to the small area behind the southern spire. There was not much space, but enough for a handful of men and a small fire.

Boats was there with two armed men. Sitting next to the fire were three redcoats. Lying by them was one of her men. Jacob, Rosi though his name was. He was alive, but had been shot in the stomach. He was in a great deal of pain and trying not to make too much noise. Before Boats came to speak with Rosi, he went over and liberally poured some liquor between the man's lips.

Boats grabbed one of the redcoats, lifted him to his feet, and walked him over to Rosi. "Beh clams terberficer" he said. He let go of the boy and took a step back.

"He says that the boy claims to be an officer," Zablonski translated.

The boy was fairly young. Probably younger than Rosi. But he was clearly well born. His skin and hair were fair. His eyes, terrified, were bright blue and danced in the flickering light. He was dwarfed by these men and had a very delicate look to him. Even better, Rosi thought, he was cute.

"I'm Captain Carol," Rosi said.

The boy looked about, expecting to be brained by one of the brutes by him, no doubt, Rosi thought. But he was brave enough. He stood tall, stuck out one leg, and bowed with awkward gallantry. Rosi noticed that one of his arms was bandaged.

"Ensign Harper," the boy said.

Rosi smiled back and flashed her bright teeth. Nice teeth had a wonderful effect on everyone here and now. "Do you have a good doctor over there."

Ensign Harper seemed a bit confused by the question. "A doctor?"

"A surgeon!" Zablonski growled.

"Ah, yes." The boy laughed. "We have a surgeon."

"Is he good?" Rosi asked.

"Better than some," was the reply.

Angie and Rosi had a long talk about this earlier in the afternoon. There was not much Angie's crew of women could do if anyone was seriously wounded. If the British had someone vaguely competent, anyone seriously wounded would have a better chance on the other side.

"How is your arm?" Rosi asked.

"A scratch. Not too bad, I hope."

"How likely is it that your surgeon would take it off?"

Ensign Harper shuddered. Rosi understood. Wounds that in her day could be treated with an antiseptic spray she could buy at a convenience store might well kill someone now.

"He's...." The ensign faltered. "He's fairly good. Tries not to cut. Better with him than others."

Rosi nodded at Jacob. "Nothing we can do about him here. He won't last the night."

Ensign Harper nodded in agreement.

Rosi went on. "You and your men can walk. You can pull a litter with him on it. You can take him back to your lines. He might make it there. I let you go, you promise to see that the surgeon sees him first. Before anyone not as badly wounded. Understood?"

The young officer gulped and nodded again.

"Word of honor, ensign."

"Word of honor, captain."

Rosi looked over to Boats. "That satisfy you, sergeant?"

"Ayuh," he answered. Rosi understood that.

The ensign hesitated. "Miss, er, captain. There's something out there. Some sort of darkness that is all around here. It's pushing in. It's pushing us forward. If your plan is trying to avoid a fight this night, you will fail. We are not going to have anywhere to go except this way. I will do my best for your man, but be prepared. Even that boy, even our officer, they don't seem to have any idea what it is or how to stop it. Something else wants a battle this night."

As Boats and the ensign prepared the litter for Jacobs, Rosi and Zablonski made their way to the front line. Just next to the stream, only a few feet from front, Rosi all but stumbled over six bodies. The sight of them startled her.

"That's war, miss," Zablonski said. "Plans's great and all these wonderful idears are, well, wonderful, but in the end, it all comes down to killing other folk. If yer not ready to kill one man so as to avoid calling another man Boss, then ye've no business fightin'. You not willin' to die fer the same reason, then ye've no business fightin'."

"Why do you do it, Sergeant Major?"

"Me? Well, I've always been a soldier, miss. Always will be. Most I'll ever be is a sergeant major. Never be an officer. I'll never be no one's boss. That might not be a good reason, but's better than most. Why you doin' this? Is this all about the boy over there?"

Rosi thought for a moment, looking down at the dead men. Her men had fought well, but had lost too many men. Only two of the bodies were wearing the redcoat of a British soldier. Rosi recognized the four dead men from her company. She did not know them very well. They were four fast friends who had joined the company fairly late. After the debacle at The Castle. Shelley and his kid brother Lenny had only lived in the area for a few years. Shelly was a schoolteacher in New Richmond. He was the most educated person in the company other than Rosi and Angie. He had been earmarked for university, but when his parents had died of typhoid a few years ago, he and his brother had moved here. Shelley had been offered the job as schoolteacher and Lenny had been given a job managing what passed for an inn about five miles out of town. It was a simple job for who was something of a simple man. The use of a horse was part of Shelley's payment. He would ride every day to stay with his brother, cook the meals for the few travelers who stayed at the inn, and keep the accounts. Lenny had been quite proud of his little brother and impressed by his penchant for using big words.

"You know something, Sergeant Major?" Rosi said, trying to keep her voice as calm as she could.

"What would that be, miss?"

"I don't want to die."

Zablonski seemed to think for a moment. "Then don't."

Rosi smiled. "I wish it were that simple."

"It is that simple, miss," the sergeant major said. "Do not die. Some day you will. Everyone will. But you don't need to die today. Go back across the stream. Climb up the bank. Run. No one would blame you. If you did, you would probably save a lot of lives. These men are here for you. If you run, most the men will run as well. Oh, the Brits will catch a few. Might even kill some. Most of us'll probably be dead by tomorrow at noon anyway. If we scatter, probably quite a few will get away. So don't die. Run."

Rosi sighed. It was tempting. If she ran away, she could find Beatitude Carol or Uncle Richard and force one of them to deal with Kirk. They might refuse and tell her that he was her problem, but they would likely do something if she opted out completely. She would never be a Guardian, but it was not as if she needed the job. It did not pay any money. She was already rich, or she would be in a couple of years when she turned eighteen.

She might be eighteen already, she realized. She did not revert back to her age when she returned from her journeys. Cuts remained. Her hair and fingernails grew. This had confused and annoyed Andy and Angie, but it had made the local beauty parlor a healthy profit.

In the real world, she was just weeks shy of her sixteenth birthday. In her world? She had spent several weeks as a slave in a caravan Uncle Richard bought her for some exorbitant price. She had spent around six months in the harem of Emperor Kangxi. Fortunately, it was towards the end of the emperor's reign and he was an old man. Rosi had been huge compared to the other women, especially her feet. She might have stood out, but the only one who paid attention to her was one of the Imperial Concubines. Rosi was never more than a *chiangzai*, a female attendant who saw to Rosi's education for the period she was there. Rosi felt that she had been kept there more as a hostage than anything else. Uncle Richard had arranged for her release. Whatever it was that he had done had taken quite a while. At one point, she spent about a month locked in a villa in the Italian countryside with a large group of petty aristocrats trying to ride out the plague. Where Uncle Richard had come up with an inoculation for the Bubonic Plague Rosi did not want to know, but she did demand twenty percent from the sale of all the furniture and artwork from the villa that Uncle Richard took with them they burned the bodies and the building to cover their theft. Rosi even had the inkling that she had been briefly married to a medieval Welsh bishop. There were about eight or nine months that Rosi could tack on to her life. Eight or nine rather dull months. Whenever she spent any extended time with anyone, it was either someone who spoke a language Rosi did not, was female, or was over seventy. Uncle Richard probably arranged for this on purpose.

"Miss?" said Zablonski, interrupting her thoughts.

Rosi blinked and looked down at the four bodies. Even though they had very little in life, they had been happy and laughing with each other every time Rosi saw them together. If she had fled a couple of hours ago, chances are that these four would still be alive. Could she let them die in vain? Would the probable deaths of dozens, if not hundreds, of men give these four deaths any meaning? Would it give them any respite in Hell? Were they in Heaven, they probably would not want anyone dying for them.

Rosi had read a lot about different wars throughout history. Every side seemed to think that God, in some form or another, was in their side. God certainly would not be on both sides. Most likely, He was on neither side. Killing your fellow man might be necessary, Rosi thought. It would, though, hardly make any worthwhile deity happy.

Even killing Kirk was probably not part of God's greater plan. God would hardly need Rosi's help if all that he wanted was to zap Kirk with a lightening bolt. Would he? Apparently, God had other things to do than futz about in revolutionary New Hampshire.

Apparently, Beatitude Carol had better things to do than maintain the proper timeline in his own backyard. From various cryptic comments and lessons Rosi had gotten over the last few months, she wondered if Uncle Richard even could interfere.

"If we don't stop Kirk," Rosi said. "Then a lot more people will die. I can only pray that it is not too late and that you will trust me a little longer. For now, move the men who were involved in this skirmish back as far as you can and replace them from the rear. If you find any more wounded Brits, send them back to their side. Move these bodies across the stream. We'll bury them tomorrow. If we can't, someone will."

* * *

THE second attack came at about one-thirty. Even though Rosi had just checked her watch, she was not sure of the exact time.

Rosi was sitting right next to the stream just beyond the glare of the northern bonfire enjoying a cool drink of water when the British attacked. This was no probe. This was an all out attack. Several grenades flew into the bonfire, which blew up and spread flaming coals all over the area.

Then the bullets came. The air was filled with staccato pings and zips. The rocks and dirt chipped and flew when they were struck. Within moments, screams followed.

"Stay low!" Rosi yelled. She ran along the line, zagging,

ducking, rolling to avoid aimed shots. The stray shots would find her on their own. "Don't fire until you have a target. They can waste the bullets!"

She glanced up and saw flashes coming from the top of the spire. A couple yells came from the other side of the smoldering embers.

"Get down!" someone cried out. It was Zablonski. He pulled her down just as several bullets flattened themselves against the old bureau someone had forgotten to throw on the bonfire. "They can see you, Miss. They can tell who you are by your hair. Stay down!" And he was gone, into the gloom.

Rosie shoved her hair into her hat as best she could. She had to move. Her position here was protected by furniture. Since Zablonski had gone in the direction of the stream, she decided to head toward the spire. Most likely, that would be where Spartacus was.

Just as she started moving, screams filled the air. A handful of grenades fell near the slit trenches and exploded. Most of the men had seen the fuses sputtering just they went off and had time to duck. That had been the purpose of these grenades, Rosi realized.

"Incoming!" she yelled. At the same moment, she saw the mass of men charging her lines. She took off in the direction of the spire. "Fire at will!" she called out several times.

Rosi was so caught up watching the charging men and trying to avoid falling into a pit that she did not see the man who ran into her. They both went straight to the ground.

"Jesus Christ!" the man yelled. He scrambled away. It was one of her own men.

"Wait!" Rosi stopped when her hand hit the stock of the man's musket. She picked it up and turned to face the enemy.

No one had made it across the line yet, in this sector, but several were making their way at an oblique angle to her.

Rosi dropped to one knee to minimize her profile and fired into the small group. One man went down. The others scattered and hit the ground.

"Don't fire all at once," she said to the men in one foxhole. She handed her musket to one of the men. "Keep a steady stream of fire going. Unless they get too close."

As she moved on, she heard a roar of voices from the other end of the line. *Line must be breached*, she thought.

Soon, this part of the line would be breached as well. A squad of four men was approaching her, hugging the spire. She was not a target of opportunity. They were all but ignoring other targets and even men firing at them.

Rosi saw them aiming at her. She saw the flash as they fired. She dove to the ground and felt the balls tug at her sleeves and hair as they passed.

When she raised her head and shook her vision clear, she could see that two men were reloading. The other two were charging her with bayonets.

Rosi lifted both pistols and, just as the men got close, she pulled both triggers.

The kick from the pistols threw her onto her back. She lay there, closing her eyes, waiting to die.

"Captain!" It was Spartacus. "Get ye up."

Lowering his own smoking pistol, he held out his hand and pulled her to her feet. "Nice shooting," he stated.

"Same to you," Rosi replied. The two front men were on the ground. One was holding his shoulder and looking a little green. The other was trying to crawl away, dragging his wounded leg. "I guess I should thank you," she murmured spotting one of the other men sitting on the ground, holding his stomach. Glancing around, she could not find the fourth man.

"Nay, captain. Don't be thanking me. Ye done fine!"

"Maybe, but I only had two shots and there was four of them."

Before Spartacus could respond, Rosi noticed the fourth man. He had doubled back and was charging at them.

"Spartacus!" she yelled.

Spartacus turned, but it was too late. The redcoat's bayonet sliced into his side. Spartacus reached around and grabbed the barrel of the musket so the redcoat could not pull it out.

Without thinking, Rosi stepped in and kicked the redcoat in the crotch. The man let go his weapon and dropped to his knees. Rosi picked up Spartacus' fallen musket and swung the butt, hitting the man in the face. He fell back. Rosi stepped forward and raised the musket to swing again.

"Captain! Captain!" Spartacus tried to be heard over the noise of the battle and the pounding in her head. "Rosi!"

Rosi dropped the musket and ran to the fallen man. "Medic!" she yelled. "Help!"

"Don't ye be worryin' about it, Miss Rosi." Spartacus gripped the musket tightly and, with a great yell, pulled the blade out.

He collapsed. Blood gushed from his side.

There was nothing Rosi could do. She dropped to her knees and held his head in her arms as the fighting continued.

"Miss!" Zablonski ran up to her.

"It's Spartacus."

"What do you want us to do?"

"He's dead."

"What do you want us to do?"

"Spartacus is dead. Can't you hear me?" Rosi screamed. "He's dead!"

Zablonski reached out and slapped Rosi across the face. "What do you want us to do? They're overrunning our positions."

Rosi took a deep breath. "Fall back!"

"Yes, miss." Zablonski turned and bellowed out. "Fall back!" He grabbed one of the loaders, Sam, who was collecting unclaimed weapons. "Get Captain Carol back across the stream."

Sam snatched at Rosi's arm. "Come on."

Zablonski rushed out of sight, but Rosi could hear him continuing to yell. "Fall back!"

Sam was scared and kept trying to force Rosi to run, but she was too tired and drained to do more than walk.

A lone British officer on horseback was urging his men on. He saw Rosi and Sam off to the side, almost forgotten by the rest of the battle. He started for them.

Sam saw the officer charging up, let go the muskets that slowed him down, and fled.

Rosi saw the horseman, picked up one of the muskets, pointed it and fired. Nothing. She grabbed it by the barrel and swung it like a baseball bat. She missed the horse, but forced it to shy away. She threw the musket at its feet so that it danced even further away.

A second musket failed to shoot as well. This one she hurled at the rider. She missed him, as well, but forced his pistol shot to go wide. Not too wide, though. Rosi felt the ball sear across her cheek. He tossed the pistol away, drew his sword, and rode in closer.

Rosi picked up one more musket and aimed it at the horse's head, she pulled the trigger. This one fired. The horse tumbled to the ground, trapping both the rider and Rosi under its great weight.

There was nothing for Rosi to do but draw her sword as well.

Sword fighting, Rosi knew, should happen in an open space. Preferably, it should happen in some huge drawing room so that the fencers could leap onto tables and swing on chandeliers, and take sips of wine between witty repartees.

This British officer was not in the mood for clever conversation. He twisted himself around and hacked at Rosi. She put her sword up and blocked it. He kept hacking at her, trying to pound her into submission. Half covered by the horse, Rosi could do little but stop the blade to avoid being decapitated. She tried to cut at him as well, with as little luck.

The officer lowered his point and thrust at Rosi's chest. She raised herself up, hoping the blade would go under her. She both felt and heard the point pierce the flesh under her arm. Screaming, she let go of her saber. The officer ripped the sword out of Rosi and prepared to thrust again. Rosi threw herself forward as far as the weight of the horse would allow and punched the man with as much strength as she could muster. Then she grabbed his wrist and used her weight to drag his arm to the ground above her head.

The officer was stronger and in better shape than Rosi, who was bleeding from a graze on the cheek and a wound in her side. With both hands, he grabbed the blade and swung the hilt at her head.

Rosi barely had time to raise her left arm to block the swing. Her forearm took most of the force of the blow as the edge of the blade caught the bone, but the officer had used enough force that the cross bar hit Rosi squarely on the temple. She went down.

Rosi was not sure how long she had been out. When she opened her eyes, she barely knew where she was. The British officer, apparently, thought he had killed her, for he had turned his back on her to extricate himself from under the horse. At the moment, he still had one leg to pull out.

Rosi grabbed up his cavalry saber and, holding it by the blade, stabbed at him in the middle of the back.

The officer cried out and tried to twist away, but Rosi kept her grip and used as much of her body as she could to hold the weapon in.

The dying man screamed and thrashed. Eventually, he stopped and lay still.

Rosi realized that she had done much the same thing only minutes earlier. So, she used the blade to slash the man's throat.

Her head throbbed.

She ripped the sleeve from the dead officer's jacket and tied it around her arm. Then she dragged her leg from beneath the horse. It took some minutes of grunting and digging with the barrel of one of her pistols. She was exhausted by the time she was free so sat there for a few minutes. Seeing some British a dozen or so yards away, she lay back and tried to be as still as she could.

* * *

EVERYTHING seemed to go oddly quiet all of a sudden. Rosi looked up and saw that the squad of British soldiers had disappeared.

That had happened fast.

Then she noticed that the darkness, the fog, had crept forward.

A glance ascertained that it was continuing to move forward. In a few minutes, it would certainly engulf her.

She looked up and saw that the black went high into the sky. Certainly higher than she could see.

She and the spire seemed to be in the center of a diminishing circle.

Well, there's only one way now.

Carefully, Rosi climbed up to the top of the spire.

There were three men at the top of the spire. They appeared to be frozen in time. Corporal Miller was on the ground. There was a fair amount of blood on him, though in the dim light that the absolute blackness gave off, it sort of looked like chocolate. Either, Miller was dead and had dropped his pistol, or he was wounded and was reaching for the weapon. Since he was not going anywhere at the moment, Rosi picked up the pistol, determined that it was loaded and primed, and shoved it in her waistband. She also took the opportunity to obtain a bag of shot and a powder horn from the fallen man.

Bartlett looked to be in the middle of turning to face the British soldier who stood a few feet behind him.

The British soldier had just fired. A puff of smoke hung in the air in front of the barrel. A small oblong-shaped musket ball was in the air, inches from Bartlett's chest.

Rosi reached out and slapped the ball to the ground. She thought about shoving the British soldier off the spire, but decided that she really did not need to. The black darkness was tightening its grip, swallowing up more and more. It had reached the edge of the spire's plateau and was inching in on all sides.

The British soldier and Corporal Morris were engulfed first. Then the dark shrank enough to cover Bartlett.

Rosi stood in the center of a shrinking circle. She reached out with her hands and her mind and tried to will the darkness to stop. She felt some resistance when it reached her, but soon she could see her arms covered in the black shadowy fog. It was both ice cold and fiery hot at the same time.

When the darkness covered her ears, she thought for a split moment that she could hear someone laugh.

The moment passed. The darkness reached her face and covered her eyes.

CHAPTER 11

ROSI expected to see the Widows. She expected to see Jesse, the self-proclaimed paranormal journalist who had tried to kidnap Rosi during the summer and force her to manipulate time for his benefit.

They were not there.

Instead, Rosi saw the battlefield, frozen in time at about the moment it had frozen a few minutes before.

Corporal Miller still lay on the ground and was reaching for his pistol. Rosi checked her waistband. It was empty. She re-appropriated the weapon and the ammunition.

The British soldier was still firing at Bartlett.

Again, Rosi slapped the bullet away. This time, the bullet went as far as her hand pushed it and then stopped when she lost contact. She slapped the bullet again. It moved as long as her hand was touching it. She experimented a couple of times. Once she was no longer in contact with the bullet, it stopped and simply hung there. After a couple of tries, she took the bullet and placed it on the ground. She had no idea what would happen to the bullet when time started up again, if it ever did. This way, the worst the bullet would bury itself into the dirt.

It did cross her mind that if she could move a bullet, she could wake up a person the same way. She was about to try with Bartlett when it struck her that she had no way of controlling how he might react, and she had a pretty good idea what he might think. If the shock did not kill him, he would think her a witch. She would most likely be able to freeze him again, but he might remember when everything went back to normal.

About the time she turned to look at the rest of the battlefield, Rosi realized that it was no longer dark.

It was still night. Clouds and stars were out. There was no

light source, but Rosi could see fairly clearly. The darkness was
there. However, it was no longer dark. It was rather a faint light
mist.

To the north, it was beginning to rain. Beyond the rain,
further than Rosi should have been able to see, a body of men
was riding like the wind towards the battle. These were clearly not
British. Were they Beatitude Carol's men?

To the south, British reinforcements were approaching the
far riverbank. These men were closer than Beatitude's.

Below, the northern line had been breached. Men were
already crossing the river. Rosi could see the splashes the soldiers'
feet made frozen in time.

The southern line was holding, but would soon face more
and more men.

The center was doing quite well. Rosi could see Zablonski
directing the men along the center to fire by rank. It was not a
particularly professional job, he had only had a week to train the
men, but it was effective. The snipers on the center spire were
doing their job as well. The British were pinned down. A handful
of bodies, redcoats, lay in the smoldering clearing. The center
would hold, until they were flanked from the north or the south.

Angie was busy on the riverbank caring for the wounded.
Zilla was down by the stream. It looked to Rosi as if she were
trying to rally men who were running away.

As hard as she looked, she could not see Kirk anywhere. He
had to be somewhere.

Rosi!

* * *

"WHAT?" Had someone said something to her?

"Hello?" Rosi looked around.

She was surrounded by people, but none of them could
speak. Or could they. She looked around. Nobody was moving.

Rosi!

There it was again. It was clearly a sound, but one that was
distant.

Rosi!

Far too distant to be coming from anywhere she could see.

Rosi!

That one was not distant, Rosi thought. That was right next to her ear. Like an annoying mosquito.

Rosi! You know what to do!

Rosi looked around even more carefully.

No one.

She leaned over to look to see if someone were hanging below the ledge of the spire.

She was relieved when she did not see someone. Her imagination was working overtime, she decided.

That was when the rocks below her feet gave way. She danced as best she could and waved her arms around, but after a couple of seconds, she lost her balance and fell forward.

Before her feet left the edge of the spire's top, her hands met resistance and she stopped.

She saw nothing, but there was something in front of her. He was not the blackness, or greyness for the moment. That burned. She had touched that before. This was firmly soft. Or would it be softly firm?

She pushed herself up so she could stand. Cautiously, she reached out and touched the air.

Again, there was resistance.

Rosi moved along the edge until her footing was firmer. Then she reached out again. Again, resistance.

Rosi!

"What!" It was more annoying than any mosquito Rosi had ever come across.

Move.

"Move?"

Forward.

"Move forward? Are you mad?"

Move.

The voice was all around her. Close. Far. High. Low.

Forward.

It would not stay in one place.

Move.

"I'll fall!"

Forward.

"No!"

Time.

"This is crazy!"

She took a step back.

The noises came flying at her, *Rosi, Time, Forward, Move, Time, Rosi,* pushing her forward. This time, she reached out and used whatever it was to keep her from falling.

Forward.

Forward?

Rosi wondered if it could be that simple. Is that all Guardians had to do?

She shut out all other thoughts and concentrated on the nothing that she was holding and pulled it towards her.

Sound and movement erupted so suddenly that she fell over in surprise.

The flash and smoke from the redcoat's musket stung her eyes and the report was close enough to deafen her.

Through the haze of light and sound, she saw Corporal Morris roll on the ground and come up to one knee and fire the nothing he held.

Bartlett continued his spin and ran himself onto the redcoats' bayonet.

Then the redcoat and Morris grappled. They clung to each other's throats. They staggered to the edge and tripped over Rosi. The redcoat stopped himself from falling. Corporal Morris tumbled over the edge and fell from view without even a yell.

"What the!" the redcoat stopped when he saw Rosi just a few feet from him. He looked around, then smiled back at her. Before Rosi had time to react, the man had lunged at her and was forcing her back onto the rock.

She scratched at his face and bit hard into his fingers.

The man screamed in pain. He reared up and backhanded her

across the face. The blow stunned her. Before she knew it, he had thrown her onto her stomach.

Screaming, she tried to crawl away, but he was too heavy on her.

Her hands grabbed dirt and pebbles and flung them behind her, which resulted in a blow to the back of the head that stunned her again.

Slowly, she pulled herself out of the blackness. She had only been out for few seconds. She could feel the man's breath on the back of her neck. She reared her head back and felt it connect with his face.

He yelled and let go of her for a moment.

He lunged after her or rather he lunged where he thought she would go. But Rosi did not try to crawl away. Instead she rolled into him. He staggered over her and rolled awkwardly. As he tried to balance himself, Rosi kicked out with both feet.

This man yelled as he fell into space.

Rosi curled up in a ball and took a moment to catch her breath.

Below her, the battle raged.

* * *

FINALLY, after what seemed like an eternity, she sat up, tucked in her shirt, and tied her belt as tightly as she could.

She looked out at the battle.

The northern line was completely routed. Many of the British had gone on across the stream and were attacking the line of wagons. Rosi could see Zilla firing from inside one of them.

A few of the British came back around and flanked the center. Zablonski had already fallen.

On impulse, when Rosi saw the body of her sergeant major, she reached out to him. When her hands met the resistance, all action and sound stopped.

Rosi rose to her knees and continued to push. Everyone, everything, every horse, every bullet began to move backwards. She waited until she saw Sergeant Major Zablonski sit up in reverse, stop, and then pull toward her.

She kneeled there and watched as Zablonski fought bravely. He rallied the men and held the line. During a momentary lull, he sat back and leaned against the center spire. One of his men said something funny. Rosi could see Zablonski start to laugh. Then he lay down. Someone had shot him in the head.

She watched as the men tried to organize themselves, as they were quickly overrun.

They died. Some quietly. Some bravely. Some cried for their mothers. Some tried to run. Some tried to surrender.

They all died.

Rosi pushed and backed everything up. She wanted to see the face of the man who killed Zablonski. After four or five times, she concluded she could not. She was hoping to find someone to hate. All she found out was that a shot was fired and that it killed her friend. It was just one of those things that happened.

The British overran the wagons, cutting down most of the men and women there. A few of the officers clearly tried to minimize the killing, but to no avail.

Zilla and Angie took what wounded they could and disappeared into the woods.

Rosi watched the battle several times. Could she find a weakness to the British plan of attack?

There was nothing she could do about their numbers.

There was nothing she could do about their superior training.

Once the British punched through one section, there was nothing she or anyone else could have done to stop them.

Rosi realized on a certain level she had done a pretty good job. She had the best position in the area. She would have liked to have been able to fall back, but that was not an option. Whatever else, the British had to be engaged. Delaying a confrontation would have made the situation far more difficult to rectify, if that was even an option. She had not seriously thought she could win the battle without assistance from either Beatitude's raiders or the New Hampshire regulars.

She knew just about every death that occurred by the stream

that night was her fault. So many of the men whom she respected and loved fell that she was too stunned, confused, overwhelmed to feel any grief.

All she could do was kneel there and watch them fall and rise and fall. They moved forward and backward. Bullets pulled out of their bodies and returned to the guns then flew back out and cut them down again.

After a while, she simply stopped it. Her company was losing, but now it was frozen in tableau.

How long could she keep time paused?

Could she keep her friends alive indefinitely just by keeping everything still?

That was not much of a life. They men would not know that there was anything going on. They would simply exist in that moment forever.

Or until she went to sleep.

Or until she died.

Then time would probably move on. Or would it.

Carefully, Rosi moved time back to the point where Zablonski was just starting to laugh. If he were to be frozen indefinitely, it would be in a moment of joy.

* * *

PERHAPS, Rosi thought. *I can simply kill all of the British.*

What a glorious idea. It would take hours. Even days. But she could do it. She could take a bayonet. She could climb down. She could cut their throats.

There were an awful lot of them. A couple hundred. And then there were the reinforcements.

But she could do it.

Then she could make her way into New Richmond and kill all the British there. Would it be possible to go out to any ship still floating and kill the men on them?

The death of so many men would certainly get the attention of other British admirals and generals. They would wonder how hundreds of throats got cut.

They might flee in terror.

They might return in greater numbers.

Was Rosi supposed to kill them as well? Would she have to kill all of the British soldiers in the colonies?

Was it even her place to do it? That would certainly be irreparably alter time. Any number of these men were supposed to have descendants in her time. Removing a few lines from the genetic tree over the last two hundred years might be something time could simply overcome. Removing hundreds would be something different.

These men had just as much right to live and die as soldiers as her men did.

Rosi simply could not do it. She could not murder that many men just to stop Kirk from screwing up time, and it would be murder.

She could, however, save lives. Some of her men would have the chance to get away.

She would start with Zablonski.

She stood up and brushed off her britches.

That was when she saw something move out of the corner of her vision. She spun around and saw Kirk moving towards her.

"What are you doing?" he called out. "How are you doing this?"

Oh, God!

How was *he* doing this? How was *he* moving and aware when all else was frozen.

"How did you expect me not to notice!" he yelled, answering her silent question. "Back and forth, stopped, sped up, slowed down. I'm surprised everyone else did not notice it. Are you mad? You have to move things forward."

"I have to fix your mistakes!" Rosi yelled back. "You are the one who ruined everything."

"How do you know I wasn't supposed to ruin everything? Perhaps I was supposed to come here to fix something that went terribly wrong all those years ago."

"That's absurd." Rosi almost laughed at how ridiculous it

sounded.

"Perhaps you or your ancestor messed around trying to keep the British out. Perhaps I was brought here to set things right. Time is out of joint, Rosi Carol. Oh, cursed spite that ever I was born to set it right." By now Kirk was running across the battlefield in Rosi's direction.

Rosi pushed and sent the battle reeling backwards.

Kirk ducked and dodged and dove around the charging soldiers and flying bullets. Within a couple of minutes, he was at the bottom of the spire. Rosi could hear him coughing up dust. In a moment, he would find the path and make his way up.

Rosi looked around. Bartlett's rifle lay behind her. She had never fired a rifle before, but the technique could not be that much different than a pistol.

When Kirk's head came into view, Rosi pulled the trigger.

He did not even flinch. "Really." He giggled. "Were you even aiming at me?"

"I...." Rosi really did not know. She had been aiming vaguely in his direction.

"Did you think that the shot would scare me and I'd run away? Huh? Now you don't even have a loaded weapon to scare me with." Kirk had finished his climb and now carefully brushed himself off. "I think I pull this outfit off. What do you think? Nothing? Not even a snarky comment? Well, Rosi Carol." He giggled again. "I am impressed. I did not think you would pull the trigger a second time. Not after all we've been through. Or will be through. It must get pretty confusing being you. But, the fact remains that you did pull the trigger. Trick me once, shame on you. Trick me twice, shame on me. You must be punished. Don't worry. It will hurt me far more than it will hurt you."

Kirk drew his pistol and shot Rosi in the right shoulder.

* * *

KIRK kneeled next to her and raised her to a seated position. He pulled out a flask and forced it between her teeth. A raw, sharp liquor poured into her mouth.

Rosi gagged and coughed. She also swallowed a lot of the liquid. It heated her up and dulled the pain in her shoulder.

"That's some mighty strong language." Kirk smirked. "Wherever did you learn words like that? You must have known a lot of sailors before you moved to quiet little New Richmond."

Kirk wandered over to Bartlett and tore the shirt off the man's corpse. He ripped the sleeves off and wadded up the shirt's body and shoved against the wound.

Rosi screamed, but let Kirk place her hand over the cloth while he tied the sleeves around her.

"It's not the best job," Kirk said matter-of-factly. He pushed her knees down and then straddled her, sitting on her legs to keep her from crawling away. He started loading the gun. He moved quickly, economically, expertly. "I didn't take First Aid, like Dan. But I suspect it will slow down the bleeding. I've been doing my research. Your blood will start clotting soon. You'll be fine. It was only in the shoulder. It's not like the bullet was poisoned. I don't think it was. This one is." He held up a small lead ball and dropped it into the barrel. The wadding followed. In moments, he was done. "So," he said. "We have some unfinished business."

Kirk jabbed the barrel of the pistol into Rosi's wound.

Rosi screamed.

Kirk threw his head back giggled.

More liquid came from the flask.

Then she felt his hands on her.

"What are you doing, you creep?" She slapped his arms away.

"Don't get your hopes up." He laughed. "I'm searching."

"Searching for what?"

"The remote."

"What remote?"

Kirk stopped frisking her. He pointed the barrel of the pistol at her shoulder again. "Don't make me hurt you again."

"Will you stop hurting me if I give you the remote?" Rosi gasped.

He thought for a moment. "Probably not."

"More drink!"

Kirk smiled. "Don't spill any," he said, shoving the mouth of the flask between her teeth. "It might burn your pretty skin.

Rosi mumbled something.

"What was that?" He leaned in closer to her.

Rosi spat the burning fluid in his face.

Kirk bellowed and fell back.

Rosi scrambled to her feet and ran to the edge.

"Stop!" Kirk called out, rubbing his eyes vigorously.

Rosi spun around. She was only inches from the edge. The river bed was maybe four or five stories down. "Stay back!" she countered.

He was pointing his pistol at her. "I will shoot you again."

"That doesn't make any sense," she said. "You don't want me to jump because it will kill me, and I won't be able to tell you anything. If you shoot me, I'll most likely fall and die anyway. Then you will be stuck here."

"I don't see you killing yourself, Rosi Carol." Kirk moved in closer.

"That's close enough, Kirk." Rosi shifted herself closer to the edge.

"Okay, okay, okay." Kirk held the pistol to one side and carefully put it on the ground.

"Not good enough!" Rosi snapped. "Toss it over the edge. Away. I will jump."

"Okay! Okay!" Kirk held up his hands in surrender. "I'll toss it away." He bent down and picked up the pistol.

"How do I know I can trust you?" Rosi shuffled.

"I don't want to be stuck in the emptiness of frozen time, now do I?" Kirk straightened up.

"Now throw it away. Over there."

Kirk half turned, then he suddenly flung the weapon at Rosi's face.

Rosi ducked down quickly. She was just able to stand up quickly enough to face Kirk as he ran up and grabbed at her.

"Are you nuts?" she screamed. She slashed at his eyes with

her fingernails. When he flinched backwards, she leapt out from the top of the spire. *This better work*, she prayed.

"No!" Kirk yelled, grabbing at her. His fingers brushed her foot.

Rosi felt herself begin to fall.

* * *

FOR a brief moment, Rosi felt the odd resistance in the air, and then she was through it. She continued to fall, but not to move.

She could feel the sensation of falling. She could tell that there was nothing holding her up.

Above her, she could see the time and place she had left. The spire she had jumped off. There was Kirk, reaching out for her. Trying to catch her or to push her, she could not tell. He was crying out as well. Somewhere, in the distance of another time, she could hear the echo of his call. He was not frozen in time. He was still moving, but he was moving in a different place and time and seemed to be still.

At the edges of her vision, she could see movement. There were people. They came and went. They were born, grew up, grew old, withered, died, and were gone. Some grew into many people, families, clans, vast civilizations that thrived, diminished, dwindled, and disappeared. Cities rose and fell. Oceans raged and dried. Stars burned out.

When she tried to see, when she turned her eyes to look, she saw nothing. Not blackness or whiteness, just nothingness.

Once again she looked up. The spire was back. It was near and far, both now and then, the speeding images returned to her peripheral vision.

She forced herself over. Was she falling towards something? And there it was, so far below, a definite something of mass and infinite size, of indescribable color, so barren and empty she could hardly call it a place at all.

Past empires, past the birth planets, past quickly spinning galaxies, she fell, speeding towards the something below but not getting any closer.

She spun herself back around and watched Kirk and the spire growing further and further away, though not diminishing at all.

* * *

RRR....
Was someone—
OOO....
Calling—
SSS....
Her?
III....
A face began to repeat itself out of the corner of her eye. It was too fast to make out anything.
R...O...S...I!
A blurry face stayed the same. The costume changed with the years. A hand reached out. It reminded Rosi of a flip book. The figure came in flashes, barely clear snapshots in the constant blur of sped up time. As she continued to fall, the flickering shape became clearer and clearer. She could not recognize a face, for if she turned to face the vision, it disappeared.
R...O...S...I!
The words flew up to her and screamed past.
"What is it?" she called out.
Help...me!
"Who are you?"
Hold...out...your...hand!
"Why?"
The arm came out of the distant vision. A hand reached for her.
Rosi flailed around. Her fingers brushed something. The other hand grasped at her several times and missed. Each time it tried, the costume changed.
Reach...out!
Finally, their hands clasped.
Rosi felt herself land. She felt the ground, if that was what it was, thud. Her teeth shook. She felt the breath knocked out of

her. Her shoulder ached, though not as much as it should have.

Gasping for breath, she forced herself to sit up.

She looked up. Kirk and the spire, if indeed they were there, were far above.

She was sitting on some sort of platform surrounded by timelines shooting up. She had the feeling that the swirling spinning timelines disappeared into some infinite chasm below.

She checked her shoulder. The wound was still there, but it looked weeks old. So much for halter-tops, she thought grumpily.

"Rosi!" someone said. "You are here?"

Rosi spun around. The voice sounded vaguely male. Near the edge of the platform was an image, half braced on the platform, the other half stuck in the swirling streams as it changed shape and costumes. He was trying to crawl towards her.

The figure looked up at her, his face distorted and fluctuating. He reached out a withered young hand. "Rosi? I could see you before." He blindly waved around his hand.

Rosi stepped forward and grabbed the brittle hand and gently pulled the man towards her.

He started to rise, as he left the streams his features began to turn young. His face took on a form. A form that Rosi recognized.

"Oh, crap," Rosi said, looking up at Jesse. She tried to jerk her hand away but he held on tight.

"You won't get rid of me that easily this time." Jessie giggled. "When you go, I go. I've been floating here too long."

"Where are we?" Rosi asked, trying to keep her distance as best she could. Even though Jesse kept a firm grip on her hand, she backed towards the edge of the platform.

"Don't go there. You'll never find your way back. Not all places and times have doorways home, Rosi Carol."

"Where are we?"

"The space in between. Neither here nor there. Neither now or then. Someplace. No-place. Never-when. My home when I can find it," Jessie sang. "When I can make my way back. Home is so long away, but the journey is everything. Never-when. Never-when. Ever-when. The places in between. The narrow interstices. This is my home, Rosi Carol. I can step out from time to time. The Widows have shown me how. But they bring me back when they wish. There is no rest in time or place for Jesse. You saw to that. You sent me here and damned the Widows to an eternity of pain and loss."

"Don't blame me," Rosi said. "You could have helped me. Instead you tried to trick me."

"There's no tricking the trickster who tricks her friends. What tricks have you pulled with those you love. Have you banished them to other-whens? Did your precious Angie choose to follow you? Will you abandon first-born Dan to time? How will you trick your way out of this fine mess?"

"How long have you been here?" Rosi was worried. She did not feel as if Jessie were a danger. He did, however, seem somewhat loony.

"Forever and a day. They let me go to tease me. Let me touch the ground and smell the sky. Let me hear the trees and dance with the wind. Never at peace. Never at peace. I step into time to see man at his worst with only a whiff of hope, but then I'm pulled back when the tide changes. Changing sides, never long enough to change to interfere to make a home. Always long enough to long for more and feel the loss. Take me home, Rosi Carol. Any home will do. Any time," he sobbed.

Rosi sighed. "I wish I could help."

"You can. I can show you how the Widow's travel." Jesse's face brightened and seemed to stop at a stable age for a moment. "How to use the interstices. No doors needed. Just slip in and out. Barely make a ripple."

"You want too much."

"Just a little home to start."

"And an empire in the end."

"I have suffered enough," Jesse cried.

"Tell me when you come from."

"Ancient Rome," he crowed."

"The real time," she insisted.

"The shogunate." He giggled.

"When you were born."

"Arthurian England."

"Nonsense." She jerked out of his grip and danced to the other end of the platform.

Jesse seemed momentarily confused when Rosi broke their connection. "I do not have your sight, Rosi Carol. There is much I can see, but in some ways, I go through time as blindly as most. I simply don't go through it in one direction. Give me a direction, Rosi Carol."

"Tell me when you came from and I will try and help you. If I can take you back to your time."

"I did not bring you here to be taken back to my old home!" Jesse roared. "There's nothing for me there. No love. No joy. Overshadowed."

"You brought me here?"

"Here. There. Then. Now. The door was there. The pieces were in the right order. But you let one piece get away. I could not find it, but I will, if you help me. I brought you here. I knew you would choose then and there to make your last stand."

"What are you talking about?" Rosi demanded to know.

"The riverbed. A romantic forlorn hope. A desperate stand. Waiting for the cavalry to rescue you at the last minute. The damsel in distress. Wasn't that your plan, Rosi Carol?" Jesse taunted.

"I...I...." It was ridiculous, Rosi knew. "I didn't have much choice. I had to force Beatitude."

"You had to make your *beau geste*," Jesse crowed. "To lead so many you claim to love to such ends. Pointless deaths. Pointless, I say. Don't interrupt. Death makes Time sick. So many pointless deaths make Time. Cruelty. War. Murder. Foolish fatal feats. Where do you think the tears in time come from? Senseless deaths. And every time you go through, it weakens the fabric. You're killing time, Rosi Carol. And for what? To protect a timeline so tied up in knots that the only way to unravel it would be with shears. The walls of Time were thin and sick when you took your friends to die on the riverbed. The perfect time for us to fetch you. To bring you here."

"You're mad," Rosi said. "How can time be sick?"

"Can't you hear his cries?" Jesse gestured here and there, pointing. "No? Not now. But soon. You will stay with me. Together we will listen to time's pain. Then perhaps, you will find me a home. For me. For the Widows."

"Perhaps I'll just leave you here," Rosi said. She reached her hand out towards one of the streams.

"Will you take the chance?"

"I'll find my way back somehow."

"And the Widows will send me after you. Time in. Time out. All the time. Time after time. No time to lose." Jesse giggled.

He really was nuts, Rosi decided.

"Then I'll go back," she said.

"And see your friends die?" he asked.

"If I must, I must."

"Then we will go together."

Jesse moved so quickly that Rosi did not even see him come near her. One second, he was on one side of the platform. In the next second, he was behind her. If he had moved, Rosi could have sworn it was away from her.

His arms were around her. She struggled, but his grip was too strong.

"We've done this," Jesse said. "So many times. So many times I've been too late. So many times your neck has broken in the struggle. Or mine. Or you weren't here. But this time was right. Is right. Let me show you how your friends die."

He picked her up in his arms. She clawed at his eyes, but he screamed and ignored here. He bent his knees and leaped into the air.

Rosi felt the two of them rising in the air past the ever-changing streams of life and death. The platform seemed to get no smaller nor the spire with Kirk any larger. They rose for an instantaneous eternity then burst into the fresh night air.

CHAPTER 12

"NO!" Kirk continued to scream.

Jesse and Rosi fell with a squishy thump into the marshy ground at the foot of the spire. Rosi landed on top of Jesse. She heard the *oomph* of the air being knocked out of him.

She scrambled away from him. He grabbed at her feet as she moved, but she was able to put some distance between them before he was up.

"Stay away from me," she said, backing away from him. She dodged around several stilled figures and ducked under a horse.

Jesse followed, but Rosi was able to move faster than him. Out of the corner of her eye, she saw Kirk climbing down the spire.

"Olly olly oxen free!" called out Jesse, dodging around a horse and snatching at her.

Rosi dodged away and ran into a clump of men charging around a small bush. She froze.

A few dozen feet away, Jesse seemed to pick up some sort of scent. He began sniffing the air and then the ground. Then he began dancing around as if he were trying to follow the trail. Fortunately, Rosi realized, the trail led away from her.

Suddenly Jesse stopped.

"Oh, my God!" Rosi heard him say.

She tried to look around the soldiers, but there were too many obstacles.

"Jesus!" she heard Kirk say.

Rosi snatched a couple of pistols from two officers that were standing near by. She was careful not to touch them. She did not to have to deal with any more people. Especially more of the enemy. The pistols were loaded and primed, so she slipped them in her belt, picked up a fallen bayonet and slid around closer to the two.

They were standing still. Looking at each other.

"Magnificent!" they both said. "Outstanding."

What did they see?

"How did you get here?" Kirk asked.

"Not yet, boyo." Jesse giggled. "Need to know and all that."

"But you will tell me?"

"If I can," Jesse promised. "We need to catch the girl first. She can help us."

"I have it pretty well set up here," Kirk said. "Now that you are here."

"She's pretty pesky," Jesse said.

"I think that together we can deal with her."

"She's tricky. She's tricked us before. She'll trick us again."

"I bet she will." Kirk giggled.

Jesse giggled as well. "If we play our cards right. But we need to make sure that we trick her before she tricks us."

"Once she gives us—"

"Gives us what?"

"The remote," Kirk said. "How she controls—"

"You don't have it at all." Jesse giggled. "There's no remote. Or, rather, she's the remote."

A look of realization crossed Kirk's face. "Of course!" he crowed. "That explains so much!"

"I knew we'd get it eventually," Jesse said.

That was when Rosi got it. "Oh, God!" she groaned.

Jesse and Kirk were the same person.

They spun when she groaned. Once she saw it, she was surprised that she had not noticed it. It might be that Jesse's scar had distracted her from the similarities.

Rosi stood up. "Stay where you are!" she said. "I'm armed."

Kirk started to drift to one side. Without looking, Jesse waved for him to stop. "She outguns us." He laughed.

"We can take her," Kirk said.

"Maybe. But not at the moment." Jesse waved Kirk over to him.

"I will shoot you," Rosi said, pulling out one of the pistols and aiming it in their general direction.

"She'll miss," Kirk stated with confidence.

"She might get lucky," Jesse replied.

"Just stand still!" Rosi ordered. "Both of you. Perhaps I'll shoot him." She pointed the barrel at Kirk. "Do you know what would happen to you, Jesse, if I killed him? I don't."

Kirk edged behind Jesse, who responded with a laugh. "My timeline exists. If you shoot him, most likely I will continue on."

"Are you sure?" asked both Kirk and Rosi.

"No. But Time has a way of getting its way, regardless of what any of us do. Rosi, I brought you here for a reason."

"I came here to fix Kirk's mistakes," Rosi said.

"I haven't made any mistakes yet," Kirk protested. "Except I didn't catch you when we took The Castle."

"She got away fair and square," Jesse said. "Time can get pretty confusing. I'm not sure if I remembered that before you attacked The Castle or after. I do know she would have gotten away whatever you tried. Indeed, I remember five or six attempts by five or six different Kirks and the only time she did not get away was the time she was killed. That was a pity. Such a waste of a pretty girl. And none of her power for us. I was quite angry. The things I did to that Kirk. I might have scarred myself for life." He giggled for several seconds. "But don't think, Rosi Carol, that you came here on your own. Oh, you sent Kirk here. That door does not lead here or now. I suppose I shan't tell you where it does lead. Poor girl. Tons of fun and not nearly as stupid as she thought she was. No, child, you opened the door to here and now. Guardians can do that, you know. Not all doors, but some they can control.

"There is something about this time that drew you here. Not sure what it was. The Widow's tried to catch you during the reenactment last summer because that was a significant event. A coming together of the past and the present and the future, the ancient, the old, the then, and your now all gathered together to create a future for you to thrive in. That is when we waited for you. You are like your father, though. You have so little interest in your distant past. So there is something about this time, this when, this place, that is linked to you and your when. I don't know. The Widows ain't been talking to me much. It was all I could do to get them to let me try this once.

"Once Kirk was here. I did not remember. There is so much I do not remember. The interstices are very lonely. I sometimes forget myself. Only when they let me out sometimes, sometimes, I do. Then I get very angry, Rosi Carol. I get very angry and I want to punish you. You are the reason that I am there with the Widows. So I am the reason that you are here, now. Did you think that you opened the door? Oh, she would have fled to her uncle. He would have known what to do. What fun would we have had then. So I brought you. I brought you. I convinced the Widows to let me open the door. Once you came on your own, your uncle would have no way of knowing when you went or how to follow you." Jesse took a couple of steps towards Rosi.

"Stand back!" she warned.

"You shan't shoot me." Jesse giggled. "You don't have it in you. You shan't shoot Kirk. He may be second son but he will have first blood. I have seen it."

"Then what do you want from me?" Rosi had the distinct impression that Jesse was somewhat insane.

"You are going to take us back to The Castle." Jesse laughed out loud. Kirk giggled.

"What do you want there?" Rosi asked. "Kirk spent almost two weeks there. What didn't he find?"

"I looked everywhere," Kirk pointed out rather snippily.

"You didn't know what to look for!" Jesse continued to laugh. "We'll open the door. We'll see through the bricks. We'll bring her back home. She'll be up to old tricks. We'll catch you. We'll snatch you. We'll break you and bind you. Don't think that we can't, Rosi Carol. We can."

"Just who is this she that you're talking about?" Kirk asked. "Who is it? Who is it? You must tell me now."

Rosi glanced at the two of them. They looked so alike. "Who

or what is hidden behind that door? I've only seen bricks."

"Then you haven't looked hard enough." Jesse sighed. "But the bricks have their cracks through which dreams have been sent. I don't know dreams. They speak to the spoken to. They speak your own language. A language of hope, love, and fears. Back there we'll go. Your questions will be answered. You'll open the door that you locked."

"I locked?"

"And only you can unlock."

Jesse and Kirk had drifted apart. Rosi waved her pistol and motioned for them to move closer together.

"Why should I help you?" she asked. Even if she shot the two of them, Rosi was not sure if she could fix much. She was not sure how to stop the British onslaught. Rosi could kill most or all of the British. That, though, was bound to spook just about everyone else here. She felt that she was supposed to fix the situation, not create that many more problems to fix. If the good guys showed up in time, then there would be a battle and, most likely, the British would end up falling back. Rosi had to get them to leave New Richmond. The more people who stayed alive, the fewer loose ends there would be to tie up.

Kirk smirked. "I'll try this, if I might."

Jesse bowed deeply. "By all means."

"Jump in if I make a mistake." Kirk bowed back.

Jesus!

"The question that should be asked is," Kirk started. "What are you planning to do? I don't mean your grand strategy. That was doomed to failure from the start. You relied too much on the timely arrival of someone who simply might not arrive."

Jesse jumped in. "But she learned something that changed all that."

"Of course she did." Kirk nodded in acknowledgement. "She thought it was all about manipulating actions and results. If the butterfly's death results in Hitler winning World War Two, simply stop the butterfly from dying. She learned she could manipulate the very flow of time itself. She could twist it, bend it to her will."

"However," Jesse said. "She did not realize that even that has its limits. But the limits are within you. Do you have the Will to do what needs to be done?"

"Stopping me is easy," Kirk said. "Simply shoot me. Go back a few weeks and shoot me the moment I open my eyes and see eighteenth century New Richmond. Rewind. Bullet. Over."

"Then, though," Jesse went on. "She is stuck here. She has to wait for herself and Angie to show up. Can she disappear into the woods and let Cromwell attack New Richmond without trying to interfere? What if she knew her new friends would be involved? They would rush to New Richmond to help. Some of them would die."

"Beatitude is bound to hear that you are here," Kirk said. "And eventually he will come to confront this new Guardian. Might this move of his bring the British back? What of Dan and Andy?"

"Beatitude let them go," Jesse said. "Because he knew you were trying to end a Confusion. If you sit around waiting for someone to tell you how to get home, he might not."

"She might not be able to reverse so far."

"She hasn't the Will."

The two giggled in concert. It was disconcerting.

"You know something, Kirk?"

"What, Jesse?"

"She likes it here. She likes everything about it. Hundreds of men willing to kill and die for her. Rosi Carol. Center of attention. Center of time. Can you beat it?"

"That's ridiculous!" Rosi cut in.

"It talks!" Jesse cried. "I was afraid you'd forgotten us."

"Forgotten what we mean to you," Kirk said.

"What you mean to me?" Rosi asked, incredulously.

"We can help you," Jesse explained.

"She does not want to be helped," Kirk said. "She was having so much fun. She was playing on the beach with her boyfriends and watching the fireworks. What a party they were having."

Fireworks? Party? Rosi was having an idea.

"But she wants to help her friends," Jesse said. "We can help her help her friends."

"How?" Rosi asked.

"The nose knows." Jesse giggled.

"The nose?" asked Kirk.

"Knows." Jesse answered. "Moses supposes his toeses are roses, but Moses supposes erroneously. 'Cause Moses he knowses his toeses aren't roses."

"As Moses supposes his toeses to be," Kirk finished.

"Excellent." Jesse giggled.

"Or," Kirk suggested. "Mosies supposies his toesies are Rosi's?"

"Most excellent." Jesse rubbed his hands together. "Now, bring her along. To The Castle!"

"The Castle!" Kirk echoed.

They started for Rosi, who turned and fled.

"Come on, Rosi!" called out Jesse. "Come on back home. You are far too young to be out on your own."

The two had split up by now. Rosi tried to keep soldiers between her and them. Unfortunately, the three of them were the only things moving. It would be hard for her to hide. She had an inkling of an idea. She could stay away from them long enough for it to solidify in her mind, then she could come up with a plan.

Fireworks.

Party.

"Come, little Rosi," called Jesse. "Help us! We can take you places. We can take you times. What an adventure you will have. Look, Rosi. Your uncle is not going to teach you what you can really do. He won't tell you who you really are. He's scared of you. We can help you. She can help you. Come along!"

They were herding her. To where and for what purpose she did not know. Just ahead of her, Rosi saw the spire. She would be safe there. She could defend herself there. She could start up time there and Kirk and Jesse could be killed in the fighting.

But so would so many others.

She made a sudden dash for the spire and began climbing as

quickly as she could.

She heard them yell and could tell they were coming closer.

A hand brushed her leg. Someone behind her fell. The two swore. They giggled. It was creepy. Then, Rosi was alone on the top.

She was safe. For a while. If they tried to climb up, this time she would not miss.

Looking down, she saw Jesse stalking around at the foot of the spire.

Kirk was sniffing around the grass, looking for something. Sniffing around looking vaguely like a dog.

Dog!

Fireworks!

Party!

Perfect. But how to do it. And would it work?

"Oy!" yelled Jesse.

There were no tears here.

"She's got something."

Or were there. She just needed to get there enough.

"Kirk! Find a gun."

Needed to badly enough.

"Shoot her!"

Rosi reached out. She felt the air in front of her press against her hands.

Kirk fired. The bullet whipped past her head, plucking at her hair.

"Find another one! Kill her!"

She dug her fingers in and pulled, forcing and dragging the air apart.

She heard another shot just as she stepped through.

* * *

INTO the cool August night lit by bursting fireworks.

Rosi took a minute to adjust her eyes to the dark. She looked down at the dry riverbed. There were clumps of grass here and there in the marsh. By the stream was a large bonfire around which danced the partiers.

Several couples wandered around the marsh. Several were drunkenly calling for what they thought was a dog.

There was laughing and shrieking and partying. It took her a minute or so to find the hulking shape and the girl it was stalking. If only she could warn herself. She knew, however, that was strictly forbidden.

Then the night erupted with light and sound.

The kids *oohed* and *ahhed*.

The Ankalagon was guided by the fireworks away from the beach. Then, Rosi saw a series of explosions that forced the beast in a large circle.

Rosi knew where she wanted the Ankagalon to go. She knew that the explosions were certainly geared to send it right where she wanted it. She was not quite sure who set the charges, though she suspected that it would be her. When she was only a few feet from the monster, it had been terrifying. Now, from a distance, it was graceful to watch. It loped and bounded and made its direction towards her.

She had always thought of the Ankagalon as some sort of large dog. Of course, dogs could not climb. And if they could, certainly they could not climb as swiftly as this climbed the spire Rosi was standing on.

This was just about the stupidest thing Rosi had ever done, but she could not think of anything else. She lay still as the beast bound up onto to top. It stood on the top of the spire and roared. Then it appeared to see or sense something below. Rosi saw it tense to spring and threw herself on it as it leapt into the air.

Below, Rosi saw herself and Kirk looking up at them. She cleared her mind and tore into the air before her.

* * *

WHEN the beast landed on the ground, Rosi rolled off and landed hard, knocking the breath out of her.

For some reason, the beast did not turn and rip her to shreds.

Perhaps it was the noise of the battle that distracted it. Perhaps it was the smell of blood and sweat and fear. Perhaps it simply felt that the red-coated prey all around it were more appetizing than Rosi was.

Rosi was not too concerned. There were times to be the least desirable person in sight and this was one of them.

She tried not to watch. Men flew in the air. They screamed. A few fought. For the Ankalagon, the people were like stuffed toys to a Labrador. It shook them, threw them, tasted them, and then moved on the next tasty morsel.

The men had no idea what they were facing. To them, it might as well have been Cerberus. It must certainly have seemed like some hellish beast.

Within a couple of minutes, the British were flying from the field.

The beast followed for some distance, but soon returned to the fresh food it had left behind.

Rosi's men, as far as she could tell, had retreated across the stream. They were terrified as well. A couple of the men, though, seemed to be keeping their wits about them, for Rosi could hear a couple of voices yelling orders.

No one on the battlefield moved. Rosi did not try to count the bodies. She kneeled there and watched the beast sate its hunger.

Rosi was drained. She was weak. Whatever it was that she was doing, tearing into the fabric of time, was taking its toll on her. And there was one more part to her little trick.

"Here, boy!" she called out, feeling stupid.

There was enough noise that the Ankalagon might not have heard her, even though it was only a few dozen feet away.

Rosi put two fingers between her lips and let loose with a piercing whistle. That got its attention. The well-aimed rock she threw at its nose did the rest.

Jevy charged her. Its breath steamed in the cool night air. Flecks of slobber flew in all direction. It eyes were dark and merciless. It leapt at her and disappeared before her very eyes.

With her last ounce of strength, Rosi slammed the tear shut. She sat down heavily.

Eventually, she hoped, someone would come out to investigate. They would find her and carry her over to the other side of the stream. The battle was far from over. Rosi had simply chased off the British who were there. At most, she would slow down the rest. If she was lucky, she would slow them down for her reinforcements to get there first.

The British might find her first. That would not be good.

Rosi slowly stood up. Just about every bone and muscle hurt.

"Going somewhere?" Rosi turned and saw Jesse standing next to her. The barrel pointed at her face looked very large to her.

Then something hard hit the back of her head and she went down.

"Ouch!" she screamed. "Christ! What was that for?"

Looking up, she saw Kirk holding a pistol like a club. "That hurt!"

"It was supposed to knock you out!" Kirk snarled.

"You watch too many movies," Rosi spat at him.

Jesse giggled. Then he slapped the barrel of his weapon against the side of her head.

"What the?" It really hurt.

After too many tries, eventually, one of them got lucky.

* * *

THE first thing Rosi noticed when her head cleared, other than that her head was really hurting, was that she was in her room in The Castle. No. She was in the place that would eventually be her room. She was tied to a hard cot. Kirk and Jesse were on the other side of the room whispering to each other.

"She's awake," Jesse said, noticing her looking at them.

"Excellent," chortled Kirk.

"What do you two want?" Rosi asked, trying to seem more defiant than she felt.

Jesse pulled open the door. Behind it was a brick wall.

Rosi looked carefully at that wall. The bricks, she could tell, went back a long way. Something other than mortar was holding them together. The bond was strong. Stronger than any glue or weld. There was a force far beyond the ranks of bricks that was fighting the bond. There were already small cracks through which the power seeped.

It was dark. It was wrong.

So very wrong.

Rosi knew the power wanted her to let it free. She knew Jesse and Kirk wanted her to set it free. She could see in their eyes what lengths they would go to to convince her to let the power free.

Rosi could also see there were infinitesimal strands of the power that were connected to Kirk and to Jesse. Somehow, these strands helped them understand and use their latent powers. Perhaps, if Rosi could break that connection, she could turn this to her advantage.

For the time being, however, she had no idea how.

"Free her," Jesse said.

"Why don't you tell me all about her," Rosi said. Her mouth hurt, but she thought that her words, or her meaning, were understood.

Jesse giggled. So did Kirk.

Rosi noticed the tendrils of power that ran from beyond the bricks to the two shimmered when they spoke.

"I built a fire," Kirk said. "I didn't want you to get a chill," he stated with a laugh.

"The time to collaborate passed a long time ago," Jesse sneered. "Now it is time for us to convince you."

* * *

ROSI was not sure how long they spent trying to convince her. After a time, she was not even sure what they were doing.

She knew it hurt. She could hear her screams, which only made Jesse and Kirk giggle all the more.

They only stopped whatever they were doing so they could

rest and so that she would not pass out, though she was sure a couple of times she did.

After an eternity of pain, of pleading, of degradation, of crying, of screaming, Rosi began to notice something. Whenever they came to her, the strands of evil darkened and tried to pull at them.

Whoever *she* was, *she* did not like them giving their attention to Rosi. *She* was jealous.

Kirk and Jesse stopped to eat. They ate quickly. They were in a rush. They were worried about something. After a hushed discussion, Kirk rushed outside and, Rosi thought, upstairs.

Jesse came over and dropped some bits of bread into Rosi's mouth. Then he poured some water on her face. She opened her mouth and swallowed as much as she could.

"Is he gone?" she asked.

"For the time being," Jesse said, sitting on the cot next to her.

"*She* prefers you," Rosi sobbed.

That got Jesse's attention. "What?"

"*She* prefers you," Rosi said again. She reached out her fingers and gently caressed his hand. "You are stronger. Wiser."

Jesse entwined his fingers in hers.

"*She* wants you," Rosi said as breathily as she could. "But *she* can't take both of you. *She* needs you. *She* needs your power. Please, Jesse. I can't take any more. You can help me. You can protect me from him. I can help you free *her*. But we have to move fast. Before Kirk comes back."

"You'll help me?" Jesse asked, excitement filled his voice. Rosi could feel him quiver.

"*She* wants me to help you."

Jesse pulled out a knife. Rosi could see in his eyes a desire to thrust the blade into her, but his greed was stronger. Swiftly, he cut the ropes holding her down and helped her up.

Rosi could barely stand, which was convenient. Her legs gave as soon as she tried to put weight on them. Jesse had to drop the knife to put his arms around her. Rosi let him hold her up.

"Closer," she said. "To the doorway."

He helped her stumble across the room. The tendrils of power were angry and frantically tugging at Jesse, but he was too distracted and excited to realize that *she* was angry.

"You are so strong," Rosi cooed. "You have been alone for so long."

"So long," he replied huskily.

"She needs you," Rosi whispered in his ear. They were close to the wall. "You are a man."

"I am a man," Jesse repeated.

"She needs a man." Rosi slipped her arms around his neck. "I need a man. I need a man."

Rosi leaned into Jesse, who leaned against the wall. She pulled his face down to hers and let him kiss her. Greedily, she kissed him back. His arms pressed her against him.

Rosi could feel the tendrils of power thrashing at her hands, at her legs, trying to force the two of them apart.

Rosi pressed against him harder.

She was furious. *She* fought against them. *She* could not believe that she was losing to this girl! So, *she* did what she had to do. *She* withdrew her presence. She pulled out.

That Jesse felt. His head snapped back. He fell to his knees.

Rosi dropped to the floor, landing heavily on her back.

"What was that?" Jesse asked.

"Payback," Rosi gasped.

"What did you do?" He grabbed her and shook her. "What did you do?" He threw her back to the floor.

"I got *her* attention." Rosi pulled her legs back. Then she kicked out at Jesse as hard as she could.

Jesse fell back against the bricks with a yelp of surprise. He kept on going through, dissolving through the cracks.

Rosi forced herself to stand. She grabbed the door and slammed it shut. Somewhere, deep inside of her, back in the recesses of her mind, with no idea how, she turned a mental key in a physical lock.

There was a click.

Rosi fell.

* * *

"WHAT have you done?"

Rosi opened her eyes to see Kirk looming over her.

Rosi smiled wearily. She was almost too tired to be scared. There seemed to be no power coming from the door, but that might not last for long.

"I sent him away," Rosi said.

A look of fury filled Kirk's face. It was quickly replaced by a look of resignation.

"You've ruined everything," Kirk said a bit too calmly.

"I hope so."

"You didn't have to ruin everything. We could have been wonderful together."

"Sorry."

"Are you?"

"Not really."

Kirk sighed. "You know what I'm going to have to do, don't you."

"Yes!" Rosi sobbed. She closed her eyes and heard Kirk walking over to the fire.

Again, there was an eternity that might have lasted seconds or days. She tried to fight, but was too weak. She screamed. She cried.

Kirk simply giggled, and forced her to his will.

Rosi knew she would serve Kirk. She would do anything for him. All he had to do was ask. Tell. Order. He did not. He was so angry he did not realize he had won.

He stepped back and looked at her. He could see it in her eyes, her slavish submission.

Kirk smirked.

Then came the sound of a shot.

Kirk fell forward on top of Rosi. Screaming in surprise and pain, he rolled off of her and stood up.

Sally's father stood on the other side of the room. "You are a monster!" he growled. Behind him stood Sally and her mother.

The father started, shakily, to reload the gun.

Kirk looked down at Rosi. "Another time, Rosi Carol. We'll finish another time."

He stepped forward and swung the poker at the three, forcing them back.

Kirk then ran for the balcony and leapt off.

The father ran for the side and looked over. He stood there and looked around for several seconds. He turned back to Rosi. "He's gone."

"Dead?"

"Nope. Simply gone."

The father came over to Rosi with a blanket and placed it over her. He rolled up some other cloths and placed them gently under her head.

"We stayed as you asked," the father said. "Didn't even try to leave. Then we hear you screaming. It went on for so long. Finally the door opened. We came down as fast as we could. Why don't you just lie down quiet. My wife'll get you some water. No food here but for bread if you can. Good. Anything'll make you feel better. You hear that?"

Rosi listened. She could hear gunfire.

"Them'll be yer friends. Out the window we saw they was coming. Trapped some British by the stables. That's why we won't go fer help. Beggin' yer pardon. They'll be here soon enough. You just drink some water and get some sleep."

Rosi did.

CHAPTER 13

"WE thought you were dead." Angie was holding Rosi's hand.

Rosi was in a bed. She could tell that. "You mean I'm not?" she whispered. It hurt to talk.

Angie laughed and gently kissed her, though it took her some time to find a spot that did not hurt to be touched.

"How is everyone?" Even asking such a simple question made Rosi's eyes water.

"We're a bit beat up, but otherwise all right." Angie adjusted her position so Rosi could see the large bruise on her forehead. "It's much better now. You've been out for days. They gave you something that kept you unconscious. Said it would help with the healing. They even left you in your old room." Angie helped Rosi sit up. The room had been transformed and looked much like Rosi would have guessed an affluent teenager's room would look like in the eighteenth century. Angie helped Rosi drink some broth that tasted divine. "Don't worry. I didn't cook it." Angie laughed. "The fresh air probably did you some good. No, don't ask. I know all you're gonna ask, so I'll just tell you."

Will and Alcott's men had shown up to relieve the beleaguered group. Even then, the British outnumbered the colonials. However, something had happened to spook many of them and that had changed so much. Now the British were on the defensive. They held on for the day and were regrouping by nightfall. The British might still have won, but then Andy and Beatitude arrived just after sunup the next morning. Cromwell fell back to New Richmond where he fled to his ship leaving most of his men behind. They might have held out, but Cromwell then opened fire on the town as he sailed off. When Beatitude and Alcott arrived, there was little left of the town and most of the British soldiers had surrendered immediately.

The truncated swimming lessons Dan had given Essex had paid off. When Dan had been knocked about by the explosions, Essex had dived under the water, found Dan, and dragged him to shore. After the British left, he took Dan to The Dancing Cavalier where Young Captain Sam dried them out. They waited there until after the British had surrendered.

Will had been furious when he arrived at The Castle. He had raged. Then he and several men took what horses they could find and rode off, vowing not to return until Kirk was caught and punished.

"We sent some men to find them, to tell them to come back," Angie said. "But no word so far." She gently caressed Rosi's hair. "I've kept you awake too long. I'm supposed to make you drink this then let you sleep."

Angie helped Rosi drink some vile tasting liquid.

Almost immediately, Rosi closed her eyes and slept.

That was pretty much the routine for the next few days. Rosi would wake up and spend a few minutes chatting with Angie and Andy. She did see Dan once out of the corner of her eye, but he was walking away. Then she would fall back to sleep. It was not until the fifth day that she was allowed to sit up properly.

A couple of days later, she even stood up and walked outside for a minute.

Andy and Angie were there all the time. Dan, it seemed, was spending most of his time helping the villagers rebuild.

After dinner on the tenth day, a young gaudily dressed man came into the room and asked Angie and Andy to take a short walk.

"I'm Beatitude Carol," he said, patting her head. Rosi felt like a puppy. "You must be Rositsa Carol. I have heard a great deal about you."

"I've heard very little about you," Rosi replied.

Beatitude laughed heartily. "That will change. You must be my great-great-great something or other."

"I suppose so."

"And you are the girl who caused so much of this mess.

Whatever was your uncle thinking?"

"Are you saying I did a bad job? I did all I knew how."

"You did fine for a first time."

"Why didn't you come earlier and help."

"I did. I sent the Fula'puli. They are much more connected than I am. I sensed your presence. We know how to make each other aware of what we are doing. I sent them to keep an eye on you. H'Cab had trouble tracking you."

"To keep an eye on me? Weren't they supposed to help me?"

"We try not to interfere with other Guardians."

"I have a question," Rosi said a little while later. "Kirk changed history. He said as much."

"That doesn't make him right. Look, time will generally work itself out the way it's supposed to. Like gravity. A raindrop will eventually hit the ground. Even if it hits a tree branch first, it will eventually hit the ground. You set things moving in the right direction. I have no doubt that when you return home things will pretty much be the same."

"What will happen to Kirk?"

"Are you worried about him? I know what he did to you. You talked while you were unconscious. It was pretty confusing. H'Cab and I were able to work most of it out, but I have no doubt your friends only got a rough idea. If your friend Will Scranton catches up to him, I have no doubt Kirk will die. Rather painfully."

Rosi blanched at the thought. She did not want Kirk to be hurt.

Beatitude went on. "If Mr. Scranton doesn't dispose of Kirk Meadows, then let us hope he is not able to confuse things much, or you will have to come back and deal with him. As I said, Kirk is your responsibility. He came here because of you, through your doorway. It is not the place for one Guardian to interfere with the manipulations of another, though it has been known to happen. These doors are peculiar to The Castle. They represent specific gateways to specific times and, yes places. Remember that time and space are intimately connected. Most of what you will deal with in your life will be localized, but not all. And, remember this, there are lots of little tears all over the place. New Richmond just happens to be a place where there is an intense congregation. Not the only place."

Rosi gulped. There was a lot to think about. Beatitude left her to sleep.

When she awakened, the sun was still out, or was it out again, and Uncle Richard was sitting nearby sipping some tea. She could smell his cigar before she saw him. When she did look over at him, he was in as foul a mood as she had ever seen him.

"You have made a mess of things," he said. "You are far from ready to go out on your own."

Beatitude laughed. "I was just telling her a few hours ago how well she had done for a first time."

Uncle Richard turned on the younger man. "It will take a lot of us a lot of time to fix her mess." He turned to Rosi. "Are you finished playing soldier? There is a lot of work to be done. A few days of gallivanting around pretending you are Lighthorse Harry Lee will hardly fit in with hundreds of years of oral tradition, legends, and collective memory."

Beatitude stopped smiling. "Give her a break, old man. Oh, by the way, hello."

Uncle Richard was clearly used to having things done his way and was nonplussed by Beatitudes reaction. "Hello. It has been a while."

"Clearly not long enough. I've explained a fair amount to Rosi. No doubt you can fill in the blanks later. I never understood your obsession with *she must figure it out on her own*. A little guidance might have helped."

"Guidance, as you call it, might well have triggered events prematurely," Uncle Richard said. "Why, by the way, did you get involved? You should have stayed out. Stayed put playing soldier to the south."

"Young Mr. Montrose made a compelling argument," Beatitude said.

"Which was?"

"That if Rosi failed, he and Dan Meadows would move into The Castle and live with me."

Uncle Richard thought for a moment. He nodded. "As it is, a lot has happened, and too many people know. Would you like to advise me on how to deal with those children?"

"Take them home," Beatitude said exasperatedly. "Even if they remember anything, who would believe them?"

"People will ask questions. New Richmond is not as isolated as it should be."

"That's your fault, old man. Don't blame a bunch of kids. Anyway, abandoning them on a deserted island would be vulgar and killing them would be melodramatic."

"Wait a second," Rosi broke in. "Are you talking about Angie and the others?"

"Yes, Rosi," Uncle Richard said, annoyed at being interrupted. "Let us deal with this."

"No. Beatitude said that this was my responsibility. He said you don't like to interfere."

"What do you mean, Rosi?" Uncle Richard snapped impatiently. "Say what you mean."

"They are my responsibility. They will be taken home, if that is at all possible."

"But—"

"No buts, Uncle Richard. Tell them whatever you want, but try anything drastic I'll...go stop The Crucifixion."

It was Beatitude's turn to blanche.

Uncle Richard smiled. It did not look right, him smiling.

"Fine, child," Uncle Richard said. "I will explain the situation to your friends. But the Crucifixion? It would not have made a difference."

"Don't start that," said Beatitude.

"It was historically unnecessary and paved the way for the excesses of a Pauline tradition that could have been avoided with an hereditary Nazarene pontificate."

"Heresy!"

"Boys!" Rosi snapped firmly. "Uncle Richard, if you

remember my first trip…I forgot a lot of things, and I'm supposed to know what's going on."

Beatitude felt that she had a point.

"But," Uncle Richard argued. "They have been through a lot. People remember in different ways their experiences. They will be changed. They will understand that something has happened."

"Then they'll know something. It's my problem to deal with. Now, you two. Out! I'm tired."

When she awakened again, it was dark, but Uncle Richard sat in a nearby chair reading by candlelight.

"I spoke to your friends," he said.

"And?"

"I impressed on them the seriousness of divulging information to individuals who were not already privy the situation. I requested that each give his word. Each did."

"And?"

"I trust them. I trust they will do their best not to speak on the subject. That is the best I can expect. I am not worried about young Montrose or Miss Kaufman, their families are local and know the score, if I may use the colloquialism. Mr. Meadows…well, we all knew that someday outsiders would find out the truth. We were outsiders once, too. It remains to be seen how they will be affected by what has happened."

They talked for a long time. Over the next few days, while Rosi steadily improved, they spoke often.

She saw a lot of Andy and Angie, very little of Dan, and a fair amount of Zilla, who came but was unable to bring any news of Will. Zablonski came into the room a couple of times. He was solicitous, but distant.

Everyone was eager to return home, but Uncle Richard suggested it would be best if Dan, Andy, and Angie's bruises and cuts were healed. Rosi would have to have some minor medical procedures because of her misadventures. She hoped she would have no scars, physical or mental.

* * *

THE day came. Beatitude gave everyone a big breakfast and handed out gifts to Dan, Andy, and Angie. Little knickknacks that Rosi was sure were worth a fortune.

"The remains of what Rosi stole from me." Beatitude laughed. "It will take years and fortunes to replace most of the stuff."

Uncle Richard took care of Sally and her family. "Plastic surgery and relocation. It is something that has to be done from time to time."

"They will be well taken care of," Beatitude assured Rosi.

"They will be carefully monitored and isolated," Uncle Richard explained.

"Thank you for that addition, old man." Beatitude scowled. He then smiled at Rosi. "They will be sent as missionaries to a small island that won't be discovered for some time."

To Zilla, well, that was Rosi's idea. Beatitude promised to buy the farm and give it to her and Will.

"You take care of yourself, child." Zilla hugged her as tightly as she could. She had sent a fair amount of time helping Rosi recuperate, but as much as she loved her new friend, she had to get home. It was time to get to work.

"I'll come back for Will if I can," Rosi promised. She slipped off her little St. Christopher. "Give this to him."

They kissed again, then Zilla left with the men Beatitude ordered to escort her home and help her rebuild her house and barn.

Zablonski had gathered together the remains of the original company. There were only twelve men left. Three or four had not been able to linger around New Richmond. Like Zilla, they had crops or jobs or families. They had lives. The rest were dead. But the twelve men who were left lined up and snapped to attention when she came out of The Castle to wave goodbye to Zilla. The rest of the company, those who had not been reassigned to their original units, stood grouped behind the twelve.

The sergeant major walked her down the line. Rosi was saddened that there were so few. That so many had died. But the men looked so serious standing there trying to keep their eyes front, saluting and bowing as she passed that by the time she was halfway down the line she was hiding a chuckle behind a huge smile. Several of them were openly agog at seeing their young captain wearing a dress. It was more of a robe than a dress. She was not about to wear all the underthings, especially not the corset. As if she needed a corset. Ha! And the dress was not laced up, but rather tied by an elaborate bow. Uncle Richard had found her a pair of sneakers, but no one could see them. But it was more clothing that she had ever worn before. How could women in this age stand it?

"Oh, my God," she said to them. "I don't even know what to say. You men kept me alive. I know that. I...I...." her tongue was getting tied up. "I love you all. I will come and see you the next time I am here."

"Captain." Sergeant-Major Zablonski snapped to attention and gave her a proper salute.

Rosi saluted back. "What are you going to do, Sergeant Major?"

"Continue on with the fight, Captain."

"And then?"

"Your...your...." He searched for the right word. "Your relative has suggested that there might be something here for me when the war is won."

"I hope there is, Sergeant Major. If you do come back, keep an eye on Zilla for me."

"Yes, Captain."

"I remember you telling me that it was not proper for a captain to hug a sergeant. Would it be permissible for a captain to kiss a sergeant major?"

"Permissible, Captain? Mandatory, I would think." Zablonski grinned and took off his hat.

He bent over. Rosi stood on her toes and pressed her lips to his scraggly cheek.

"Thank you, Sergeant Major," she said to him quietly, giving his hand a quick squeeze.

Rosi turned and practically fled inside, followed by a rousing series of cheers from the company.

"You can not come back for Will," Uncle Richard said sternly, taking her arm and leading her to her room.

"Why not?"

"Because he has his life to lead. He will have a family, or not. He will succeed, or not. He will grow old, or not. It is not your place to interfere, to confuse what will and has happened."

Rosi supposed she understood.

They went down to Rosi's room, where Uncle Richard had put out some clothing for Angie and Rosi. Dan and Andy's clothing had been saved by the Fula'puli.

"We will be arriving about an hour after Dan and Andy left," Uncle Richard explained after the girls had changed.

Uncle Richard nodded. Rosi reached out and touched the door, which swung open.

* * *

THE first thing all the kids did when they came out the other side of the door was to rush outside Rosi's bedroom and look across the harbor at the town. It was late at night. The harbor was lined with lights. They could even see an airplane flying above.

Right away, Rosi noticed that even though she had always considered her rooms unnaturally quiet it was surprisingly loud. She had never noticed the noise before.

Taking Angie's arm, Rosi hobbled up to the front door to say goodbye to the others.

The first thing Andy was going to do the next morning, he explained, giving her a hug, was to go straight to the Historical Society and see what the reports said about the Battle for New Richmond.

The first thing Angie was going to do was to take a long, long, long hot, hot, hot shower, and then sleep for about a week and then eat some real food. She would give Rosi a call then.

Andy and Angie took each other's hands and went outside to wait for Dan.

"So," said Rosi.

"Yeah," said Dan.

"I never did get to say Happy Birthday."

"Oh, that's right."

"Sorry," she said.

"No. It's all right." Dan fidgeted.

Rosi hesitated for a moment. "I...."

"What?"

"I didn't—"

"Didn't what?" Dan asked.

"What you—"

"What I?"

"Thought I...." She let herself drift off.

"I thought?" Dan looked confused.

"With Will." She blurted out. "I didn't. I really didn't."

"Did you—" Dan stammered. "Will you, I mean, do you...."

"What?"

"Love him?" He could not look at her when he asked.

"Love him?"

"Yes."

"He was...." She sought for the right word. "There."

"That's all?" Dan sounded shocked. "He was there?"

"I mean, you weren't." She could feel her eyes burn as she tried to blink back the tears.

"No," Dan admitted.

"Love? What is love?" asked Rosi.

"You tell me," he insisted.

"Is it wanting?" she asked.

"Yes."

"Needing?"

"Yes."

"Holding?"

"Yes."

"Crying?"

"Yes."

"Laughing?"

"Yes."

"Is it desiring, hating, caring, regretting, missing, knowing, trusting, doubting, and despairing?"

"Yes, yes, yes."

They held each other's eyes for a long moment.

"I suppose, then, that I did," she said.

Dan turned and started to leave.

"If that's what love is then I love you, too," Rosi said to his back.

"Perhaps," Dan replied.

"Please stay," Rosi said, reaching out and touching his arm.

"Not today." Dan left.

It was beginning to rain outside. This was good, for it would explain why his face was wet.

Rosi was tired.

She felt nauseous.

She sat down and stared at the door.

Uncle Richard came up quietly. "It will be light soon."

"Yes, Uncle Richard."

"This life is not about fun, games, or boys."

"No, Uncle Richard."

Uncle Richard held out his hand. Rosi took it and stood up.

"You do realize that you miscounted," Uncle Richard said.

"What do you mean?"

"There was someone else here."

Rosi thought for a moment. "Lois? What happened to her?"

Uncle Richard thought for a moment. "She's not in The Castle."

"And that means that we—" Rosi paused. "I have to find her."

"Well, before you are ready, we have a lot of work to do."

Together, they entered The Castle.

THE END

About the Author

EDWARD EATON has studied and taught at many schools in the States, China, Israel, Oman, and France. He holds a PhD in Theatre History and Literature, and has worked extensively as a theatre director and fight choreographer. As a writer, he has been a newspaper columnist and theatre critic. He has published and presented many scholarly papers, and also has a background in playwriting. In addition to academic and creative pursuits, he is an avid SCUBA diver and skier. He currently resides in Boston, Massachusetts with his wife Silviya and his son Christopher. Publications include the young adult novels *Rosi's Castle*, *Rosi's Company*, and *Rosi's Time* plus the dramas *Elizabeth Bathory* and *Orpheus and Eurydice*. For more information or to contact the author, visit: www.edwardeaton.com.

Rosi's Doors Series:

ROSI'S CASTLE
[Book I]

ROSI'S TIME
[Book II]

ROSI'S COMPANY
[Book III]

50665533R00139

Made in the USA
Middletown, DE
02 November 2017